To Luke
Best w
Pat Spence
x

True Blue

(The Blue Crystal Trilogy)

Book Two

Pat Spence

ISBN-13: 978-1514203507

ISBN-10: 1514203502-

True Blue

Amazon reviews

I loved the first book in this series but this one knocked my socks off. Twists and turns around every corner, some expected but others I couldn't have imagined. Definitely recommend it and look forward to the next instalment (conclusion?). Erica

If you enjoyed Blue Moon, you will absolutely love this book, so much happens, lots of twists and turns but at the centre of the book is Emily and Theo and their love for each other. I loved Seth in this book, he was comical and really entertaining. When reading the book I felt like I was watching a movie as I could picture everything going on, that's the beauty of Pat's writing. If you like your books paranormal you will not be disappointed. There are shifters, gross dark things and other paranormal entities... Tracey

Excellent - keeps you gripped and interested all the way through – even better than Book One. Read it all too quick so looking forward to Book Three now!! Judith

This fantastic novel will not disappoint. Gripping ending to run your imagination wild! Can't wait to discover the long awaited outcome... Sarah

What an awesome imagination Pat Spence has. Like her previous book, it's not my usual read, but again here is a true page-turner! I can't wait for Book 3, I have absolutely no idea how it ends for Emily, her friends and the de Lucis family. Who on earth took that crystal? Denise

For Bob, somewhere down the crazy river…

'Sweet Helen, make me immortal with a kiss.'

Faustus by Christopher Marlowe

CONTENTS

PART THREE: **RESCUE**

PROLOGUE:

Two figures peered through the oppressive darkness, surveying the scene before them. The smell of decay hung everywhere, ingrained in the ancient walls. Undisturbed for many years, the air lay heavy and stale.

It was a natural underground cavern, enhanced by man at some point in the past, the sweeping vaulted ceiling of the main chamber giving the impression of a vast subterranean cathedral. Stacked on shelves hewn into the rock lay the rotting remains of centuries old coffins, spewing out their bony contents onto the ground beneath.

The smaller of the two figures carelessly flung open the lid of the nearest coffin, inhaling deeply the cadaverous odour that spilled forth.

'Enough,' commanded the other. 'Let them be. We have not come to wake the dead, but to find a resting place for the living.'

The smaller figure indicated a raised plinth at the far end of the crypt, on which stood a large lead tomb.

'Perhaps there…'

The larger figure crossed to the raised area and, moving the heavy lid to one side with apparent ease, examined the inside.

'Perfect. Remove the occupant. Make space for the girl.'

The sighing of a thousand souls seemed to fill the chamber, causing the air to tremor and long settled dust to rise in clouds.

'Silence,' commanded the larger figure, raising its arms, its raspy voice rippling through the darkness.

'There is work to do. My time is nigh…'

PART ONE: TEENAGE LIFE

1. **Classroom**

I put my foot down on Martha's accelerator and felt her surge forward. Arriving early at college, I parked and walked slowly to my English seminar, hovering nervously in the classroom doorway. I wasn't looking forward to seeing my friends. Last time I'd seen Seth and Tash had been at Hartswell Hall when they'd witnessed the power of the blue crystal for themselves. My fingers went to the small blue crystal hanging round my neck and stroking its smooth, cool facets, I felt better.

'Emily, you have some explaining to do!' Tash's voice came from down the corridor and I turned to face her. Seth was with her and neither looked happy.

'What's going on, Em?' he asked. 'Why did you go back into the Clock Tower? And what happened to Kimberley Chartreuse? She was fit.'

Not any more, I thought.

'Sorry,' I said, looking down. 'I couldn't come with you.'

I was saved from further explanation by the arrival of our English tutor.

'Why are you standing out here?' demanded Miss Widdicombe. 'Come into the classroom. At least pretend to show willing.'

She ushered us in and we sat at our desks.

'We'll continue this at break-time,' said Seth in a whisper.

I nodded. That gave me a couple of hours to get my story right.

'Okay, I thought we'd take a look at one of our set texts for next year,' announced Miss Widdicombe. 'Who's heard of Doctor Faustus by Christopher Marlowe?'

'I have,' called out Seth, sprawling on his chair, his legs too long to fit under his desk.

'And?' asked Miss Widdicombe.

'It's about a guy who makes a pact with the devil,' said Seth. 'He sells his soul for knowledge and magic.'

He looked across at me and I felt a prickling sensation at the back of my neck.

'Very good, Seth,' said Miss Widdicombe. 'The play is actually a sixteenth century morality tale ...'

Her voice droned on, lulling me into a daydream. I began to imagine how life would change when I stepped into the crystal's blue light ... how I'd stay seventeen forever.... see the world's through Theo's eyes... be with him for eternity.

'Carry on, Emily.' Miss Widdicombe's voice broke into my thoughts.

'What?' I stuttered.

'Carry on reading. Oh, for goodness sake, concentrate! Seth, show her...'

Seth pointed out the passage, but before I could speak, he began to read the words in a dramatic voice:

'Till swol'n with cunning of a self-conceit,

His waxen wings did mount above his reach,

And melting, heavens conspired his overthrow...'

'Thank you Laurence Olivier,' said Miss Widdicombe disparagingly. 'Don't call us, we'll call you.'

There were a few sniggers around the classroom and she looked at us with a resigned expression. 'Can anyone tell me what these words mean?'

'Yeah,' said Seth, lazily, flicking his long dark fringe away from his face and slouching down in his chair even further. 'It's referring to the story of Icarus, the Greek guy who flew too close to the sun. His wings were made of wax and they melted and he fell back down to earth. Kapow!'

He made a whistling sound with his mouth, like a bomb flying through the air, and slapped his palms together, making a splatting sound.

'Without the sound effects, thank you,' said Miss Widdicombe. 'But you're right. It's a story about reaching too high and suffering the consequences.'

Seth raised his eyebrows and glanced at me. He might be playing the clown, but he didn't miss a trick. He knew I was playing a dangerous game. I saw Tash looking at him and frowning. She could sense a storm was brewing.

It began at break-time. I sat in the cafeteria opposite Seth and Tash. Thankfully, Theo and Violet weren't there.

'Okay, Emily,' said Seth, sitting back on his plastic chair. 'Shpill the beansh.'

'If that's a Sean Connery impression, it's pretty bad.'

'Sean Connery? Columbo, if you don't mind.'

'Seth!' said Tash. 'Can we stick to the point?'

'Okay, Mish Moneypenny.'

Tash rolled her eyes. 'Emily, that story you told us about the blue crystal bestowing eternal youth on those who bathe in its rays… It's true, isn't it? Kimberley Chartreuse believed it. That's why she held us at gunpoint. What happened after we'd gone?'

Tash's complexion was pale, contrasting with her long, red Pre-Raphaelite hair and emphasizing her big green eyes.

Seth flicked back his fringe. 'You have to tell us, Emily. Last we saw of Kimberley, she was holding the crystal and getting younger before our eyes.'

'She didn't make it,' I said brusquely. 'The crystal killed her.'

'Youza!' said Seth, his eyes wide. 'Was it gory?'

I avoided his question. 'Look, stuff is going on Hartswell Hall. But the more I tell you, the more you're in danger. It's better you don't know.'

'Emily,' said Tash, softly. 'We appreciate you protecting us, but we need to know.'

I studied her face. 'Okay. You're right. The story about the crystal is true. But as long as you keep quiet, you'll be safe.'

'Safe from who? The de Lucis family?' asked Seth.

'No. Not the family. Worse than that. The Lunari.'

'What, that fictitious shadowy secret sect?' said Seth with a laugh. 'Try saying that quickly…'

'Seth!' said Tash sharply.

'Sorry,' he said, putting his hands up. 'It's hard enough getting your head round a mysterious crystal with magical powers, but a supernatural sect? Come on.'

'Believe me, Seth, they exist,' I said. 'And they are a bunch of psychotic killers you don't want to cross. I met them yesterday.'

'OMG, they were at the hall?' asked Tash.

'That's why you had to leave. I couldn't let them find you there,' I paused. 'The problem is, you were seen. And now they're watching you.'

'Meaning what?' asked Seth.

'Meaning you're okay as long as you don't say anything. Otherwise….' I did a slicing movement across my throat with my index finger.

'OMG, this is scary,' said Tash.

'Great,' said Seth, sarcastically. 'We've only got some weirdo spooks on our tail, who'd kill us soon as look at us. Cheers, Emily.'

I sighed. 'You wanted to know.'

'But, what about you, Emily?' asked Tash. 'You know about the crystal. How come you're still alive?'

This was the bit I didn't want to say.

'I've done a deal with them.'

'What do you mean?' asked Seth, suspiciously.

'I'm going to join the de Lucis family. Bathe in the light of the crystal at the next full moon and become one of them.'

'No, Emily,' gasped Tash. 'This is wrong. I always knew there was something bad about Theo and Violet.'

Seth looked at me coldly. 'She's right, Emily. You can't do it.'

I smiled ruefully. 'You won't change my mind.'

'You're going to sell your soul for eternal youth,' said Seth in a flat voice. 'Like Faustus. I knew it.'

'No. It's not like that,' I said. 'I want to do it. I want to be with Theo.'

Seth snorted in disgust. 'Golden boy! He's pressured you into this, hasn't he?'

'Absolutely not. He doesn't want me to.'

'He doesn't?' asked Tash, surprised. 'Why not?'

'The initiation ceremony is dangerous. He knows I might not make it.'

'You mean like Kimberley Chartreuse?' asked Tash, 'What did happen to her?'

'The crystal was too powerful. When I got back to the Clock Tower room, the ageing process had started to reverse. One minute she was young and beautiful, the next she was an old crone. She withered before my eyes. Turned into a pile of dust.'

5

'OMG,' said Tash, 'I didn't like her, but she didn't deserve that.'

'Gross City!' said Seth. 'Wish I could have seen it.'

'No you don't,' I said. 'It was horrible. All bone and flesh and melting collagen.'

'But the same could happen to you,' said Tash.

'Without the collagen,' pointed out Seth.

'It could,' I admitted, 'but I touched the crystal and I'm still here. Chances are I'll survive.'

'It's too risky, Emily. You can't do it,' said Tash.

'I have no choice. If I don't, the Lunari will kill me. And this way, I get to be with Theo.'

'Theo!' echoed Seth. 'Everything was fine until he came on the scene.'

'I want to be with him,' I said slowly. 'Whatever it takes.'

Seth said nothing, just looked away, his face flushed.

'I don't want us to fall out,' I said, 'but there's nothing you can do. My mind is made up. I'm going to join the de Lucis family at the next full moon.'

'Shouldn't you wait for a blue moon?' asked Tash.

'No, they only happen every three years or so and it would be far too powerful. A full moon's enough to initiate me.'

'And if we try to stop you....' began Seth.

'The Lunari will kill you,' I said.

'Great,' said Seth. 'Do nothing and we lose you to the de Lucis family; stop you and we all die. We're damned if we do and damned if we don't. We can't win.'

'But, Seth,' I said, quietly, 'You're missing the point. I don't want you to stop me. I want to be with Theo.'

'Even if it kills you in the process?' asked Tash.

I looked at her steadily. 'It's a risk I'm prepared to take.'

2. **Family Talk**

Hartswell Hall nestled in the warm spring sunshine, its honey-coloured Cotswold stone shining with a golden glow, and even the carved gargoyles seemed to smile rather than display their customary leers. The grounds overflowed with spring flowers and the deep grassy lawns created a luxurious green carpet beneath the lofty cedars. An atmosphere of tranquility and peace pervaded the air, giving the impression of contentment and sleepy harmony.

Inside, the scene was somewhat different. The de Lucis family convened in the library, Violet and Theo sitting on the large leather Chesterfield sofa, Joseph standing behind. Opposite sat Viyesha and Leon, while Pantera stood by the door, regal and haughty as ever. Edgy and taut, Aquila hovered by the window, staring out on the gardens, an angry scowl etched into his swarthy features.

Viyesha looked around the room, her expression serene, belying the emotions beneath. As ever, she was immaculate in a pale blue shift dress, her shimmering blonde hair pinned back, her pale skin as smooth and flawless as polished alabaster. She addressed them softly, her mellifluous voice calming and caressing.

'Thank you for coming, everyone. It's been an eventful weekend and we must plan accordingly. For the moment, we have appeased the Lunari and they have left, satisfied we can deal with the situation.' She paused, gathering her thoughts.

'The events of yesterday must never happen again. To compromise the crystal's safety is unforgiveable and could bring about the demise of us all. I take the blame for leaving Emily alone and unprotected. I should have let you stay with her, Theo.'

'You did what you thought was best, mother,' he answered. 'Violet and Pantera were here. You thought Emily was safe. You couldn't have known that woman would be armed with a gun and knowledge of the crystal.'

'I'd like to know how a low-life private detective was able to provide her with information about the crystal,' said Leon, sitting back.

'You said you visited him,' said Joseph. 'What did you find?'

'Nothing but a grubby office littered with waste paper, pipe tobacco and used coffee cups. The sewer rat had long since scarpered, going back underground with the flotsam of his world.'

'Aquila, do you think you can flush him out?' asked Viyesha.

Black eyes glittering and features contorted with rage, Aquila spoke in vicious, guttural tones. 'This would never have happened if I had removed the girl. I lay the blame at Emily's door.'

'I agree,' said Pantera, moving in to the room. Her dark skin gleamed and her eyes flashed with anger. 'Our problems begin and end with the girl. She is not welcome here, even if she survives her initiation. It was she who allowed that woman to touch the crystal and harness its power, and it was she who let in a feeder.'

She lowered her voice and stared at Viyesha. 'Such an act would have been punishable by death in our previous world. Now we are in a civilised country, you have grown soft, Viyesha. Your powers of perception are diminished and your ability to act has deserted you. It is a weakness that could prove fatal.'

'A feeder should never have got into the hall, let alone the Clock Tower,' said Theo, through clenched teeth. 'I put the blame at your door, Pantera. You're supposed to guard the crystal. If anyone failed, it's you.'

Pantera could barely contain her rage. 'How dare you accuse me. It is you who have placed us all in danger by bringing an outsider into our midst. If it weren't for me, the feeder would have latched on to the crystal and achieved human form. When I arrived, it was already leeching the life out of your girlfriend. Thanks to me, she survived. Don't forget, it was I who destroyed the feeder and saved the crystal.'

'Enough!' shouted Leon, jumping up. 'This is getting us nowhere. We must unite, not fight. Enough recriminations. Fault lies on all sides.'

He addressed Pantera: 'I will not have you and Aquila fracture our family stability. Emily is no ordinary girl. Why else would Badru give her a stay of execution? He sees her power and wants to see how she will transform. You must accept her.'

'Seems to me,' said Joseph, trying to lighten the atmosphere, 'that we need to focus on finding the private detective.'

'You're right,' said Theo. 'He's getting his information from somewhere, which makes him the real danger. It was thanks to him Kimberley Chartreuse met her demise.'

'Speaking of which,' said Viyesha, looking troubled, 'have we contained the story? It was most regrettable.'

Leon smiled ruefully. 'I don't believe her absence will attract any attention. I understand she has a twin sister all too keen to take her place.'

'Oh, the fickleness of the celebrity culture,' laughed Joseph. 'Don't you just love the twenty-first century?'

Viyesha looked thoughtful. 'It is the second casualty since our arrival. There can be no more mistakes. For the moment, we will close the hotel to guests.' She paused, and spoke decisively: 'Looking back achieves nothing. We must move forward. I propose two things. Firstly, we must protect Emily until she is initiated. And that includes you, Aquila and Pantera.'

Both scowled, but remained silent.

'Theo and Violet, stay close to her at college,' said Viyesha. 'Aquila, watch over her at night. Ensure she remains safe. Joseph, stay vigilant in the grounds. If you see anything suspicious, alert Leon or me. There are enemies everywhere. Secondly, we must find Mr Nelson. If he is prepared to sell his knowledge of the crystal to any who will pay, he has to be stopped. Leon, do you agree?'

'I do. We must find him before he inflicts further damage. He has to break cover at some point. Aquila, search for him in daylight hours. Pantera, scour the city streets at night when your senses are strongest. Follow your instincts and track him down. If you find him, strike quickly and remove him once and for all. If the Lunari believe we are unable to protect the crystal, they will install sentinels of their own. This beautiful house will become a prison and our family life changed forever.'

'That will not happen,' said Viyesha decisively. 'We can protect the crystal without the Lunari dictating our every move. She addressed her daughter: 'Violet, you're quiet. Do you agree?'

Violet looked at her mother, a troubled expression on her face.

'I'm worried about my friends,' she said.

'You mean Seth and Tash?' asked Theo. He laughed scornfully. 'You don't even like them. And there's certainly no love lost between you and Tash.'

Violet ignored him. 'Badru said he'd be watching them. And you know how ruthless he can be. How did he know they were here yesterday?'

Pantera snorted. 'Someone has to have ears and eyes and report back to our brothers. I saw them leave. I simply relayed the fact.'

'How stupid was that?' exclaimed Violet. 'You know what the Lunari are like. The very fact you mentioned them makes them a threat. Oh, well done, Pantera.'

'Enough,' said Viyesha, holding up her hands. 'If they know nothing, they are safe. Emily assures me they have no knowledge of the crystal. We have more important issues to attend to and I must prepare the Clock Tower Room for Emily's initiation. Now, is there anything else?'

She looked around, receiving headshakes from her family members and scowling acknowledgements from Aquila and Pantera. Crossing her thumbs in front of her cupped hands, she said quietly: 'We hold eternity in the palm of our hands.'

The others followed suit, echoing her words. Silently, they stood and filed from the library. Theo and Violet were last to leave.

'What was all that about, Vi?' Theo asked, 'Why are you looking out for Seth and Tash? I don't get it.'

She looked at him coldly. 'You wouldn't. You have eyes only for Emily. Why should you worry about her friends being in danger?'

Theo looked at her strangely, and smiled.

'Oh, I get it. This isn't about Tash, is it? It's Seth. You have feelings for Seth. Well, well, little sister. You are a dark horse.'

She looked at him coldly. 'I don't know what you're talking about. We're not all as weak as you when it comes to controlling our feelings.'

She turned, and with a toss of her long, golden hair, walked quickly across the reception area towards the central stairway without looking back.

3. **Energies**

I sat at home with my mother that evening. She'd made my favourite meal, lasagne and Greek salad, and although I appreciated the gesture, I didn't have much of an appetite. Too much was going on in my head and the breakfast room felt empty with just the two of us there. It had only been a couple of weeks since Granddad died and we felt his absence keenly. My mother turned on the television trying to fill the silence.

'Emmerdale?' she asked.

I shrugged my shoulders. 'Yeah, whatever. I don't mind.'

The news was finishing. It was that bit at the end where they add a feel-good story or showbiz gossip, and I froze when I saw Kimberley Chartreuse's image fill the screen. No, I thought, it's not possible. They can't know what happened to her.

'And now for the latest news from the world of show business,' announced the presenter. 'Ex-glamour model, authoress and multi-millionaire businesswoman, Kimberley Chartreuse, has announced her immediate retirement, raising questions about her health. It's rumoured she may be having a breakdown or suffering from a terminal illness, but sources close to her remain silent. However, die-hard Kimberley fans need not despair, as they haven't quite seen the last of her.'

I stared, aghast. What was going on? I'd seen her disintegrate into dust.

'Her place will be filled by her identical twin sister, Janey Juggler, and by all accounts, it's impossible to tell the difference,' said the announcer gleefully. The screen was filled with another Kimberley look-alike, speaking to camera, all big hair, white teeth, bronzed skin and heaving chest.

'My sister decided she'd had enough of the limelight,' she drawled in a pseudo trans-Atlantic accent. 'Her agent called and asked if I'd like to take her place, so what's a girl to do? I accepted, of course.'

'I can't believe they've put a story like this on the national news,' said my mother, changing the channel. 'Do they think we're interested?'

'Obviously they do,' I murmured, not giving anything away. If only people knew the real story! It would have made international headlines. I shuddered when I remembered the last few seconds of Kimberley's untimely death. Then reality hit me. That might be me in two weeks' time. In fact, it was less than two weeks until the next full moon. If I went the same way as Kimberley, these might be my last few days alive. I looked at my mother with tears in my eyes, thinking how much I loved her. I couldn't bear for her to be left alone, not so soon after we'd lost Granddad.

'How was college today?' asked my mother brightly, trying to make conversation.

'Okay,' I answered, pushing the bad thoughts out of my head. 'Double English Lit with Miss Widdicombe was a pain, but Art was great. We're starting a new project: 'Interpret the theme of duality using recycled materials.' I thought I'd do a collage depicting light and dark, with crushed up light bulbs, newspaper, egg shells and bits of wood.'

It occurred to me that I might not be around to see the completion of my art project and I pushed that thought away too. I had to be positive.

'Actually, mum, could you get me some shavings from the wood yard?'

I was referring to the local timber company, where my mother worked as an admin assistant.

'Speaking of the wood yard,' said my mother, a dreamy look coming into her eyes, 'there's someone I'd like you to meet. His name's Juke.'

'Ah, the mystery man,' I said, with sudden interest.

'May be,' she replied, looking pleased.

It had been so long since my mum had been on a date, let alone had a relationship, it was hard to get my head around her having a boyfriend.

'Juke,' I repeated. 'Are you going to tell me about him?'

She smiled self-consciously. 'Well, he's really nice. Good looking and chivalrous.'

'Chivalrous!' I laughed. 'What kind of a word is that, mum? Is he, like, a knight on a horse?'

'Of course not, don't be stupid,' she flushed slightly. 'I mean he's kind and thoughtful, like nothing's too much trouble.'

'He's got dreadlocks,' she added as an after-thought.

'Dreads!' I exclaimed. 'OMG, what is he, an aging hippy?'

'No. He's very cool. In fact, you can meet him. He's coming round tonight.'

Hearing my mother describe her new man as cool was bad enough. But having to meet him made me feel very uncomfortable. What if they held hands? What if they kissed?

'Really? He's coming here? I might not be around. Theo's coming over. We're going out for a drive. In fact, he should be here by now. Let me text him.'

I quickly typed a message into my phone:

'Hi Light Boy, Where r u? How kwik can u get here? Need 2 c u. x'

He replied instantly:

'Faster than speed of light. At front door. xxx '

Right on cue, the doorbell sounded.

'There he is,' I said with relief, getting up from the table.

I went into the hallway, forcing myself to walk slowly. Anticipation was everything. I felt my body tingle and my breath quicken. How could one person have this effect on another? I'd hated being apart from him today, every minute had seemed like an eternity. Any second now and I'd be in his arms, feeling his energy around me, protective and all consuming. I opened the front door, a smile on my lips, and there he was. My Theo, standing on the front door step, dazzling, intoxicating and beautiful, dressed in a white linen shirt with the sleeves rolled up and torn, pale blue jeans. He smiled, just as a brief burst of evening sunshine lit the sky, illuminating him and giving him an ethereal glow. For a moment, I simply stood there, drinking in his physical perfection, his smooth skin, shining blond hair and azure blue eyes. Then I was in his arms and reality ceased to exist. He was my world, my future, my destiny. I felt his lips on mine and as we kissed, his energy filled my being with a white hot, molten intensity. I surrendered to the moment, until I remembered we were still on the doorstep and that Mrs Brown opposite might be watching. I pulled away.

'I've missed you today, Theo, so much. But we can't do this on the doorstep.'

He grinned. 'Better invite me in.'

I pulled him in and closed the front door. Once again I was in his arms, savouring the feel of his lips on my neck, cheeks and mouth, his warm, protective energy surrounding me like a cloak, enfolding and caressing. Never before had I felt so totally loved and adored. All doubts about my forthcoming initiation melted away. This is what I wanted, for now and eternity. Always to be with this beautiful, shimmering creature, who gave every moment an intensity I'd never known before.

'I thought we could put Martha through her paces,' I said huskily, breaking away and referring to my newly refurbished, freshly painted cream Mini that stood on the pathway, gleaming and sparkling, like a tantalising temptress. As much as I could have stayed in the hallway kissing Theo all evening, I wanted to cram as much as I could into my limited time as an ordinary 17-year old girl.

'If that's what you want to do,' said Theo, drawing back.

For a brief moment, I looked into his eyes, mesmerised by their light and colour. It was like falling into a kaleidoscope, the myriad of flecks and hues constantly alternating, azure turning into sapphire, cornflower into cobalt, indigo into cyan… electric, dazzling, bewitching. I felt myself drowning in the endless blue, never wanting to surface, losing myself forever in their unfathomable depths. I forced myself to look away and break the spell.

'Yeah, I do. Let's go.'

Grabbing my blue Hollister jacket, I called back to my mother: 'Theo and I are going out for a drive. Catch you later. And Juke if he's here.'

'Juke?' questioned Theo.

'My mum's new boyfriend. She met him at the wood yard. He has dreads.'

'Dreads?' said Theo, in disbelief. 'What is he? A 90s throwback?'

'Shush,' I said, as my mother put her head around the breakfast room door.

'Hi Theo,' she fluttered at him.

'Hi, Mrs Morgan, how are you?'

'All the better for seeing you.'

'Mum,' I said uneasily, 'stop being so embarrassing.'

'It's okay, Emily,' said Theo, smiling. 'I can cope with it.'

'You're as bad as she is,' I said, incredulously. 'Perhaps I should leave you two together.'

'Go on,' said my mother, laughing. 'I can dream, can't I? Now, don't be late and don't drive too fast.'

'Okay,' I said, knowing that not being late was achievable, but not driving fast was impossible, given that my newly souped-up Mini was fitted with a V8 engine and my boyfriend was a supernatural speed freak.

I graciously allowed Theo to drive and sat alongside him, breathing in the scent of Martha's newly-fitted white leather upholstery. Theo turned to me, smiling wickedly, with a gleam in his eye.

'Are you ready? Better hold on tight.'

I squealed as he put his foot down and Martha shot forward. In no time, we were out of the village and tearing along a stretch of motorway that was thankfully free of speed cops, Martha eating up the miles with an appetite she'd never had before her refurb. I could swear she was actually enjoying it.

'It's like she's alive,' I shouted to Theo over the noise of her throaty engine.

'Typical woman,' he shouted back. 'Loves power.'

I pressed the button on the new Fender sound system and the sound of Bastille singing Of The Night filled the cabin. I turned up the volume to max and the sensation was electric. The low, powerful growl of the engine combined with the awesome acoustics and the blur of fields and trees flashing by was mind-blowing. Add to that I was sitting next to the most exquisite, intoxicating creature, who loved me with a passion, and I felt I was the luckiest girl in the world.

We left the motorway and Theo drove along country lanes, the evening sun dying before our eyes in a last blast of orange and pink, darkness creeping upon us, velvety and black. It was a clear night without a cloud in the sky and soon the stars appeared as tiny pinpricks, and a new crescent moon hung suspended, silvery and bright. Theo pressed a button and Martha's panoramic sunroof slid back, revealing the heavens above us in all their glory. He turned

Martha off the road onto a narrow farm track and brought her to a halt. We reclined the seats as far back as they would go and lay alongside each other, gazing up at the open sky. I pressed play on the sound system and the sound of Counting Stars by One Republic filled the air. Theo's hand found mine and we lay there, our fingers intertwined, breathing in the clear night air, encapsulated in our own world, the solar system above us. We didn't speak or kiss or cuddle. We didn't need to. Just holding hands was enough, Theo's energy passing into my fingertips and pulsating round my body, like a mercurial life force. I don't think I had ever felt so complete, fulfilled or perfectly at peace. I felt I held the universe in my hands, right there and then, lying next to Theo in my small cream Mini, in a country lane.

The song came to an end and it was time to go. Theo started the engine and he drove us home, my hand lightly on his thigh, needing the physical contact. All too soon, the journey was over and we were back on my driveway. Theo killed the engine and we sat in silence. I turned to him.

'That was amazing. Thank you.'

He looked at me tenderly and smiled.

'If you think that was amazing, wait until you're initiated. Once you've bathed in the crystal's light, every experience will be intensified a hundred times over. Your senses will come alive and you'll see, feel and hear things you never knew existed. What you're experiencing now will fade into insignificance. Everything will be sharper, brighter, more intense than you ever imagined.' He stopped. 'As long as you make it. If anything happened to you…' his voice dropped to a whisper and I felt his pain like a frozen shard entering my heart, 'I couldn't carry on, Emily.'

'Theo, I'll be fine. I promise,' I said softly. 'Don't forget, I've already touched the crystal and I was okay.'

'It will be more powerful at the time of the full moon,' he said in an anguished voice. 'We have to face it, there is a chance you might not survive.'

'What does it feel like?' I asked, fighting the dizziness that threatened to creep into my head. 'What does the first time feel like?'

'I can't say,' he answered. 'It was different for me. My parents were light bodies, so I already had the genetic make-up. I just needed charging up, as it were. But from what I've heard, the first time isn't always pleasant,' His voice dropped a tone. 'No one can prepare you for the experience, Emily.'

'What did you hear?' I asked, feeling a shadow of fear pass over me.

'They say it's like a white hot burning sensation that consumes every part of you, every sinew and every cell,' he said. 'You feel like you're burning up, but you're freezing cold. The pressure on your system is intense, as your heart, your brain, all your internal organs fight the process. By all accounts, you feel like you're going to break apart. You have to remember, your whole molecular structure is changing and it affects every part of you, every atom. Some say it's an agonising, unbearable experience and takes months to get over. Some come through it unscathed. Others don't make it at all. Can you see now why I'm afraid for you?'

I gulped as I took in his words. So far, death had been an abstract thought and I hadn't really bought into it. Now, just as I was feeling invincible and indestructible, just when I'd fallen in love and life was full of possibilities, I was being forced to consider how it might feel.

I strengthened my resolve and spoke with conviction: 'Theo de Lucis, I'm going to make it. You just watch me. I'm made of strong stuff. Now, are you going to come in? Mum will kill me if you don't, and all chat this will be irrelevant.'

'Okay,' he smiled. 'I'd better come in.'

I opened the front door and heard the sound of a man laughing, followed by my mother speaking. They were in the lounge.

'OMG,' I whispered to Theo. 'It's her boyfriend. She's with Juke. Shall we go and say hello? What do you think?'

'I think we should check him out,' said Theo. 'You go first.'

I cautiously pushed open the lounge door and peeked in. My mother and Juke sat together on the sofa, sharing a beer and a joke, and I felt a stab of jealousy. It seemed wrong to see an outsider occupying the safe, secure place that belonged to my mother and me. I saw my mother's happy face. I had to admit, it was good to see her laughing. She'd had a tough time over the last few weeks and needed to lighten up. He was just the tonic she needed.

'Hi,' I said brightly, stepping into the room. 'You must be Juke.'

I'd never seen anyone quite like him. At first glance, he looked like an eco-warrior, more at home on a protest march or at a hippy festival than sitting in a nice house in a middle class village. He was early forties, I guessed, with tanned, leathery skin and long bleached blond dreads, interwoven with beads, hanging down either side of his face. He wore an old denim shirt with a leather thong knotted at his throat, and black jeans, tucked into shabby leather boots. A battered old rucksack was thrown carelessly to one side of the sofa. I stared, fascinated by his lived-in physicality, noticing the clearly defined biceps beneath his shirt, and his calloused, powerful hands. I could see why my mother was attracted to him. He was different, exotic. This was a man who'd peeled back the outer layer of life and looked beneath, tuning in to a rhythm I barely knew existed.

'And you must be Emily,' he said with a faint Aussie accent.

He smiled and immediately his eyes were surrounded by a myriad of laughter lines, his tanned, crinkly skin emphasising their twinkling deep blue. Although I fought the impulse, I couldn't help but like him. He might be rough around the edges, but there was a warmth and genuineness to him. He stood up and approached me, holding out his hand.

'Pleased to meet you.'

'Likewise,' I said, shaking his hand.

There was a musky, earthy smell about him that wasn't unpleasant, just very different from Theo's cut-glass glamour and sleek sophistication. He gripped my hand in a powerful handshake that spoke of strength and determination, and just as he let go, I felt a residue of energy skim past me, cool and wispy, like a faint silver skin. It was over in a split second, and whatever it was dissipated immediately into the air, but I definitely felt it.

'This is Theo,' I announced.

'Good to meet you, mate,' said Juke, grasping Theo's hand.

'Hi,' said Theo, eyeing him suspiciously.

I watched to see what would happen and sure enough, I saw the same flimsy silver film leave Juke's fingers, once again rippling into the air, before dissipating quickly. It was over in a flash, but I knew Theo had seen it, and judging by his face, it had spooked him.

Juke looked at him for a moment longer than was necessary, his eyes moving around, as if he was sizing Theo up, then grinned and said: 'Fancy a beer?'

'Yeah, come and sit with us,' said my mother, indicating the sofa on the other side of the room.

I wasn't sure I liked the 'us' my mother was referring to, and for the first time in my life, I felt like a parent. Who was this man? Was he suitable for my mother? She obviously liked him, but what did we know about him? Was he going to love and leave her? Or would he stick around? I remembered how my Granddad had grilled Theo and I followed suit.

'I gather you work at the wood yard, Juke,' I said, going into interview mode. 'What do you do?'

He grinned at me, his leathery face folding into deeply etched laughter lines, and his eyes flashing sapphire blue.

'I drive a fork lift truck,' he answered. ' I spend my day moving bits of wood around.'

'I see. And where do you come from?'

'Melbourne. In Australia.'

'Yes, I know where it is. How long have you been in the UK?'

'Emily, what is this?' said my mother. 'Stop asking so many questions.'

'No worries,' said Juke. 'She's just checking me out, looking after her ma. I understand.'

I glanced at Theo and tried to stifle a smirk. No worries! This man was the original Aussie cliché. But Theo failed to see the joke. His face was expressionless.

'In answer to your question, Emily,' said Juke, 'I've been in and out of the UK for the last twenty years. I'm a traveller. I follow my dreams, go where the fancy takes me, and where I can get work. Meeting your mother at the wood yard has been an extra bonus.'

He winked at her and my mother flushed and giggled. She was behaving like a teenager. How embarrassing was that?

'Emily, I need to go,' said Theo, quietly. 'It's getting late.'

'Okay,' I said, surprised, but aware that something wasn't right. 'If you're sure.'

Theo turned to Juke. 'Nice to meet you. See you again.'

He clearly couldn't wait to get out of the room.

'Yeah, catch you later, mate,' said Juke.

Once again, I had the impression he was sizing Theo up. Something was going on between them and I intended to find out what it was.

'Goodnight, Mrs Morgan,' said Theo, stooping to kiss my mother on the cheek, which made her flush even deeper.

'I'll see you out,' I murmured, following him into the hallway and closing the lounge door behind me. I turned to face him.

'Okay, spill!' I said, in an urgent whisper. 'I saw that ectoplasm stuff come out of his fingers. What was all that about?'

'You did?' asked Theo, sounding surprised.

'Yes, I did. I'm sensitive to these things. And I saw him looking at you. What was he doing?'

'He's an energy sensor,' said Theo. 'He tunes in to people's energies.'

'You mean like Violet?' I knew his sister had the gift to see auras. She'd seen mine was bright blue.

'Similar. His second sight is really strong. I can feel it.'

'He's not dangerous is he?' I asked, suddenly scared for my mother.

'I don't think so,' said Theo. 'He's not dark matter. There's a brightness about him. But it's no coincidence he's suddenly shown up. I need to tell the family. Come back with me, Emily. You'll be safe at the hall.'

I thought how happy my mum looked, so alive and carefree. I hadn't seen her look like that for so long and I didn't want to burst the bubble. Not yet. I thought about Juke's eyes. You can tell a lot from looking into a person's eyes.

'I like him. He has good energy. We'll be fine.'

'Emily, you can't be too careful. Juke knows what I am. He recognised me the moment he saw me.' Theo's voice was tight and strained. 'We don't know what he wants. And whether he knows about the crystal.'

'I'm staying here,' I said firmly.

'Okay, but I'm sending Aquila to watch over you. If he's not outside already.'

'Oh, great, just what we need. A big black scrawny eagle watching us through the windows.'

'Emily, there are enemies everywhere. We have to be on our guard, especially for the next couple of weeks.' Theo sighed unhappily. 'This is going to be the longest fortnight of my life.'

'That's saying something,' I joked, 'given how long you've lived.'

'Exactly,' he said, without smiling.

4. **Nightmare**

Mr Nelson tossed and turned on his makeshift bed, his mind feverish and troubled. Once again, he was having the recurring dream. As before, he was in a long, dark tunnel, the walls slimy and damp with mildew and moss, an overwhelming stench of dampness permeating the air, making it hard to breath. Old water dripped down from overhead, slicing into his head like needle-sharp knifepoints. He tried to move faster, but his feet were caught in the fetid sludge that ran along the base of the passageway. It was an ancient sewer, rancid and putrid, with years-old matter all around him.

On he went, his feet squelching in the viscous mess, trying to breathe but nearly gagging on the sulphurous blasts. Ahead he could see a faint glimmer of light and knew he had to keep going. The alternative was unthinkable, falling beneath the bilge and suffocating as the ancient excreta of people long dead filled his airways. Perspiration broke out on his brow and his heart hammered against his ribs as if demanding to be let out. Slowly, the light got closer, but every step was a massive effort as his muscles tired and his lungs screamed for air.

Then, mercy above, he was reaching the light and salvation was at hand. Taking what could have been his last breath, so thick and heavy were the fermenting fumes, he fell rather than climbed out of the old brick passageway. Immediately, the air was cleaner and he took deep, rasping breaths with the desperation of a drowning man. Gradually, his faculties returned and he looked around.

He was in a large, cavernous chamber, as he knew he would be. Not that he was able to see much, as an oppressive dark mist swirled around, filling the vast proportions he sensed rather than saw, making everything appear filmy and black. He walked forward slowly, his eyes adjusting to the low light. Through the mist, he could just make out huge arches rising above him, creating a lofty, vaulted ceiling and massive stone pillars on an industrial scale disappearing into the emptiness above from the broken rubble that littered the floor. It was a disused, discarded, forgotten world, full of broken dreams and abandoned hope, and he felt despair and desolation creep into his head with spidery fingers.

He knew he wasn't alone. There were always others around. They were just too flimsy and wraithlike to make out, too lacking in substance to have any form. Dark shadows watching and waiting, ready to prey on his fear and panic. Except he didn't feel fear and panic, which was probably why he survived. He had been summoned for a special purpose. He was the chosen one, with a role to perform and a destiny to fulfil. He knew this because the Dark One had told him. He'd been here on many occasions and each time the Dark One had shared secrets with him, giving him power and knowledge others could only dream of possessing. It was the Dark One who'd told him about the blue crystal, of its amazing power to bestow eternal youth on those who bathed in its light, how the rich and famous paid handsomely to enjoy such privilege and how it had been stolen from its resting place many centuries earlier.

He knew he played a vital role in the plan to restore the crystal to its rightful owner, bestowing life and humanity on those who lived in the darkness, capable only of leading shadow lives. He would be their saviour and messiah. The Dark One had told him so. If he made a few bucks along the way, sharing the information with those desperate for eternal youth, there was no harm done. Well, apart from that unfortunate woman. He hadn't realised the crystal could be quite so destructive. If he'd known, he'd have warned her. Of course he would, he told himself, thinking of the wads of cash that lay beneath his stinking mattress. He probably shouldn't have betrayed the Dark One's trust, but how would he ever know? Besides, there was a plan to put into action. He assumed that was why he'd been summoned.

A movement to his left made him turn sharply. This was a cavern of secrets and perils. You had to be on your guard, protect yourself against the horrors that lurked in the filmy darkness.

'You have come,' spoke a voice, somewhere from the depths of the chamber. It was a slithering, sibilant voice that hissed rather than enunciated, echoing throughout the underground chamber, leaving a remnant of threat and menace hanging in the air. 'Come closer that I may look into your thoughts. Approach....'

Mr Nelson moved forward as he was bid, fear and excitement coursing through his veins. Perhaps this time he might see the face behind the voice, glimpse the creature that had promised him so much, whose destiny lay within his making.

'I see you shared our secret with another,' hissed the disembodied voice. 'That was unwise. How can I trust you not to do the same again?'

'Just a little business…' began Mr Nelson, in his flat Black Country accent, but got no further.

'Silence,' screeched the voice, with the sound of a hundred nails being dragged across a blackboard, searing Mr Nelson's insides and making him put his hands to his ears.

'I know what you are, you stinking piece of filth. You think you can follow your own agenda, when I have asked you to work for me. Am I not giving you enough? Have I not promised you the world and more? Perhaps I should let you feel the power of my wrath.'

As he spoke, Mr Nelson experienced the sensation of being torn apart by wild animals; the stretching, tearing, cutting and biting searing every part of his body with an agony so intense, he dropped to his knees, screaming in pain. No sooner had it started than the sensation stopped.

'Enough,' said the voice. 'I need your loyalty not your duplicity. Do I make myself clear?'

'Yes,' said Mr Nelson, his voice catching in his throat, attempting to get back to his feet. 'Sorry. It's just my line of work. Old habits die hard, you know. You have my unerring loyalty, I promise.'

'Very well, the time has come for action. I need the crystal. I have waited too long in the shadows, without form or function, and Viyesha has enjoyed the wealth and power that was rightfully mine for too long. Bring me the girl. The family cannot stand back and let her endure the tortures of the void. Once I have her, I will exploit their weakness.'

The voice was getting louder and closer, and appeared to be coming from over his right shoulder. Mr Nelson turned sharply, trying to see through the darkness and discover the identity of this tortured soul who craved the crystal so desperately. Momentarily, the dark mist lifted, giving him a fleeting vision that chilled his blood and very nearly made his heart stop dead in its tracks. He couldn't see the owner of the hissing, reptilian voice, but he could see what the chamber contained. Surrounding him on all sides and suspended high up in the vaults, he saw row upon row of strange black creatures, dark and malevolent, their glittering eyes watching him carefully. As his eyes focused on the legions of black entities all around him, he was filled with a loathing and dread so powerful he thought his head would explode. He felt he was experiencing all the negative thoughts of the world concentrated in this one place; thick, crushing and unrelenting, extinguishing any warmth and vitality he might possess. And underneath the misery and pain was a vitriol and menace, so evil and malevolent, he could feel the poison seeping into his soul.

The oily, sibilant voice spoke again, whispering into his ear, so close Mr Nelson could almost feel its presence touching his shoulder. Only now he was too afraid to look.

'I will have human form once again. Eternal youth and beauty will once more be mine. Bring the girl to the crypt at St. Michael's and All Angels' Church. That is the entrance to my world. Once I have her it is only a matter of time until I have the crystal… Bring me the girl…'

The voice began to fade into the swirling dark mist and, overcome with nausea and fear, Mr Nelson felt himself falling back. Deeper and deeper he fell until he landed with a jolt, the impact causing him to open his eyes wide. He looked around, eyeing his derelict surroundings with relief: the damp, peeling wallpaper; the dirty, stained carpet; the unwashed coffee cups and overflowing ashtrays; the empty whisky bottles and beer cans littered around him. It wasn't great here in the squat but this was a squalor he could cope with, was quite at home with, lying on this miserable old sofa, springs and stuffing coming out from all angles. It was one of many safe houses he used ever since he'd seen Leon de Lucis sniffing round his office and knew they were on to him. He needed to lie low for a while, but that wasn't a problem. It wasn't the first time he'd had to disappear for a while.

Slowly, he got up and stretched his body, trying to rid his mind of the dream's disturbing images and force the overpowering negativity from his head. He reached for his old Columbo-style raincoat that he'd placed beside him before he'd fallen into his drunken stupor, and realised it was missing.

'Typical,' he groaned to himself. 'They'll take the coat off your back, soon as look at you. What would anyone want with my grubby old mac? Good job I have a few more stashed away.'

Putting the issue out of his mind, he focused on the task in hand.

5. **Enemies**

Early the next morning, just as the first light of dawn was breaking, the de Lucis family convened once again in the library. As before, Aquila and Pantera were also there. It was a brief meeting, but none the less serious for its brevity.

'Theo tells me we have an energy sensor in the village,' Viyesha informed them. 'Violet, have you detected any abnormal energies around the hall?'

'No, I haven't,' she answered. 'Who is this person?'

'Emily's mother has acquired a new boyfriend,' explained Theo. 'He recognised what I am straight away, which really threw me. He's definitely not dark matter, but we need to tread carefully. We don't know why he's here.'

'I agree,' said Leon. 'This is more than coincidence. If he knows about us, he may know about the crystal.' He addressed the chauffeur, who stood scowling by the door. 'Aquila, you were on guard outside Emily's house last night. Did you see anything to cause alarm?'

'No,' Aquila spat out the word, as if it had a bad taste. 'Nothing happened. The energy sensor stayed for half an hour after Theo left. Then he returned to his lodgings. No cause for alarm.'

'Nevertheless, remain vigilant,' instructed Leon. 'Keep an eye on him, especially when he's in contact with Emily. He's here for a reason and we need to know what it is.'

'Pantera, did you have any luck finding Mr Nelson last night?' asked Viyesha, looking towards the housekeeper.

'No. I picked up his scent in his office, rancid it was too, enough to turn the stomach of the most hardened predator. That man is bad all the way through. I searched the streets but found nothing. He's around. I know it. Give me time. I'll find him.'

'Okay, everyone,' said Leon, 'let's keep our guard up. Joseph, be especially watchful for anyone approaching the hall through the gardens. If there's any cause for suspicion, act quickly. We cannot afford to make mistakes.'

'You can count on me,' said Joseph, with his customary smile, spreading sunlight and goodwill across the group.

The group broke up, aware that events could become critical at any moment. Only Pantera and Aquila remained in the library, talking under their breath.

'Do you think the energy sensor is a threat?' asked Pantera.

Aquila smiled uncharacteristically, giving prominence to his beaked nose and revealing stained, yellow teeth. 'We can only hope so. If he took the girl, he'd do us all a favour. The Lunari would never allow us to bargain for her release. They'd regard her as an unfortunate casualty.'

'So, if you see something...' said Pantera.

'You have my assurance. I will do nothing. One way or another, we will rid ourselves of this irritation and restore the family to what it once was.'

Quietly, they left the library, each feeling a sense of hope they hadn't experienced for some time.

6. **Seth's Proposition**

We crowded round the noticeboard in the school reception area, trying to get a glimpse of the poster that had been pinned up.

'What is it?' I asked Tash, who had managed to push to the front and read the details.

'True Blue Impromptu Prom,' she said, coming back to join me at the edge of the crowd. 'Next Saturday, in the school hall. Miss Widdicombe is organising it as a thank you to the Lower Sixth for doing so well this year.'

'Miss Widdicombe?' I said in disbelief. 'She thinks we're all hopeless. She's always saying so.'

'Well, whatever,' said Tash. 'Maybe we're not as bad as we think. Oh, hang on, I get it. The band playing is Blue Walrus. That's her son's band. She's doing this as a showcase for him.'

'Pukka band, from what I've heard,' said Seth, fighting his way out of the crowd and joining us. 'They've been getting some good reviews locally.'

'What d'you think?' asked Tash. 'Worth going? Or perhaps it's beneath you, Emily,' she added spitefully, 'now you've decided your future is with Theo.'

I ignored her taunt. 'Why not?' I answered. 'It might be fun.'

'Count me in,' said Seth. 'Any excuse to show my moves to the ladies.'

He spun round like an out-of-control robot and we both stared at him.

'Move like that and you'll empty the dance floor,' said Tash. 'Dancing is definitely not your thing.'

'Under appreciated and misunderstood, that's me,' he said, grinning amiably. 'You don't recognise talent when it's right under your nose, Tash.'

'More like a bad smell,' she pointed out.

'Cruel,' he answered back. 'Just as well I know you love me really.'

'In your dreams, bad boy.'

I watched them banter, feeling strangely distant. Since I'd told them of my plans to join Theo, a gulf had opened up between us.

They were still my friends, but everything had shifted. I was about to enter a different world and that meant leaving them behind. I don't know how I would have felt had the tables been turned: let down, betrayed, scared, angry. They were all those things, I knew, but I had no choice. I had to join the de Lucis family. It was my only chance of staying alive and it meant I would be with Theo forever. For eternity. This is what happened, I guessed, as you grew older. Sometimes you had to make the choice between love and friendship.

'Is there a theme?' I asked, determined to go to the prom, and wondering if I'd have time to get a dress.

'Yeah, it says the theme is blue. Wear anything, as long as it's blue,' said Tash. 'To go with Blue Walrus, I suppose.'

'Are you going, Emily?' asked Seth. 'Won't it all be a bit too 'normal' for you?' He made inverted comma signs with his fingers. 'I mean, there'll be no blue crystal to bathe in, no eternally young beings, no Hollywood superstars. You know, all those things you've become used to at a party.'

I gave him a withering glance.

'Don't even go there, Seth,' I warned him. 'Look, we have less than two weeks to make the most of our friendship while I'm still like this. Are you going to keep pushing me away?'

'Emily,' said Seth, putting his arm around me and giving me a hug, 'you don't get it, do you? We don't want to lose our friend. You're too precious.'

Luckily, the bell for first lessons sounded and I was able to make my getaway, so they couldn't see the tears in my eyes.

Late morning, events took an unexpected turn. I was sitting in the cafeteria on my own, enjoying a free period. I'd seen Theo briefly, first thing, but he had a personal tutorial and a morning of lectures, and we'd agreed to meet at lunchtime. Violet had been shadowing me all morning, but couldn't escape her Philosophy teacher, who wanted to discuss her latest essay and, reluctantly, she'd left me alone. Seth and Tash both had lessons, so I took the opportunity to sit, with a hot chocolate, trying to get to grips with Faustus. I didn't really want to read about a man who made a pact with the devil, selling his soul in return for power and knowledge. Was I any better? Was I clutching at dreams that would inevitably fall to dust in my hands? It didn't make me feel good and I pushed the book away, staring out of the window. I took out my iPod and put in my earphones, listening to my new find, Jagaara. I was soon lost in the hypnotic rhythm of their song, Heartbeats, and totally failed to notice Seth sliding onto the seat next to me.

'Penny for your thoughts. On second thoughts, keep them, I don't want to know.'

'Seth,' I cried, with a start, pulling out my earphones. 'Don't do that, creeping up on me. You nearly gave me a heart attack. I thought you had lessons this morning?'

He grinned. 'I do. I'm playing hooky.'

'Why?' I asked.

'Because I needed to see you, Emily. That's why.'

'Oh Seth, we're not going through all this again, are we? My mind's made up.'

He held up his hands. 'Okay, I get it. But I don't want to talk about that.'

'You don't?' I asked, surprised.

'Nope. I have something far more important to discuss.'

'Okay,' I said, intrigued. 'I'm all ears….'

'Now, that is a weird thing to say, when you think about it. How can a person be all ears? The visual image is disturbing to say the least.'

'D'you want to discuss the vagaries of the English language or is there something you really want to say?'

'It's like this, Em,' he shifted awkwardly. 'This prom thing. D'you wannna go with me?'

His words took me by surprise. I hadn't even mentioned the prom to Theo, who would have been my first choice of partner.

'With you?' I said, sounding rather more condescending than I intended.

'Yeah,' he said defensively. 'What's so strange about that?'

'Nothing, absolutely nothing,' I backtracked. 'I'm just surprised that's all. I mean, I haven't definitely decided I'm going yet. And there is Theo to think about.'

'Oh, yeah, golden boy. Are you going with him?'

'We haven't discussed it.'

'I was just thinking about what you said this morning,' Seth explained. 'You know, about making the most of our friendship before you change. And I thought, why not? It'll be the one and only chance I ever have to take you to a prom.' He smiled sadly. 'You know I've always liked you, Emily. And I can't compete with Theo. But I can offer you a normal life. It's worth thinking about.'

'Hang on,' I said, hardly believing what I was hearing. 'Are you asking to take me to the prom or spend the rest of my life with you? You're a fast mover, Seth, I'll say that for you.'

'Prom. Rest of your life,' he placed his hands one on either side, as if weighing up the two options. 'What's the difference?'

'Er, rather a lot. Where's all this come from?'

'Seems to me you're at a crossroads in life,' he said, looking uncharacteristically serious, 'and you need to think very hard about which way you'll go. With me, you could be normal. No weird initiation ceremony, no risk of premature death, well, unless that's what you wanted. I'm sure I could arrange something.'

I still wasn't quite sure what he was saying.

'Let me get this straight. You're asking me to go to the prom. But you're also asking if I want a relationship with you?'

'Yeah. That's about it. We've always got on well. We know each other inside out. Well, not literally. That would be weird. Gross, more like.'

'Seth, shut up. Why ask me now?' I demanded. 'Why couldn't you ask me, say, six months ago. It was all different then.'

'Because six months ago, I didn't know I'd feel like this.'

'So, it's only the thought of losing me that's made you realise you have feelings for me?'

'Yeah. No. I guess I've always had feelings for you. I just didn't recognise it. Will you at least think about what I've said?' He looked at me with his big, brown puppy-dog eyes and my heart melted.

Seth, the boy next door, the boy with whom I'd grown up, shared secrets and discussed things I'd never mentioned to anyone else. It felt like I'd known him forever. I thought about all we'd done together over the years: made dens in the garden, gone cycling round the village lanes, played monopoly for ten hours once when it hadn't stopped raining, hung out in the park, swopped books, texted each other. He was the boy I always thought I'd end up with, thinking if I waited long enough, my feelings would be reciprocated. Then Theo had come into my life and everything else had paled into insignificance.

'Oh, Seth, why did you wait until now? Why couldn't you have said something before?' I said sadly.

'Look, I'm offering you an alternative,' he said, passionately. 'A different way to Theo. Doing normal things. I mean, we could even get married.'

'Whoa,' I said, opening my eyes wide, 'stop there. You've gone from asking me to the prom to proposing. Get a grip, Seth.'

'Well, I don't mean now. Obviously. Maybe some point in the future. I don't know.'

He looked at his watch. 'Gotta go. Tell me you'll at least think about it. The prom, that is. And the other bit, too.'

He stood up, all lanky arms and legs, and threw his backpack over his shoulder.

'You and I, Em, together we could go places.'

'And what about the Lunari?' I asked him. 'There's the slight problem that they might just kill us off.'

'Got that covered,' said Seth. 'We'll go to the police, tell them we're being threatened. The Lunari wouldn't dare do anything if they knew the police were watching, it would draw too much attention to them. And what's the one thing you don't want when you're a secret society? Public interest. So, sorted.'

'You've thought this through, haven't you?' I said.

'Yep, all came to me while Mr Green was boring us with the theory of relativity,' he paused, then spoke in his movie soundtrack voice: 'Emily Morgan, your future lies before you. Which road will you take? A life of laughter, fun and normality,' he lowered his voice, 'or one of shadows, weirdness and supernatural horror?'

I laughed. 'When you say it like that....'

I broke off when I saw a familiar face walk into the cafeteria. It was Theo.

'You'd better go,' I informed Seth. 'Theo's here. I will think about it. I promise.'

Seth saluted, and quickly walked towards the exit. I saw him mutter a brief word to Theo as he passed, and watched in horror as he did a vampire impression behind Theo's back. I suppressed a giggle, not knowing where to look.

'You look happy,' said Theo, sitting opposite me and taking my hands in his.

Immediately, I felt his energy pulse into my fingers, passing up my arms and into my body. It was the most amazing sensation. How could I possibly think about not being with him? Nothing else could ever come close to what he gave me. And yet, the thought of a normal life with Seth, the person who probably knew me better than anyone, except maybe Tash, was certainly tempting. I put the thought away and looked into Theo's eyes, falling into the deep pools of blue and never wanting to surface.

'I'm happy because you're here,' I answered. 'You make me feel amazing. I've never felt like this before about anyone.'

'The best is yet to come, Emily,' he said. 'Like I told you last night, this is nothing compared to crystal living.'

As he spoke, sparks of energy flew from his hands, filling my body with well-being. It was like being hooked up to a massive battery and feeling the energy direct from the source.

'Now, about this prom,' he said. 'Would you like me to escort you?'

I looked at him, not sure what to say. Did I owe it to Seth to go with him, while I was still human? Or should I go with Theo, as a sign of trust in our future and what was to come?

As if life wasn't complicated enough already, I had another dilemma on my hands.

7. **Undercurrents**

'I suppose you're going to the prom with Theo,' said Tash, sitting next to me, as I drove Martha to college. Seth had a dental appointment and wasn't coming in, which gave me a little breathing space.

'Yeah, probably,' I said non-committedly. I hadn't made a decision yet and I didn't feel like telling her about Seth's proposal, which was why her next words threw me.

'D'you think Seth would take me?'

'Seth?' I repeated stupidly. 'Why would you want Seth to take you?'

'Because I have no one else to go with. We don't all have beautiful boyfriends waiting in the wings.'

I ignored the dig and considered her question. I couldn't tell her Seth had already asked me. That seemed too cruel.

'I don't know, Tash. Is there nobody else you'd rather go with? What about Lewis Sheldon? You like him. Or Stuart Leonard? You've always had a thing about him.'

'Yes, but I can't ask them, can I? How desperate would that look? And they might say no.'

'Okay, you've got a point. I suppose Seth is the only boy you could ask and it wouldn't be taken the wrong way.'

'Exactly. So, d'you think I should ask him?'

'Tell you what, let me have a word with him first and see how the land lies.'

'Okay. Good idea,' she said, brightening up. 'I've seen this amazing blue dress in Top Shop, which would look fantastic. After college, I'm going into town to get it. I just don't want to be all dressed up and have no one to go with.'

'Leave it with me,' I said, sounding more confident than I felt. What was I going to say to Seth? And what would Tash say if she knew Seth had already asked me?

'Do you want me to come into town with you?' I asked.

'Would you?'

'Of course. You are still my best friend, you know.'

At last, Tash and I seemed to be on firmer ground. Except the web was to become even more tangled later that day.

It was a fairly ordinary day, if the word ordinary could ever be applied to my life again. I'd seen Theo briefly first thing and he seemed more relaxed than he'd been recently. He told me he was looking forward to the prom.

'It's the first prom I've ever been to,' he confided.

'You're kidding,' I said, amazed. 'The first prom in three thousand years? Where have you been?'

'I don't know,' he said. 'Just not the kind of places where people have proms.'

'Well, this isn't the full deal,' I explained. 'It's not like the big end of college prom, with limousines and ball gowns. This is mainly for Miss Widdicombe's son's benefit, from what I can gather. You know, give The Blue Walrus a chance to perform. Rumour has it there are some A&R people from a record company coming to watch.'

'Whatever the reason, I'm looking forward to it,' said Theo, 'and I'm especially looking forward to going with you.'

'Yeah, me too,' I said, wondering what I was going to say to Seth, wondering why I was even considering Seth's invitation, let alone his proposal to spend the rest of my life with him.

'I thought Aquila could take us in the Jaguar,' he said. 'You know, arrive in style.'

'What about Violet?' I asked. 'Won't she want chauffeuring?'

He grinned. 'I got there first.'

'We could always go in Martha,' I suggested. 'That would be cool.'

'Whatever you want. I don't mind, as long as I'm with you.'

The bell for lessons went at that point and we didn't get the chance to talk any further. Just when I thought it couldn't get any more complicated, Violet waded in and muddied the waters still further.

She joined Tash and me at lunchtime in the cafeteria, looking stunning as usual, in trendy Aztec leggings and a pale coral cable-knit sweater, her long blonde hair shining, as if she were fresh from a shampoo commercial. Everybody watched as she walked through the cafeteria to our table, looking cooler than was humanly possible, all the girls wanting to be her, all the boys wanting to be with her.

'Hi guys,' she said in her beautiful, clear voice. She sat down with us.

'No Theo?' she asked, with a frown.

'He's on his way,' I said. 'He just texted to say his tutorial's running late.'

'And Seth?'

'Day off. He's gone to the dentist.'

'Oh.' She looked a little disappointed. 'Still, while he's not here, can I pick your brains, Emily?'

'Sure,' I answered, wondering how someone like me could possibly advise someone like her.

'It's the prom,' she said, causing my insides to knot slightly. 'I was wondering if Seth would take me. Do you think there's a chance? I was wondering if you could have a word.'

'You'll have to get in the queue, Blondie,' said Tash, stepping in. 'Chances are he's going with me.'

'With you?' Violet couldn't hide the surprise in her voice. 'I didn't know you two were an item.'

'We're not,' said Tash defensively, 'but we're very good friends. And that's what counts.'

'Not when it comes to the prom,' answered Violet. 'I wanted to know if Seth would take me as a date, not as a friend.' She emphasised the word 'friend' to make it sound like something second rate.

I looked around me, wondering what I could say and was thankful to see Theo walking through the cafeteria.

'Here's Theo,' I said, loudly. 'Can we discuss this later?'

'Everything all right?' he asked, sitting next to me and placing his coffee cup on the table.

'Yes, fine,' I said, feeling suddenly tongue-tied. All roads led to the prom at the moment, and I began to wish that Miss Widdicombe had never arranged it.

'I have to go,' said Violet, getting up and tossing her golden hair behind her.

'I'll leave it with you, Emily,' she said cryptically, glancing sideways at Tash, then holding her head high and walking out of the cafeteria as if she owned the place.

'Leave what with you?' asked Theo, sipping his coffee.

'Oh, nothing, just talking about clothes for the prom,' I said lightly, not wanting to meet Tash's eye. I needed to think how to handle this.

'You'll all look gorgeous whatever you wear,' said Theo diplomatically, causing Tash to snort.

'Oh save it, Goldilocks,' she said rudely. 'I can honestly say I wish you and your family had never moved into the village. Everything was fine till you came along.'

I shook my head at Theo, warning him not to say anything.

'Some of us have lessons to go to,' she said, picking up her shoulder bag. 'I'll see you later, Emily. Okay?'

'Yeah, catch you later.'

She stomped bad-temperedly away from our table.

'What was all that about?' began Theo, looking baffled.

I intertwined my fingers between his.

'Don't ask. It's girls' stuff.'

I looked into his blue eyes and once again I was lost, with no chance of being saved, by Seth or anyone.

After college, Tash and I caught the bus into town.

'Honestly, can you believe the cheek of the girl?' asked Tash. 'Just because she's beautiful and has supernatural powers, she thinks she has first call on Seth. I mean, why on earth would he want to go to the prom with her? He doesn't even like her, does he?'

'I don't know,' I said miserably. 'I'm as baffled as you are. Can we concentrate on the dress, please?'

'Okay, here it is.'

We were in Top Shop and Tash picked out a long, royal blue dress hanging on a rail.

'I saw it online,' she explained. 'I'll try it on.'

Tash was blessed with a near perfect figure. She was tall, willowy and curvy in all the right places and proved to be the perfect clothes hanger for the slinky blue dress. She came out of the changing room looking like a goddess. The fabric clung to her body, showing off her figure and contrasting with her stunning red Pre-Raphaelite hair perfectly. She put on some high platform shoes and towered above me.

'Eat your heart out, Violet,' she said, preening in front of the mirror. 'What d'you think, Emily?'

'You look fabulous,' I said, and meant it. 'Can you afford it?'

'Whatever it costs, I'll pay,' said Tash, 'I aim to steal the floor a week on Saturday.'

'All this rivalry with Violet,' I said. 'Are you really interested in Seth? I thought you just wanted someone to take you to the prom. If Violet is really interested in him, wouldn't it be nicer to let them go together?'

'You don't get it, do you Emily?' asked Tash.

'Obviously not. What?'

'I don't like Violet. I never have and never will, especially if her family takes away my best friend. Why should I possibly do her any favours? As far as I'm concerned, it's every woman for herself. And if I can get Seth to take me to the prom and she doesn't like it, tough.'

She tottered back into the changing room, pulling the curtain behind her abruptly. I bit my lip, not knowing what to say. Something was going to go wrong. I felt it in my gut.

That evening, my mother announced Juke was coming over. We sat at our usual places in the breakfast room, eating a delicious meal of salmon marinated in ginger, lime and chilli, with a green leaf salad and new potatoes.

'This is really nice mum. Ever since you fell in love, you've been cooking lovely food,' I complimented her.

'Thanks, Emily, doesn't say much for my culinary efforts before, does it?' she laughed. 'And just for the record, I'm not in love, to quote the words of the song.'

'What song's that?' I asked.

'10cc. Before your time. But did you hear what I said? I'm not in love. And don't you go saying anything to Juke. He makes me laugh, he's different, and I'm well aware he's not going to stick around, so my heart is well and truly out of bounds.'

She began clearing our plates away, banging them together a little too noisily, and I knew I'd hit a nerve. She really liked him and I knew she was worried she'd get hurt. Twenty minutes later, the front doorbell sounded and there was Juke on the front step, all dreadlocks, twinkling eyes and tanned skin, a guitar case slung over one shoulder. The late evening sun shone behind him, giving the appearance of a strange, shimmering energy hanging around him. He leant forward and kissed my cheek and I had the same sensation of silvery-white phosphorescence skimming over me as before. It wasn't as powerful as the energy charge I got from Theo. This was more gentle and caressing, making me feel relaxed and laid back.

'Hi, Juke, come in. I see you've brought your guitar with you. I didn't know you played.'

'Yeah, the old guitar comes with me everywhere. I thought your mum might like to hear some music.'

'I would too,' I said, impressed. 'D'you sing as well?'

He smiled lazily. 'It has been known.'

'Hi Juke,' said my mother, appearing in the hallway, looking flushed and excited. 'Come on in, I'll get you a beer.'

Half an hour later, we were sitting in the lounge, listening to Juke sing and play his guitar. It was amazing, like nothing I'd heard before. He started off with a couple of old Aussie folk songs: Waltzing Matilda and Tom Traubert's Blues, then went into some Dire Straits, and was just starting a Jake Bugg song when the doorbell sounded.

'That'll be Theo,' I said, jumping up. 'He texted to say he'd be round soon.'

I wasn't sure how he would take to meeting Juke once again, but guessed he'd prefer to keep him in sight rather than letting him go off the radar. I still couldn't see Juke as a threat. He seemed too kind and friendly. I ran to the front door, preparing to look into those deep blue eyes and feeling that familiar tingle all over me. To my surprise, it wasn't Theo. It was Seth.

'Hi, Em,' he said, lounging against the doorframe.

'Hi, Seth. What are you doing here?'

'Well, I do live next door,' he pointed out.

'I wasn't expecting you, that's all.'

'Can I come in?' he asked.

'Yeah, sure, we're in the lounge, listening to Juke play his guitar.'

'Cool. Who's Juke?'

'My mum's new boyfriend. He works at the wood yard.'

'Oh yeah, you mentioned something about her having a new man.'

He walked into the hallway, and stopped to face me, his dark fringe falling over his face.

'Have you thought any more about what I said? I gave you some space today.'

'Is that why you weren't in?' I asked.

He wrinkled his nose. 'Partly. I had a dental appointment. And I hadn't finished my Geography essay. It seemed kinda better to stay away. So, anyway, have you made a decision?'

He looked at me hopefully, his eyes soft and chocolate-brown, making part of me melt. If only this had happened a year ago. Six months ago. Even a few weeks ago, things could have been so different.

'Er, no, I haven't, Seth. I don't know what to do. You've taken me by surprise.'

'That's me. Unpredonkable as ever.' He grinned.

'Still studying the urban dictionary, then?'

'Is it that obvious?'

'Yes. Look, why don't you come in and meet Juke?'

'Okay. Coola boola.'

I led him into the lounge and introduced him. 'This is Seth, he lives next door

'Hey man, pleased to meet you,' said Juke, shaking Seth's hand. 'I'm Juke Wellington.'

'Juke Wellington?' I queried.

'Yeah, my parents were jokers. And they liked jazz.'

Seth was delighted when he heard Juke's accent.

'Hey man, you're an Aussie,' he said, his eyes lighting up. 'Where ya from, dude?'

'Melbourne,' answered Juke, laughing at Seth's urban uncoolness, 'although I spent a lot of time in Sydney and the outback. My granddad used to live with the aborigines. He taught me to live off the land, so I still do it from time to time. Good for the soul.'

'Fair dinkum,' said Seth. 'Or should I say no worries?'

'Seth,' I said in embarrassment, 'shut up, will you?'

'Say what you like, mate. It's a free world,' said Juke smiling.

'Cool,' said Seth, grinning at his new friend.

I raised my eyes to the ceiling. He was incorrigible.

'You staying for a beer, Seth?' asked my mother.

'Thanks, Mrs M, that'd be great.'

My mother threw him a can and Juke picked up his guitar again.

'You got a favourite, Seth?' he asked.

'Can you do Love Me Again by John Newman?'

'Sure,' said Juke.

He proceeded to do the most fantastic acoustic rendition of the song and I thought Seth was going to fall over in admiration. He stared at Juke like a lovesick teenager, which I suppose he was. He was certainly experiencing a major man-crush.

'Amazing-dazing,' he said, when Juke finished.

I poked him in the ribs.

'Shut up, Seth, you are so not cool.'

Seth was unperturbed. 'Tell us about the outback, Juke,' he said, star-struck.

Juke laid down his guitar and sat back on the sofa. 'When I was a kid, I used to go and visit my granddad,' he began. 'He lived in in the interior, a god-forsaken place with nothing but a few rocks and tumbleweed floating around. He taught me which plants you could eat, where to find water, that sort of stuff. But most importantly, he taught me about Dreamtime.'

'I've heard of Dreamtime,' said Seth. 'It's the spiritual belief of the aborigines.'

'That's right,' said Juke. 'It's not about past, present or future. Dreamtime is just there, all around you. It's creation, it's the values you live by, it's belonging to a place, it's your relationship to the land. It's about connecting with your spiritual ancestors, seeing spirits in the rocks, trees and landscape.'

'Is it very old?' I asked.

'Sure, it's been there since the beginning of time,' answered Juke. Everybody's got their own Dreaming, it's what gives you your identity. Dreamtime links it all together.'

'I've heard it's possible to enter Dreamtime,' said my mother. 'Isn't that what the shamans do?'

'They can do,' said Juke. 'If you get into a trance-like state and raise your consciousness, it's possible to get in to Dreamtime.'

'Have you ever done it?' asked Seth, Juke's new number one fan.

'It has been known,' said Juke enigmatically.

I looked at my mother. She was engrossed. This was what she loved. She'd always been fascinated by paganism, ancient beliefs, spirituality and the whole new age movement. She couldn't have found a better boyfriend. He was so far removed from any of the men in the village it was untrue. Again I wondered what a mystical creature such as Juke was doing here. He had to be here for a reason, and yet I couldn't come right out and ask him. It didn't seem the right thing to do.

'Can we have another song?' asked Seth.

Juke picked up his guitar and played a few cords. 'Sure, buddy, what did you have in mind?'

'D'you know Best Day of My Life by the American Authors?'

'Sure.'

Seth looked like he was in seventh heaven, playing pretend drums on the table, as Juke began to sing, and my mother was totally besotted. When we got to the chorus, we all joined in, laughing as we got the tune wrong. It was turning into a brilliant evening, thanks to the music, the company, the beer and the laughter, and I realised I hadn't had so much fun in ages. Theo was my soul mate, I was sure, but it was all so intense and so deep with him, we never seemed to lighten up. Just for the moment, it felt good to relax, draw back and enjoy friends and family. No sooner had the thought entered my head than the doorbell sounded again. I knew it would be Theo and for a brief second my heart grew heavy. I didn't want this happy moment to end and I knew it would as soon as Theo entered the room.

I went to the front door and let him in.

'We're in the lounge,' I informed him. 'Juke's playing the guitar. We're having a singsong.'

'A singsong?' he asked and raised his eyebrows.

'Yeah, it's the kind of thing normal people do,' I said with an edge to my voice.

'Are you alright, Emily?' he asked. 'You seem tense.'

'No, I'm fine. Come in.'

I led him into the lounge, noticing his look of surprise when he saw Seth sitting alongside Juke on the sofa.

'Hi, Theo,' said Seth, looking like the cat that had the cream.

Juke nodded and continued playing guitar.

'Come and sit here, Theo,' said my mother, patting the sofa next to her. 'Would you like a beer?'

'Sure,' he said, looking as if he'd rather have teeth pulled than join in a singsong, especially with Seth. I sat at Theo's feet, my back leaning against his legs, but despite my gesture of intimacy, I could sense his unease. So could Seth, and I could feel the rivalry growing between them. Now on his second beer, Seth was losing his inhibitions and, never one to be subtle, was talking to Juke about music and bands as if he were his long lost brother. Theo was excluded and, given his suspicion of Juke, it made for a very uncomfortable atmosphere.

'Hey, you like The Stones, man,' said Seth enthusiastically. 'That is so cool, they are like my number one band, even though they're all ancient.'

'Nothing wrong with being ancient, mate,' said Juke, good-naturedly. 'Is there Theo?'

'No, ancient is good,' said Theo warily, watching Juke closely.

'You're not a Stones man, are you, Theo?' asked Seth, 'Not your bag.'

'I don't mind The Stones,' he answered. 'I have eclectic taste. I like all styles.'

The undercurrents were swirling thick and fast and I wasn't sure what was going on. All I knew for sure was that since Theo had entered the room, the atmosphere had changed. Juke seemed aware of the tension between Theo and Seth and was watching both with amusement. Theo was noticeably edgy in Juke's presence.

Then the evening nosedived spectacularly.

'Going to the prom, Theo?' asked Seth, now on his third can of beer.

'I think you've had enough, Seth,' said my mother, catching my expression.

'Yes, isn't it time you were going, Seth?' I said, nervously, looking at my watch.

'No, I'm good,' he answered, oblivious to our suggestions. 'I've asked Emily to the prom.'

I didn't dare to look at Theo.

'I'm not sure I'm going, Seth. I haven't made my mind up yet,' I said diplomatically, not wanting either to lose face.

'I thought we were going to the prom,' said Theo quietly.

'We were. We are. I don't know,' I sounded pathetic and I knew it. 'Seth asked me before we'd discussed it.'

'See, you're not the only option Emily has,' said Seth, enjoying Theo's discomfort.

'Seems like you'd better decide where your loyalties lie, Emily,' said Theo, standing up as if to go. 'If you're having second thoughts, I need to know.'

'I'm not having second thoughts,' I began, and realised everyone was looking at me. 'Can we discuss this tomorrow? This is so not the right time.'

'You're right,' said Theo, coldly. 'This is neither the time nor place. I'll see you tomorrow at college, Emily.'

He walked to the door and I went to follow him.

'I'll see myself out. You need to get him home.' He looked at Seth with dislike. 'Good night, Mrs Morgan, Juke.' He nodded in their direction and left the room, closing the door behind him. I heard the front door open and slam shut.

'Oh, well done, Seth,' I said, turning to face him. 'That's really upset the apple cart.'

'I told you, Emily,' said Seth, putting his arm around my shoulder and hanging over me, 'you don't have to be with him. I can offer you a whole different future.'

'Yes, I know, Seth. Come on, it's time to go home.'

I gently pushed him towards the door.

'Night, Juke, thanks for the songs, bro,' he called back.

'Night, Seth,' answered Juke. 'Take care, mate.'

As we left the room, I heard Juke say to my mother in a low voice, 'Young love, eh? Who'd want to go through all that again? Especially when choices made today can have such far reaching consequences.'

There was no mistaking the edge in his voice.

8. **King Pin**

King Pin could hardly believe his luck. He put on his new raincoat, delighted to find it fitted like a glove. It was just the right size and couldn't have fitted his portly figure any better if he'd had it tailored. It really had been his lucky day. Not only had he found a Marlboro packet with half a dozen smokes inside, but also half a bottle of Jack Daniels, just lying in the park, waiting for him to find. Why someone would leave a half bottle of JD behind was beyond him, but he didn't question it. Just thanked his lucky stars, grabbed it quick and stuffed it in one of his carrier bags to be consumed later.

No-one knew why he was called King Pin, least of all him. The reason was long since gone. He was one of life's strays who roamed the streets and alleyways, not caring whether he had an identity or not.

He'd carried his spoils around for half the day, his willpower getting progressively weaker. Now he needed somewhere to sit and enjoy them. The park bench was okay, but it was very public. He'd got used to abuse over the years, people spitting and swearing at him, the odd kicking or beating up. It went with the territory. You couldn't expect to live on the streets and live unscathed. But just recently, he'd become the target for a local gang who hung out in the park. They'd enjoy relieving him of his liquor and smokes, and giving him a good thrashing into the bargain.

So mid evening, he'd let himself into the doss house. He'd planned to sit and drink, enjoy a smoke, maybe watch some TV if the old set was still working. He'd been surprised to find a man asleep on the sofa and had watched him for a while, tossing and turning. The man was maybe sleeping off some bad score. Who knew? Who cared? What he did like was the man's raincoat, which he'd found draped over the back of the sofa. King Pin put it on, discovered it was a perfect fit and decided to leg it before its owner woke up to find it missing. Three gifts in one day. The gods were truly smiling on him.

He decided to find his favourite park bench after all. It was a warm night and the whisky would warm him even more. The gang was nowhere to be seen and he sat enjoying a smoke and a drink until pretty soon the world became a fuzzy, mellow yellow place. He pulled his new raincoat round him, feeling happier than he had in weeks. As a deep, dreamless sleep claimed him, a dim thought ran through his head, recalling boyhood days studying Shakespeare: 'If 'twere now to die, 'twere now to be most happy'.

It was to be his last coherent thought.

The large black panther padded through the park, nostrils distended. Suddenly it stopped, ears pricked, yellow eyes no more than slits. At last, a faint whiff of the scent wafted past on the gentle breeze. The animal inhaled deeply. There was no mistake. This was the prey it sought. It didn't take long to find the sleeping figure. With a powerful leap, the panther pounced, teeth bared and claws extended. The attack was quick and deadly. It took no more than a couple of minutes to rip the sleeping man to shreds in a frenzy of biting, tearing and clawing, leaving a bloodied mess that barely resembled a human being at all.

When they found his remains early next morning, the local police were sickened by the savagery of the attack and dubbed it The Ripper In The Park murder. By this time, the panther had long since gone, believing its mission to be successful.

9. **Protecting the Secret**

Early that morning, Pantera reported back to the family, delivering the news they'd been waiting for. She told them how she'd found her prey.

'He was sleeping off the effects of a drinking binge,' she informed the family. 'He knew nothing. There was no struggle and by the time I'd finished, there was little left of him.'

'You have done well,' said Viyesha. 'I would not normally condone such violence, but in this instance, we had to act quickly to eradicate the threat.'

'I hadn't intended the attack to be so frenzied,' admitted Pantera. 'Instinct took over and I gave in to desire. All my anger at this piece of filth compromising the safety of our crystal came to a head. I had to make sure he was properly removed.'

'Sounds like you've achieved that,' quipped Joseph. 'Remind me never to get on the wrong side of you, Pantera.'

'Shame we couldn't do the same with the girl,' snarled Aquila, scowling at them all. 'If anyone deserves it, she does.'

'Silence, Aquila,' said Leon, sharply. 'I will not tolerate this aggression against Emily.'

'And you'd have to get through me first,' said Theo angrily.

'Tch, you are little more than a child,' spat out Aquila, 'What do you know?'

'More than you, obviously,' joined in Violet. 'You think violence is the answer to everything.'

'Aquila, that is enough,' said Viyesha, in her calm voice. 'The immediate threat has been removed, and I believe the crystal is safer as a result. However, we must still be on our guard. We know the Reptilia will come, and we know they will send feeders. We cannot allow them to gain access to the crystal. I am wondering whether it would be prudent to install a custodian. It is not my choice, but I fear the crystal's location may be discovered and further threats will come. What do you think, Leon?'

'Perhaps just a sentinel?' he suggested. 'Someone to keep watch, leading up to the initiation ceremony.'

'A temporary sentinel. Yes. Pantera, I'll leave this in your hands. Ask the Lunari to send us someone, as a precaution, no more. Do not give Badru cause for alarm. How about the energy sensor, Theo? Any developments?'

'Nothing to report,' answered Theo. 'He hasn't done anything, other than to make music. For the moment, he's keeping his cards close to his chest.'

'Very well, you and Aquila keep watch. I think that's all for now. The day is beginning, we must get on.'

Theo was leaving the room when his mother called him back.

'Come and sit with me, Theo.'

She patted the place next to her on the Chesterfield sofa and, obediently, he joined her.

'You're not yourself, Theo. What is it?' she asked tenderly.

'It's Emily. I think she's having second thoughts.'

'How do you mean?'

'She's thinking of going to the prom with Seth. And last night when I went round, I found her and Seth sitting with her mother and the new boyfriend in a cosy family scene. I didn't belong there and Emily was distant with me. I think she might be changing her mind.'

Viyesha put her hand on his arm and instantly he felt calmer.

'Theo, listen to me. You're asking Emily to make a massive commitment, to give up everything and take a huge step into the unknown. She's bound to have doubts. It's less than two weeks to her initiation, when the world she knows will cease to exist and she'll become something she cannot even comprehend right now. And she knows the danger. Can you possibly imagine what that feels like? To think that you might never see your family and friends again, that you might cease to exist?'

'No,' he said sadly. 'I guess I can't. And I've told her how agonising the initiation process can be. I don't suppose that's helped.'

'She's frightened, Theo. She doesn't know what's going to happen. It's only natural she's considering an alternative. This boy, Seth, from what I know, has been her friend for many years. He represents all that is safe and familiar in her world. She feels at home with him, on safe ground. You must allow her to work through these feelings. If she wants to go to the prom with him, you must let her. He's not the threat you perceive him to be. Don't forget, to love someone means letting them go to make their own decisions. She will come back to you, I have no doubt. You two are as one, destined to be together. You have to let the mortal side of her come to terms with her destiny, so that she is absolutely sure when she comes to her initiation.'

'When you say it like that, mother, it kind of makes sense. But it's not easy to see her like this, knowing she's considering a mortal pathway, when I'm offering her immortality. What he can offer doesn't even come close.'

'I know, my love, be patient. You will be with Emily, as before.' She smiled. 'You need to show some superhuman understanding.'

'That's what I'm finding difficult. I might be superhuman, but I still have feelings and insecurities, just like any human.'

'That's because you're in love. Just because you're immortal, doesn't make you any less insecure. If anything, you have a heightened sensitivity. Remember, the more you crowd Emily, the more you'll push her away. Give her space, give her time and she'll come back to you. I promise.'

She paused, considering the situation. 'Perhaps she needs to see the crystal again. Remind her of the unique position she finds herself in.'

'But isn't that dangerous? What about Aquila and Pantera?'

'They need not know. We must do this quickly, before the sentinel arrives. Why not invite her over this evening? Tell her I want to see her. She cannot refuse that.' She smiled at Theo, looking calm and serene, although her next words held a touch of menace. 'Emily has to join us, Theo. She has no alternative. The Lunari would be swift to take retribution.'

She leant forward and placed a kiss upon his forehead. 'Don't worry, my love. All will be well. I will do all in my power to make it so.'

Theo smiled, looking more relaxed. 'Thank you, mother.' He glanced at his watch. 'I must go. I have college.' He rose from the sofa and walked towards the door.

'More than anyone, you deserve happiness, Theo,' called Viyesha after him, 'Emily's destiny is not with Seth, I assure you.'

He turned and said jokily: 'I don't suppose Violet would be too happy if it was.'

'What do you mean?' asked Viyesha.

'She has feelings for Seth. It's obvious. She's infatuated.' He grinned and opened the door, disappearing into the hotel reception area.

A brief frown appeared on Viyesha's perfect brow. 'Is she indeed?' she murmured to herself. 'Given the Lunari's interest, that is of far greater concern to me than Emily's doubts.

She got up and walked to the window, deep in thought, her golden hair illuminated in the morning sunshine, giving her beauty a strange, mystical quality.

Looking out over the gardens, she said quietly, 'This infatuation can go no further. I will see to it.'

10. **Decisions**

I wasn't looking forward to seeing Theo at college that morning. The price I had to pay for being with him was almost too much. How could we sustain this for eternity? What if we got bored with one another? What if it didn't work out? And what did eternity mean exactly? How would I feel when all around me started to age and everything that was familiar began to crumble away while I stayed seventeen? Not for the first time, I wondered if I should have taken Philosophy 'A' level instead of Business Studies. If I'd got used to discussing such esoteric issues, maybe I'd be better prepared now. It was all very well understanding profit and loss, finance and marketing and other such issues, but what good would it do me? I needed to see the bigger picture, and for me that meant seeing my current existence as a tiny speck on a vast track that literally went on forever.

Seth didn't show that morning. I guessed he was sleeping off the effects of too much beer and I was glad not to see him. I needed to get my thoughts in order. I loved Seth absolutely, and had always done so, ever since we'd played on the front driveway when he first moved in. But did I want to spend the rest of my life with him? I knew what he was doing and the very fact he was putting his own life on the line showed me how much he really loved me. But was it a romantic love? Was it an all-consuming, passionate love that took my breath away and made me feel weak inside? I didn't think so. With Seth, I could laugh and joke, be myself, feel happy and relaxed. With Theo, I became someone else, sophisticated and confident, empowered by his energy to realise a potential I didn't even know I had.

And then there was the question of the Lunari. By choosing Seth, I was potentially imposing a death sentence on both of us. What would it be? A savage attack one dark night, an unexplained car crash with tragic consequences, or a strange disappearance that was never solved? I had no doubt the Lunari were capable of anything. With such issues going through my brain, it was no wonder I was a little short with Tash.

'So, did you ask him?' she said, getting into the car.

51

She looked stunning in a tight fitting green tunic dress, with a dark green bomber jacket and shiny green platforms, setting off her beautiful red hair and green eyes to perfection.

'Ask who, what?' I said absently. 'What are you talking about?'

'Seth?' she said, impatiently. 'Did you go round and have a word with him last night, about him taking me to the prom?'

'Oh. No, I didn't. Sorry.'

'Didn't you see him?'

'Well, yes I did, but my mum's boyfriend was there, and I didn't really get the chance.' How could I tell her both Seth and Theo had asked me to the prom?

'It's all right for you. You've got a boyfriend,' she said, pointedly.

'I thought you didn't want me to be with Theo. You said it was too dangerous.'

'I still think that,' she said, 'but you've made it quite plain you're not going to change your mind. So, what can I do? I don't want to stop you and die in the process.'

'Well, that's very noble of you,' I said sarcastically, thinking how one friend was prepared to put his life on the line, while the other was happy to let me get on with it.

'Don't get me wrong,' she said. 'I really don't want you to go ahead with this whole initiation thing. But if your mind is made up, there's nothing I can do, is there? So can you have a word with Seth before Violet muscles in?'

I groaned inwardly. How was I going to handle this? It seemed so unimportant compared to the bigger issues facing me.

'Yeah, okay. Leave it with me.'

Her next words had far greater impact.

'I'm going to book in for some Botox before the prom, so I look really good.'

'You're doing what?' I asked, looking at her incredulously. 'Tell me you didn't say what I think you just said.'

'You heard. I'm booking in for a bit of Bo. Just here and here,' she indicated a place between her eyebrows and two further areas either side of her eyes. 'May be some round my mouth, too. To stop any frown or laughter lines showing.'

'You have to be joking,' I said, sitting back and staring at her. 'Whatever for? You're seventeen. You don't have any lines. You have a beautiful face, Tash. Please don't do this.'

'Not as beautiful as Violet, though. How can I compete with a supernatural girl, who has perfect skin and bathes in the light of a magical crystal to keep her looking beautiful forever? She has an unfair advantage, you have to admit.'

Now I saw where this was going.

'Do you really think someone like Seth would even notice? You know what he's like. He's hardly the most sophisticated creature in the world. The finer points of female beauty go right over his head.'

She was adamant. 'I've seen the way he looks at Violet, and I've heard his comments.'

'Yes, they're the same comments all the guys make. Violet's beautiful to look at, but she's kind of scary, too. None of the guys at college would dare go out with her. It's all talk. She's just too perfect.'

Tash looked at me disparagingly. 'Emily, you can never be too perfect. Anyway, you can't speak. You'll soon be bathing in the light of the blue crystal and enjoying eternal beauty forever more. As that isn't an option for me, I've got to find an alternative. I'm booked in to have a spray tan over the weekend and I'm having nail extensions and my hair straightened next week.'

'Nails, hair and spray tan are one thing,' I said, 'but teen toxing? It's not right, Tash, and you don't need it. You have no lines. Do you really want to inject poison into your face and not have a normal expression? This could backfire spectacularly. It's more likely Seth will think it's ridiculous. What does your mum say?'

'She doesn't know.'

'And where will you have it done?'

'There's this beauty salon down a back street in Balsall Heath. They don't ask any questions apparently.'

'Sounds well dodgy. I'd give it a miss if I was you.'

'Well, you're not and I won't. I might even have collagen in my lips.'

'Tash! Remember what Kimberley Chartreuse was like? You don't want to become like her, Botoxed up to the hilt and running out of options in her mid-thirties. It's a slippery slope, believe me.'

She stared ahead. 'Well, I'll think about it. As long as you have a word with Seth.'

'Okay, I will. I promise.'

I parked Martha in the college car park and we walked towards the main building just as Aquila's black Jaguar drew up by the front entrance. This was not good timing. Theo and Violet got out and I felt suddenly tongue-tied.

Theo was friendly but distant: 'Hi, Emily. Sorry, I have to dash. I have a personal tutorial first thing and I need to get my notes ready.'

'Okay,' I said, my heart sinking. 'I'll see you at break?'

'Yeah, possibly.' And he was gone, lost among the hordes of uniformed school children going in to Hartsdown High School.

Violet, on the other hand, acted like she was my best friend.

'Hi, Emily,' she said, her face lighting up.

'Hi Violet,' I said, sounding brighter than I felt.

She looked stunning in a sapphire blue cowl neck top under a denim jacket, dark blue leggings and huge navy platform shoes. Two beautiful blue crystal earrings caught the light, flashing and dancing, matching her eyes. She wore a matching bracelet and pendant necklace, similar to the one I wore. The whole effect was of a shimmering, shining vision.

'Oh, hello, Tash. Hardly noticed you there,' said Violet, and laughed affectedly.

'Sorry, did somebody speak?' said Tash looking around, 'I thought there was an animal in pain somewhere.'

'I'd forget the put downs, if I were you,' said Violet. 'You're never going to win Tash. And when it comes to choosing one of us to take to the prom, there's no competition, you might as well face it. You're a loser.'

'Oh, for heaven's sake,' I said, standing between them, 'There are loads of gorgeous guys in the lower sixth. Why don't you each pick someone else and make life simple?'

They both looked at me as though I was mad and I realised there wasn't going to be an easy solution to this situation.

'D'you mean back down?' asked Violet. 'That is so not going to happen, Emily. When I want something, I usually get it. And by the way, I don't know what you've done to upset Theo. He's not happy today.'

'Theo and I are fine,' I said curtly. 'Come on, Tash, let's not be late for Art.'

I took her firmly by the arm and led her away, leaving Violet in a hazy cloud of blue, surrounded by a crowd of school kids gawping at the vision before them. She would have been more at home on a Parisian catwalk than Hartsdown School.

'Honestly, did you hear her?' said Tash, fuming. She put on a spoilt little girl voice, imitating Violet: 'When I want something, I usually get it.' She snorted. 'I'd like to punch her lights out, self-indulgent little rich girl.'

I thought if I explained the situation to Seth, he might come up with a solution, and found him later that morning, hanging round the locker area, looked decidedly the worse for wear.

'Hi Seth, how's the hangover?' I said, watching as he tried to cram too many books into his locker. He shut the door quickly, trying to keep them in, but wasn't fast enough and they all spilled to the floor.

'Oh, sugarflakes,' he said, looking at his books lying across the floor.

'Here, I'll help you,' I said, stooping to pick them up, 'Guess you're not feeling too great today.'

'I'm fine,' he said, flicking his hair back from his face. 'All the better for seeing you, Emily. That was a great night last night. And Juke, wow, what a cool dude. He can play that axe.'

'I think 'axe' refers to an electric guitar,' I pointed out. 'He was playing acoustic.'

'Acoustic, schmoustic, who's splitting hairs?' said Seth, 'He can play his instrument and he has a great voice.' He looked into the distance for dramatic effect. 'A world traveller, how cool is that? That's what I'm gonna be. Today Hartswell-on-the-Hill. Tomorrow, the world.'

'Seth, you can barely find your way to the next lesson, let alone across the world. You wouldn't stand a chance.'

'That's the thing with us world travellers,' he pointed out, 'we don't have a destination, we go with the flow. Wherever we lay our hat, that's our home. Paul Young 1983,' he informed me. 'That would be a collective hat, of course.'

I ignored this latest piece of pop trivia.

'So, you're going to be a world traveller? What about wanting to spend the rest of your life with me? Where do I fit in?'

'Oh yeah. D'you fancy being a world traveller, too?' he asked, hopefully.

'Not really, no. I prefer to have my feet under the table. We may have an irreconcilable difference here.'

I began to realise that Seth didn't know what he wanted, much less a future with me. It had been a grand gesture on his part and he meant well, but he couldn't deliver. I had to see his proposal for what it was: an attempt to do the right thing and keep me safe. He was a sweet boy, but he wasn't a sure bet for the future and I still had the small issue of the prom to sort out.

'About the prom,' I said.

'Ah yes, the prom.' He put on a lovey, actor's voice. 'I take it I will have the pleasure of your company for that evening?'

I stared at him.

'Noel Coward,' he informed me, 'just in case you didn't get it.'

'I didn't and I don't think you will have the pleasure of my company.'

'Why not? I thought you said yes.'

'No, I didn't and it's probably not a good idea for a number of reasons. For a start, Theo's not happy about it, and secondly, you have two other admirers both vying for your attention.'

'I do?' he said, looking surprised.

'Tash and Violet both want you to take them to the prom,' I informed him.

'They do?'

'Yes, Tash because she hasn't got anybody else to take her and Violet because, well, unbelievable though it sounds, she likes you.'

'You mean gorgeous, model-like, out-of-this-world Violet, who could pick any guy in the world, has a thing for me?'

'It would appear so.'

'Cool bananas. She has taste.'

'She's deluded, more like. So, I'm not such an attractive proposition after all?'

He looked at me closely. 'Hm, that's a difficult one. Most beautiful girl in the world against oldest friend... Ego versus conscience… Personal gratification against doing the right thing. I guess doing the right thing ought to win.'

'Oh, thanks. That makes me feel great. Like I say, I'm better off going with Theo.'

'No, don't do that, Emily. I really do want to take you to the prom. I want to show you there is an alternative to being with Theo, and if I can't persuade you to change your mind, at least I can share a special occasion with you before, you know…' He trailed off.

'I know, and it's a lovely gesture. Thank you.'

'Oh, come on, Emily. Can't we do this one last thing together? I mean, if it all works out, Theo has you for eternity. All I'm asking for is one evening. And Theo shouldn't even be going, anyway. He's upper sixth. They have their own prom in a few weeks' time. Come on, I'm prepared to forgo the company of a goddess and risk the wrath of Tash for you. Sounds like a movie, doesn't it?' He put on a deep American accent: 'The Wrath of Tash. Dangerous and deadly.'

'Look, I might not even go myself. I'm feeling really weird about everything. I don't feel much like celebrating at the moment. There's too much to take in, too many big issues to get my head around.'

For once in his life, Seth focused and looked serious. 'Emily, you don't have to do this initiation. It's obvious they're forcing you to do something you don't want to do.'

'No, they're not, Seth. That's just it. I made the decision. Viyesha gave me every opportunity to back out and I carried on. I committed to this course of action. It's what I want to do.'

As I said the words, I realised I'd answered my own doubts. I did want to be with Theo and I would go through with the initiation, whatever the risk.

'Look I've got to go,' I said to Seth. 'I'll catch you later.'

I picked up my bag and began walking down the corridor.

'At least say you'll think about the prom,' he called after me.

'Okay,' I called after him, 'but you need to think what you're going to say to your two admirers.'

Let them fight it out amongst themselves, I thought. I had other things on my mind. I looked for Theo in the café at break time, but he didn't show and I couldn't see him anywhere else. I checked by his locker and walked past the rooms where he usually had his tutorials, but there was no sign. I tried calling him but his phone was on voicemail and I couldn't think of the right words to say. Was he avoiding me? I didn't know.

In the end, I texted him:

> 'Need to see you. Meet me by the netball courts at 12.30 if you want to talk. xx

At 12.30, I waited nervously in the area where the wall curved behind the Games Block. It was the place where Theo had led me that day when we first got together and had special significance for us. I found it hard to believe it was only a few weeks since. It seemed a lifetime ago. After fifteen minutes, I began to wonder if he wasn't coming. It wasn't like him to be late. My mouth felt dry and my heart was hammering against my ribs as my anxiety increased. Where was he? Please God, don't let things go wrong between us now. And then I saw him, walking towards me, his shoulders drawn down, face looking tight and worried. He looked so sad and vulnerable, my heart went out to him and I realised, for all his supernatural allure, he was still a boy with feelings and sensitivity. Even his energy seemed diminished and I knew I'd hurt him.

'Hi,' I said, as he approached me, looking all the more desirable for his sudden fragility. I wanted to take him in my arms and tell him that everything would be okay, that we'd be together and nothing would ever keep us apart. But of course, I couldn't. I didn't know that for sure.

'Hi, Emily. I guess you're having second thoughts,' he said quietly. 'That's what was going on last night, wasn't it?'

'Yeah, I guess so,' I admitted. 'It's all such a big deal. I felt overwhelmed and then Seth said there was an alternative…'

'You mean, he asked you to the prom?'

'Yes. But I hadn't accepted his invitation. He just jumped to the conclusion.' I paused for a moment, and decided it was a time for honesty. 'He also offered to spend the rest of his life with me.'

'I see,' said Theo, looking pale and drained. 'So, you really are having doubts. Have you come to any decision?'

'Yes, I have. You have to understand what a huge step this is for me, Theo. Seth was giving me an alternative in the world I know. Not because he really wants to spend the rest of his life with me, but because he cares about me. He doesn't want me to throw away my life on something I might regret.'

'And is that what you think you're doing with me? Throwing your life away?'

I looked into those tender blue eyes, and saw centuries of pain, hurt and fear, intermingled with love and hope shining back at me, and I knew unequivocally and beyond all doubt what I had to do.

'Theo,' I said gently, 'I'm yours. Always have been. Always will be. For now and eternity.'

A slow smile spread across his face, banishing the rainclouds with radiant sunshine. The energy flowed, white hot and bright, and I felt it surround me, caressing and nurturing, like the warmest sunshine on the most beautiful day. I smiled back at him and then our lips were touching and I was lost in the most sensual, overpowering, all-consuming kiss I have ever experienced. I felt passion and longing rise within me, and pushed myself closer to him, feeling myself blend into his being, enmeshed in his energy, our souls touching and becoming one. My hands gripped his shoulders, feeling the strength of his arms around me and absorbing the power and love that flowed from him. I felt the centuries melt away, thousands of years passing by in an instant, taking me back to a place and a time long since forgotten, and I knew I'd come home. This was where I was supposed to be, this was my destiny, my true love.

My hands fumbled with the buttons of his shirt as I yearned to touch his flesh and let desire take over. But no sooner had my fingers touched the alabaster smooth skin beneath his shirt, than he pulled away, a look of panic and torment etched on his face.

'No, Emily, you mustn't... I can't....'

'What do you mean?' I looked at him, uncomprehending. 'Surely this is the most natural thing between two people who love each other, who are committing their lives together, not just for the future, but for eternity? What's the matter?'

'You don't understand,' he said, running his fingers over his face.

'Well, I guess it's a bit public,' I said, trying to make light of the situation. 'I suppose we ought to wait until we're somewhere more private.'

'No, you don't understand,' he repeated. 'I can't... Not now. Not before you're initiated.'

I stared at him. 'But Theo, we both know I might not make it. This could be my only chance to have this experience. Surely, you wouldn't deny me that?'

He shook his head. 'I'm sorry. We can't…'

I tried again. 'But why not? I don't understand.'

He took my face in his hands and looked deep into my eyes, making my insides flip once again. I'd never experienced longing like this. Never had my insides felt so molten and hot, waves of desire flowing through me.

He sighed. 'I'll explain tonight, I promise. Viyesha has invited you to Hartswell Hall. She wants to talk to you. She said she'll show you the crystal again, if you wish. And I will tell you the truth, I promise. I owe you that… Just come to Hartswell Hall tonight.'

11. A Taste of History

My conversation with Viyesha made my concerns about the prom seem childish and insignificant. She sat in the ballroom, dark blue candles lit all around her, looking exquisite in the flickering light, dressed in a long, pale purple shift dress that emphasised her slim figure and toned skin. A large purple crystal nestled against her breastbone, with matching droplet earrings and bracelet, sparkling and shining in the candlelight.

'Emily, how lovely to see you,' she said, rising as I walked into the room.

'Hi, Viyesha, you look amazing,' I said, spellbound, my eyes drawn to the large purple crystal. 'What a beautiful crystal.'

'Amethyst,' she said, 'Powerful, protective, transmutes energy into love.'

She came forward and kissed me on either side of my face. Immediately, I felt peaceful and at one with the world. This gift she had for conveying tranquillity and wellbeing never ceased to amaze me. I loved being in her presence, I loved the calmness and serenity that she bestowed. Who needed drugs or alcohol when you had Viyesha?

'Come sit with me, Emily,' she said, gliding back to the large purple sofas placed either side of the ornate fireplace at the far end of the ballroom.

Even though it was spring, a fire blazed in the hearth, the flames emitting a flickering brightness, adding to the atmosphere created by the candlelight and giving the room a warm and welcoming feel. I followed her and sat on the sofa opposite.

'Would you like a drink?' She indicated a blue crystal decanter containing a blue liquid, sitting on a central coffee table, two blue crystal glasses alongside it. 'Blueberry juice, nothing more. From our gardens. A wonderful anti-oxidant that nourishes the body.'

'Thank you,' I said, and she poured some of the deep blue liquid into the crystal goblets. I sipped mine. Of course, it tasted divine.

'Forgive me for asking you here this evening,' began Viyesha, 'but it's less than two weeks to your initiation and I felt we needed to talk. It's a big step you're taking, Emily. I understand that. And I also understand if you're having doubts. That would be entirely natural. You're young and we're asking you to make a huge leap of faith into a world beyond your comprehension when you've barely begun to comprehend your existing world.'

'I don't think I'll ever understand the human world, Viyesha,' I admitted, 'let alone a supernatural world. I find people very hard to fathom, I don't know what makes them act the way they do.'

Viyesha laughed. 'Some things don't change in any world, supernatural or otherwise, Emily. We may have eternal youth, but we are still governed by feelings of love and jealousy and insecurity. That, I promise you, never alters. Now, tell me, have you been questioning your decision?'

'Yes, I have,' I told her. 'I'm afraid. I don't want to die. I can't believe that these may be my last few days if I don't survive the initiation. I don't want to leave my mother behind. She's only just lost my Granddad. She couldn't bear losing me, too. And I'm not sure I'm ready to live for eternity. I don't know what that means. It's such a huge concept to grasp, it almost has no meaning. It's like winning ten million pounds on the lottery and not being able to get your head around it. D'you know what I'm saying?'

Viyesha looked at me kindly and spoke softly.

'Yes, Emily, I do. I have seen many go through it and I know the psychological adjustment it entails. I believe you will survive the initiation. The signs are good. You have already held the crystal and felt its energy, and suffered none the worse. Unlike that poor unfortunate creature, Kimberley Chartreuse, whose immune system crumbled under its power.'

I shuddered at the memory.

'But Theo says the crystal will be more powerful at the full moon.'

'Yes, it will. But it was still powerful when you touched it. If anything was going to happen to you, it would have happened then.'

'He also said it's an agonising process and that people can take months to get over it.'

'That is true. It's not a particularly pleasant process, as your whole body chemistry is changing; every cell altering, renewing and strengthening. But agonising is possibly too strong a word. And given that you have already touched the crystal, your body is already attuned to its energy, so I don't believe you will suffer particularly. Some people have been known to enjoy the process. You may, too.'

'I hope so,' I muttered and sighed.

'Some people feel instantly reborn. They feel amazing, as if they hold the universe in their hands, which of course they do. Although that is often the more difficult transition to which they must adjust.'

'What scares me more than anything,' I admitted, 'is to see my friends and family ageing around me, while I stay seventeen. And what about the future? What will I be doing in two hundred years' time? I can't get my head round it.'

'That's because you're seeing things from a human perspective,' she answered. 'Once you've changed, you will see time from a completely different viewpoint. I promise, you won't feel like this. And just because you hold eternity in your hands, doesn't mean you enjoy the present any less. All any of us have is today. We don't know what the future holds, so you must learn to enjoy the present, mindful of every moment, experiencing every second as it happens.'

She paused and took a sip of the blue liquid from her blue crystal glass.

'I can promise you one thing, Emily. You will see the world with a fresh intensity. Whatever you see, hear, touch, smell or feel will be like nothing you have experienced before. It will be as if your senses are coming alive for the very first time and you encounter a magical world, where every small happening is a microcosm in its own right. To hear ants conversing, buds bursting forth and grass growing is the most amazing sensation. To see the colours of the sunset in all their true radiance, to inhale a thousand different scents in the garden, and feel the cellular composition as you touch another's skin is simply beyond your sphere of existence at present. That is the true wonder that awaits you. Time, as always, keeps on turning, and we take each day as it comes. Before you realise it, days have turned into weeks, weeks into months, months into years, and years into centuries. And still the wheel keeps turning.'

She smiled at me. 'Small steps, Emily, that's what you must take, experiencing the wonder as you go along. You can do no more.'

'But my friends and family....'

'You will learn to let go of your human attachments as they fall away. After all, you will have a new family around you, who loves you and will keep you safe. And you'll have Theo by your side, giving you the most wonderful gift of all: true love for eternity, with the world as your playground. What more could you ask?'

I looked at Viyesha, marvelling at her deep blue eyes, with the same sparkling intensity as the blue crystal glasses on the table. She was far-seeing and intelligent, and I wanted to ask her, while I had the opportunity, about the many things she'd seen during her lifetime. I wanted to know about the people she'd met and historical events she'd witnessed, the civilisations and cultures she'd encountered that had shaped mankind, and the changing landscape of the world as it moved through the centuries. She had all this knowledge and I wanted to hear about it while I could still see it from a human perspective.

'Tell me of the things you've seen, Viyesha,' I asked her. 'Tell me what it's like to live through history. You know what really happened.'

She observed me for a second, and started laughing.

'Oh, Emily, it is so refreshing to talk with you. Yes, it's true I've lived through the world's historical events. But much of it was seen from a distance. For many years, I dwelt in the desert caves of Egypt, staying away from conflict and unrest. After Tutankhamun died, I fled, afraid for my life. Leon joined me and we lived as hermits, afraid to show ourselves, for fear our beliefs, our longevity and our fair colouring would prove our undoing. We fared better under Rameses the Second. He was a good ruler: tolerant, artistic and much loved. He built beautiful temples and established a city, Per-Rameses, close to where modern day Cairo is today. He was a great warrior, too, and negotiated peace with Egypt's great enemies, the Hittites.'

She paused and sipped once again from the blue crystal goblet.

'There is so much I could tell you, Emily, of the Carthaginians, the Golden Age of India, the Chinese dynasties, Ancient Greece and the founding of Rome… the Peruvian cultures, the Vikings, the Magyars and the wonderful civilisation of the Maya. Later came the Ottomans and the Mongols, followed by the Incas, the Aztecs and the Conquistadores… then the colonisation of America, the rise of Russia and the British Empire …. So many great cultures have we seen rise to power, seemingly invincible, only to fall into dust. Not that we took part in any of this, you understand. We were only ever bystanders, watching and observing, always on the side-lines, never getting involved, never changing the course of destiny. For that is the nature of destiny, Emily, to continually rise and fall … a cyclical dance on the wheel of fortune that keeps on turning…' She laughed self-consciously. 'Forgive me. I talk too much. How can I recall three thousand years of history in just a few minutes and expect you to have any comprehension of what we have seen. It is impossible.'

'It's amazing,' I said, totally in awe of the goddess before me. Prior to this, I'd taken the de Lucis family at face value. Now, I began to get a sense of their history.

'Not that we've been around all the time,' said Viyesha, 'Occasionally, we opt out and withdraw from the world. Everyone needs time away from the madness to restore their sanity.'

'You mean like meditation?' I asked.

'More than that,' said Viyesha, 'We discovered we had the ability to slow down our bodily systems, reduce our heartbeat and lower our temperature, enabling us to survive for long periods without waking. When you have eternity at your fingertips, an extended sleep is sometimes necessary.'

'How long did you sleep for?' I asked incredulously.

'Sometimes, hundreds of years at a time. Where do you think the legend of Sleeping Beauty began? In the 17th century, we retired to a castle in deepest Rumania. As we slept, the forest around the castle walls grew thick and dense, preventing outsiders from entering. When the time came, the guardians reawakened us.'

'You mean Aquila was the handsome prince?' I said, aghast. I couldn't think of anyone less suitable for the job.

Viyesha laughed. 'Storytellers will always embellish.'

'But what about the blue moon?' I enquired, 'Didn't you need to re-charge your energy?'

'It would appear not. When a light body is in such a state, it neither regenerates nor ages. It remains suspended in time. So we were able to give our systems a total rest.'

'I suppose a hundred year sleep is no more than a quick nap, relatively speaking, when you live for eternity,' I reasoned. 'Is that something I'll be able to do?'

'Eventually.' She smiled at me, as a mother to an inquisitive child. ' It's all about mind control, Emily… being able to lower your brain waves and enter the alpha state, allowing your body to switch off and your mind to rest. In such a state, you can survive for a long time without sustenance or water and suffer no ill effects. If you wish, your mind can still see, even though your body sleeps. Remote viewing, I believe they call it: allowing your astral body to leave your physical body and travel to other places, observing what is happening with your mind's eye.'

I stared at her, lost for words, trying to take in all that she had told me.

Viyesha clapped her hands and sat back into the sofa. 'Enough, Emily, you ask me too many questions. I wanted to put your mind at rest, not blind you with science.'

'No, you haven't,' I assured her. 'There are things I need to know.'

Viyesha looked at me conspiratorially. 'Would you like to see the crystal again?' she asked, a gleam in her eye.

'Surely, that's not possible,' I said, my eyes opening wide at the prospect. 'What about Pantera and Aquila? They won't like it.'

'As long as you're with me, they won't know. After today, it won't be possible, as we'll have a sentinel in place.'

'A sentinel?' I echoed.

'A guard provided by the Lunari. I've requested one, to give us extra protection until you are initiated. We cannot risk any more dark matter getting near the crystal. But tonight, I thought you and Theo could see the crystal together.'

My eyes shone at the prospect and right on cue, the door opened and Theo walked in.

'What d'you think, Emily?' he asked, walking up to the sofa where I sat. 'Mother says we can see the crystal. Do you want to?'

'I will if you will,' I said, grinning at him. He smiled back, sparks of energy lighting up his eyes.

'Very well,' said Viyesha. 'Let us go to the Clock Tower room.'

She arose and we followed her out of the ballroom, barely able to conceal our excitement.

12. **The Blue Crystal**

We followed Viyesha up the main stairway, my hand in Theo's. From the first floor landing, she led the way up the old servants' stairway, on to the upper landing, the plush blue carpet thick beneath our feet, excitement building at the thought of seeing the beautiful blue crystal again. Along the corridor we walked, and up the old stone spiral stairway until we reached the heavy oak door with its strange carvings and large keyhole.

Viyesha prised open a brick on one side of the door, taking out the big iron key hidden behind it. She placed it in the lock, turned it and pushed open the door. I stared into the hexagonal Clock Tower room, still expecting to see the remains of Kimberley Chartreuse over by the window, but thankfully, it was empty. Theo turned to look at me, his eyes sparkling and excited, and I don't think I had ever loved him more.

'Are you ready, Emily?' he breathed softly.

'Absolutely,' I said resolutely. We were in this together, forever. For eternity.

Viyesha walked to one of the far walls and loosened another brick, revealing a lever, which she turned. Immediately, a portion of the wall slid to one side, revealing the silver casket covered in ancient symbols, nestling in its alcove. She took hold of the casket and carried it into the centre of the room, placing it on the floor in the centre of the hieroglyphics etched into the worn old floorboards. Slowly she opened the lid.

Although I had seen the crystal on two occasions before, nothing prepared me for the brilliant blue light that shone forth from the open casket. I'd forgotten how powerful and blinding it could be, even now, in its waning state. The ancient symbols on the floor glowed faintly, and my eyes went to the beautiful blue crystal, its many facets sparkling and glinting. Unlike before, this time I was able to look at it, marvelling at its structure and beauty, seeing for the first time the large blue hexagonal points that rose into the air, and the smaller, sparkling crystalline shapes that nestled at its base. It was quite simply the most beautiful, magical thing I had ever seen in my life. I felt the small crystal pendant around my neck vibrating against my breastbone in tune with the larger one.

Viyesha picked up the crystal and immediately rivulets of blue energy ran over her fingers and hands, up her arms and onto her shoulders. She closed her eyes, breathing in deeply as if absorbing its energy, her face bathed in the brilliant blue light. Slowly she opened her eyes and spoke to me.

'Emily, come, take the crystal.'

'I can't,' I protested, 'it's too dangerous.'

'Trust me,' said Viyesha, holding it out to me. 'You'll be fine. As long as you hold Theo's hand and take the crystal in your other hand.'

I glanced at Theo.

'Do as my mother says,' said Theo. 'You'll be okay. I promise.'

Cautiously, I stepped forward holding Theo's hand in my left palm, feeling his fingers cool and smooth in mine. I stretched my right arm out towards Viyesha and she carefully placed the crystal in my hand. The sensation I experienced was like nothing I had ever felt before. I watched as shards of blue light leapt from the crystal onto my hand and up my arm, travelling through my body at speed, running down my other arm and into Theo's hand. If was as if Theo were pulling the crystal's energy through my body into his.

'As long as the crystal's energy passes through you, there's no danger,' said Viyesha. 'Theo is drawing the energy through you, so there's no possibility of it short circuiting and causing you harm.'

I gasped as I felt the full extent of the amazing force pulsing through my body. To begin with, it felt both warm and cool, gently caressing my skin like an angel's touch. The feeling intensified as the crystal's energy grew more powerful. I saw the mark on Theo's arm, the infinity sign crossed by a circle, glow bright blue, and began to feel I was on fire with cool, soothing flames that flicked and licked my skin, making every cell come alive, yet creating the most overwhelming sense of peace within me, as if I were lying beneath gentle sunshine, feeling warm sand trickle between my toes. It was the most heavenly, delicious sensation, made all the more precious by Theo's closeness. I felt connected to him in a way I'd never experienced before. I knew what he was feeling, what he was thinking, what he was experiencing, as if we were part of the same energy circuit, linked physically, mentally and telepathically.

It was perfect and I never wanted it to end, an exquisite connection that joined us body and soul, but all too soon Viyesha spoke.

'Enough. Even though the crystal is at its least powerful and you have Theo's strength to protect you, it is not advisable to continue any longer. You must respect its power. Hand it back to me, Emily, but keep hold of Theo's hand until the blue flame has disappeared.'

I did as she bid, handing back the crystal, feeling for the last time its smooth cool facets beneath my fingertips and watching as the shooting blue flames licked my skin. Viyesha replaced the crystal in the silver casket and closed the lid, and it felt as if a shadow had passed in front of the sun. Everything became dark and monochrome and there was a flatness all around me. I felt crushed, cold and alone, without warmth or nourishment, as if the source of my life had been taken away. Theo squeezed my hand and colour began to seep back into my grey, empty world. I felt Theo's warmth and energy spreading into my left hand and up my left arm, restoring circulation to my lifeless limbs, bringing me back into the land of the living. I turned and smiled at him, seeing his clear blue eyes and shining blonde hair with a new intensity. His skin looked translucent, glowing with health and energy and I felt more alive than ever before.

Viyesha placed the casket back into the niche in the wall, allowing the partition to close and concealing the precious contents once again.

'Come, we must leave,' she said softly. 'I would not have the others know what has just transpired. This is our secret, Emily, giving you a taste of what is to come for you and Theo.'

She led the way out of the Clock Tower room, locking the door and replacing the key in its hiding place behind the loose brick.

'Quick, go down the stairs,' she instructed. 'Theo, take the lead.'

I followed him down the old spiral stairway, hearing our footsteps echo on the worn stone steps. When we reached the upper landing, Viyesha whispered quietly 'Go into the ballroom and sit by the fireside. I'm sure you have things to discuss.'

I stared at her, feeling a wave of affection pass over me, aware of what she had risked to show me the crystal and help calm my doubts.

'Thank you, Viyesha,' I whispered.

She smiled and I saw such love flow from her eyes, I felt emotions stir deep within me and tears begin to form. At that moment, there was no doubt in my mind that she loved me as her own.

'Go,' she repeated. 'It would not do to be discovered here.'

Theo took my hand. Together we ran along the blue-carpeted corridor, down the old servants' stairway and onto the main landing. Once again, there was no one around and we made it back into the ballroom, without being seen. The candlelight still flickered and the embers in the fireplace glowed, giving a warm, romantic feel to the room, and we fell onto one of the sofas together, Theo's arm around me, holding me to him.

'That was awesome,' I murmured. 'I have never experienced anything like that in my whole life.'

'And that's just a taste of things to come,' he murmured into my neck, his breath warm against my skin.

Then his lips were on mine and we were kissing in a frenzy of passion and desire, intensified by the crystal's residual energy still pulsing through our veins. I felt his hands on my shoulders, around my face, touching my arms, drawing me closer to him, so that our bodies were enmeshed as one. Desire pulsed through me and I knew it was reciprocated but I was also aware there was a problem and broke away, frowning.

'Theo, I want more. You know I want more. I want to experience you as a human, so I have something to compare with when I become superhuman. And if I don't make it through the initiation, this might be my last chance.'

He pulled back and looked at me with eyes so desolate and sad I could barely breathe. I saw centuries of pain and grief flash before me.

'What is it, Theo?' I asked. 'You said you would tell me. What's stopping you taking things further?'

He sighed so desolately I thought it would tear him in two.

'I will tell you, Emily, but it is not easy to speak of, and once you know the truth, you may not think so highly of me.'

'Go on,' I demanded, wondering what could be so bad to cause him such suffering.

He sat back on the sofa and stared into the distance.

'The story begins three thousand years ago, when I was a young man in the reign of Rameses the second in 1275 BC.'

This wasn't quite what I was expecting and I felt my jaw drop as I listened to his words.

'I was nineteen years old and had just been initiated into the Order of the Blue Crystal. I was getting accustomed to the new levels of power and energy that the crystal had given me, and felt I could conquer the world. I felt wonderful, invincible, unstoppable, and I was also in love. A year previously, I'd met the most exquisite girl. She was the daughter of my parents' friends and had been working in the temple as a handmaiden since the age of seven. When she was sixteen, she chose to leave the sanctity of the temple and returned to live with her parents. It was during a celebration paying homage to the God Osiris that I first met Ahmes, whose name means child of the moon. She was fair skinned and pale, with blonde hair and blue eyes, like ours, which is why she'd been singled out to become a handmaiden. She looked like you, Emily, the likeness is incredible. That day at college when I first met you, it was as if I was seeing Ahmes again for the first time in centuries.'

'She's the girl on the crystal cameo pendant you wear, isn't she?'

'Yes.'

'So what happened?' I asked, intrigued to find out what fate had befallen the exquisite Ahmes.

Theo smiled sadly.

'Ahmes fell in love with me, too, and it was decided that we would marry. She knew of the blue crystal and it was deemed suitable that after her seventeenth birthday, she too would be initiated into the Order and join me in eternal youth. I cannot convey the happiness we both felt. To be young and in love, with the prospect of being together forever, was the most powerful feeling you can imagine.'

He stopped for a moment, and I knew he was reliving what had happened.

'Yes,' I prompted him, gently.

'Ahmes was to marry me on her seventeenth birthday, and two weeks later, when there was a full moon, she was to be initiated.'

'Do you mean she didn't survive the initiation?' I asked.

'She never made it to the initiation,' said Theo, bitterly. 'We had the most wonderful wedding feast, with dancing and celebration, the best wines and all manner of exotic fare. Ahmes was dressed in a white silk gown, her hair flowing loose, interwoven with lotus flowers. The connection between us was electric, the desire flowing between us too powerful to resist.'

He stopped and looked at me with tears in his eyes.

'Emily, you must understand, I had no idea that my body chemistry had changed during the initiation. I didn't understand the power of the energy that flowed through me, how destructive it could be to an ordinary mortal.'

'You killed her....' I gasped in a whisper.

'I didn't mean to, you have to believe me,' he said desperately. 'When we retired to our wedding bed, I thought we had eternity before us. Instead, we had just minutes. Desire took hold of us and it should have been the best night of our lives, but the consummation of our love proved fatal to her. The power within me was too strong, it was the equivalent of ten thousand volts going through her body. She didn't stand a chance.' He put his head in his hands. 'Now do you see why I can't let anything happen between us? Why I need to protect you? I've carried the guilt for over three thousand years, knowing that I killed the woman I loved, and now you've come back to me, I can't let that happen again.'

I stared at him aghast and couldn't quite take in what he was telling me. It was just too awful and shocking to comprehend, and certainly not an image I wanted in my head. He sat there, head in hands and I simply couldn't imagine what torment he'd gone through since that day over three thousand years ago. I tried to find the right words.

'Theo,' I said gently, pulling his hands away from his face, 'look at me. You killed her with love. You didn't know what was going to happen. You cannot carry this guilt with you any longer. If we're to have a chance, you have to put it behind you and focus on our future.'

Although I didn't dare admit it, I was glad Ahmes was dead, because, had she lived, I wouldn't be with Theo now. There again, if

I was the reincarnation of Ahmes, her story was my story, which put a different spin on things. Either way, I was out of my depth.

Hiding my confusion, I spoke resolutely. 'Theo, I'm not going to die. I intend to survive and be with you for eternity. And if that means waiting, so be it.'

It wasn't what I wanted, but I didn't have a choice. Theo looked at me, tears in his eyes.

'Oh, Emily,' he said, pulling me to him. 'You have come back to me. I always knew you would. And this time, nothing can stop us. We'll be together forever.'

He wrapped his arms around me and I felt his heart beating rapidly beneath his white linen shirt. I breathed in the scent of him and knew that I had found my soul mate. I might not have any memory of being Ahmes, but I knew we belonged together, like two halves of the same whole. Instinctively, I felt that some deep-seated ancient link, which couldn't be broken, bound us together. This boy was my past, my present and my future. I had never been more certain.

'I'm yours, Theo,' I whispered into his ear, 'body, mind and soul, for as long as we have together. And I think it's going to be a long time.' I pulled away and smiled at him, then decided I might as well use the situation to my advantage. 'Which is why I need you to let me go to the prom on my own, with my friends. It's one last evening together when I can celebrate being human before the countdown to my initiation. What do you say?'

He nodded. 'Okay. Does this mean you'll be going with Seth?'

'No,' I answered. 'It means I'll be going with Seth and Tash. I just want to have fun with them for one last time before everything changes. Can you understand?'

'Of course...' he began to say, when he was interrupted by the sound of raised voices in the reception area and the ballroom door was flung open with such force it bounced back on its hinges, making the candlelight flicker. It was Violet. She stood in the doorway, trembling with rage.

'Here you are, Emily,' she said angrily. 'It's not enough for you to have one boyfriend, is it? You have to have another and spoil my chances of happiness.'

'Violet, what are you talking about?' I asked, perplexed.

'I'm talking about Seth,' she shouted. 'You knew I wanted to go to the prom with Seth. I even asked you to put a word in for me. Now mother tells me he's asked you to go with him.'

She strode through the ballroom and came to stand by the purple sofa where we sat, looking beautiful and magnificent in the low light.

'You already have Theo. How selfish can you get?' she demanded.

'It's not like that,' I protested. 'Seth asked me because he wanted to have one last evening with me before I'm initiated and join your family.'

'But you could have said no,' she pointed out. 'Especially as you knew I was interested.'

'The thing is, Violet, I didn't know what I wanted. This is a massive step for me. You can't blame me for looking at the alternatives.'

'So Seth was an alternative?'

'Yes. No. I thought maybe he was for a brief moment. But now I know he's not. I know I want to be with Theo.'

'Sorry, I'm getting confused here,' she said, a sneer contorting her beautiful face. 'You want to be with Theo, but you're going to the prom with Seth?'

'And Tash,' I said.

'Oh, great. It gets even better. Even she's getting more of a look-in than me. What's she got that I haven't?'

'Nothing, Violet. You're missing the point. These are my oldest friends.'

'Leave it, Vi,' said Theo, 'I'll take you to the prom.'

'Just what I need,' she said sarcastically. 'I'm so desperate, my brother has to escort me. Oh, forget it.'

Angrily wiping away the tears that were forming in her eyes, she stormed out of the ballroom, slamming the door behind her and making the candlelight flicker once again.

I glanced at Theo. 'Why would your mother do that? Why would she tell Violet that Seth had asked me to the prom? And how did your mother know in the first place?'

'I think that's my fault,' he murmured. 'I told her Violet was interested in Seth and that she wouldn't be very happy when she found out he'd asked you to the prom.'

'I still don't understand. Why would your mother deliberately hurt Violet?'

Theo sighed. 'It's called being cruel to be kind. The family don't need any more emotional entanglements. It's too dangerous. The last thing they want is Seth turning up at the hall, especially now the Lunari are watching. If Badru felt the crystal's safety was comprised, he'd have no compunction killing both Seth and Violet. He's done worse in his time. In my mother's words, it was a situation that needed nipping in the bud. She did it to protect them.'

'Poor Violet,' I said. 'She must hate me. First I go off with her brother and now it seems I'm taking Seth away from her.'

'She'll get over it,' said Theo dismissively. 'She'll have a crush on somebody else next week.'

I threw a cushion at him.

'Typical boy! No empathy. What are you like?'

'A typical boy,' he grinned, then said in disbelief, as the ballroom door opened once again. 'Oh, what now?'

This time Viyesha stood in the doorway.

'Theo,' she said urgently, 'the sentinel has arrived.'

'That's good isn't it, mother?' he said, glancing over to the doorway.

'I'm not so sure,' she answered. 'It's Bellynda LaDrach.'

Surprise registered on Theo's face. 'Great. Just what we needed.'

'Who's Bellynda LaDrach?' I asked.

'Only Badru's right hand woman,' answered Theo, 'otherwise known as The Dragon Woman. And believe me, she really does breathe fire. She is one lady you don't want to cross.'

Right on cue, I heard a loud, imperious voice echoing across the reception area.

'Will someone take my luggage? Call this a hotel? I've seen better service in a rat hole!'

She had an East European accent similar to Aquila's and, even though I hadn't yet seen her, I disliked her immediately.

'Viyesha,' she hissed, 'come help me.'

Viyesha raised her eyebrows at us, sighed and disappeared from sight.

'Might as well get it over,' said Theo, through clenched teeth. 'Come on, Emily. Come and meet Bellynda LaDrach.'

13. Bellynda LaDrach

We walked into the reception area and I encountered the most incredible woman I had ever seen. She was nearly two metres tall and dressed from head to foot in black leather. I stared at the biker's jacket, complete with studs and chains, skin-tight black trousers and long leather boots. In her hand, she held a black motorcycle helmet and I noticed her long, pointed nails were painted black. A swathe of black hair fell across her shoulders and she had the same hooked nose as Aquila. Her eyes were a deep glittering yellow, her skin a dark olive and her mouth a slash of black lipstick. A bored expression was fixed on her face and she had the impatient, superior air of one who does not like to be kept waiting. She was at once fearsome yet charismatic, repugnant yet awesome, like a great black lizard. With the name dragon woman planted in my head, thanks to Theo's description, I was sure her tongue would be forked and could almost see clouds of smoke coming from her nostrils. She tossed her hair dramatically over her shoulder and fixed her strange hooded eyes on me.

'So, this is the new initiate,' she hissed, stepping forward and extending her hand in a rapid movement. 'Bellynda LaDrach.'

I shook her hand, finding it smooth and cold.

'Emily Morgan,' I said in a small voice, feeling insignificant in the presence of such a flamboyant creature. As soon as I touched her hand, I had the impression of hardwired cruelty and knew instantly she was as ruthless and predatory as a crocodile.

'I see you've arrived using your usual mode of transport,' said Viyesha, pouring calm on the troubled waters that swirled around the reception area. 'What's your latest machine, Bellynda?'

The lizard-like creature smiled at Viyesha, revealing a row of sharp, yellow, pointed teeth.

'A Kawasaki Ninja ZX-14R,' she said proudly. 'Fastest motorcycle on the planet: a high compression, fuel-injected powerhouse. One of the sweetest mules you could ever straddle. Silky smooth torque, suspension set up for twists and turns. 1400cc over 200 horsepower and a top speed of 186 mph. What you'd call a mean machine.'

'A bit like yourself, Bellynda,' said Joseph, walking down the main stairway.

'Ah, Joseph, I see you still have that sense of humour,' she said drily.

'Never goes away, Bellynda,' he said, coming forward and kissing her on the cheek. 'I'd like to say it's good to see you, but I'm not sure I can.'

'No, I must say I am baffled by your presence,' said Viyesha. 'When we asked Badru for a sentinel, we didn't expect him to send his second in command. Surely he cannot spare you?'

'Strange. I thought Pantera asked for me specifically,' said Bellynda, drumming her long pointed nails on her motorcycle helmet.

'Did she?' asked Viyesha, looking thoughtful. 'Maybe Badru misunderstood. We had a recent incident with a feeder that we don't want to repeat. We simply wanted a sentinel to stand guard by the Clock Tower Room. Especially while I prepare the crystal for Emily's initiation.'

'I am well aware of everything that has transpired here,' snapped Bellynda. 'Badru is concerned. He felt my presence was necessary. We cannot allow any more.... mishaps.' She hissed out the last word, as if making a point. 'Ah, Leon,' she said, drawing back her lips in an ugly smile, as he walked into the reception area. 'The lion stirs. How are you, my beauty?'

'All the better for seeing you, Bellynda,' he said diplomatically, kissing her on both cheeks. 'This is an unexpected pleasure, we were not expecting you to grace our establishment.'

'Very tasteful,' she said dismissively, looking around. ' I think I shall be quite comfortable for the duration of my stay.'

'And how long is that likely to be?' asked Viyesha, smiling.

'That depends on what occurs,' said Bellynda, looking at me. 'Whether you can control your new initiate and her friends and whether we have any further trouble from the Dark Ones. I will remain until I am convinced all is secure and safe. Let's just say, for the duration...'

I swallowed. I disliked this creature intensely, all too aware of the power she wielded and the deference that the family paid her.

'Now, perhaps you will show me to my quarters,' snapped Bellynda. 'I have been on the road for hours. Even I need a rest.' She addressed Joseph. 'My machine is in the courtyard. Park her somewhere safe. I don't want her disappearing.' She threw him the keys. 'No test driving, okay?'

'Spoil sport,' said Joseph, catching the keys. 'You're sure you don't want it servicing after such a long journey?'

She eyed him for a moment, considering, and to my surprise, agreed.

'Okay. You know I wouldn't trust that to anyone else but you, Joseph. It's a deal. Service it and I may let you take her for a spin.'

Joseph beamed at her. She turned to Theo.

'As for you, speed freak, you don't know the meaning of the word. I can show you what speed's all about.' If I wasn't mistaken, she was flirting with him. My dislike intensified even further.

'I look forward to it, Bellynda, but there's not much you can tell me about speed.' He laughed scornfully. I watched him and couldn't mistake the gleam of excitement in his eyes. It would seem Bellynda had a way of wrapping people around her little finger. Especially the men of the house.

'Okay, I challenge you,' she said, delighted. 'You against the Kawasaki. Do you accept?'

Theo considered for a moment, and smiled. 'Bring it on.'

Bellynda laughed. 'Hoorah! This visit is getting more interesting by the minute. Now, I need to rest.'

'I'll take your luggage, Bellynda,' said a voice behind me. 'As housekeeper, it's my duty.' I turned to see Pantera walking into the reception area. There was no mistaking the look of triumph in her face.

'Pantera, my old friend,' said Bellynda, striding forward and kissing her. 'You summoned and I came.'

'I am very pleased to see you,' said Pantera. As she embraced Bellynda, she glanced my way and there was no mistaking the menace in her eye.

She picked up the small black leather bag that constituted Bellynda's luggage, and walked to the foot of the main stairway.

'Up here, Bellynda, if you would care to follow me.'

Bellynda smiled and I shuddered to see the row of sharp, pointed teeth between her black lips. 'But of course. Lead the way Pantera.'

As she passed me, her eyes flickered on me for a brief second and I knew her arrival did not bode well. I felt for Theo's hand, desperately seeking the energy connection between us. He didn't disappoint me, but when I looked in his eyes I couldn't help noticing the distraction there. Bellynda had played him and he'd fallen for it, and that made my position all the weaker as a result.

14. **Teen Toxed**

Next day at school, Seth seemed oblivious that he was the cause of so much heartache.

'D'you think I should ask Violet to the prom?' he asked, slouching on to the seat next to mine in the cafeteria.

'No!' I said sharply. 'That's a bad idea. I thought you'd asked me, anyway.'

'Yeah, but you're you and Violet is...'

'What?' I said edgily.

'Well, she's amazing. The prettiest girl in the college. She'll do wonders for my street cred. Imagine what the guys'll think. And the girls. I'll go right up the pecking order.'

'I hate to break it to you, Seth, I got it wrong. Theo's taking her to the prom.'

'Her brother? That's a bit weird isn't it?'

I shrugged. 'It leaves you free to go with me, which is what I thought you wanted. In fact, I thought all three of us could go together. You, me and Tash. What d'you say?'

He considered. 'Hm, two girls on my arm. I suppose that looks pretty cool.'

'Seth, do you ever think beyond looking cool? I can't believe you sometimes. What about wanting to spend the rest of your life with me?' I looked at him incredulously. He was so immature.

He studiously started to re-tie his shoelace.

'Seth?'

'Yeah, I heard you. The thing is, Emily...'

'Yes?'

'Like I said yesterday, I'm not sure what I want. I kinda like the idea of swooping down to save you from Theo's clutches. Like Superman.' He stuck his arms out in a Superman pose. 'Super Seth to the rescue.' He put his arms back down. 'It's just the bit after that. I'm not sure I can do it.'

'You mean the forever-after bit?'

'Yeah. I don't think I can do the whole settling down thing. Sorry.'

I grinned at him. 'Just for the record, Seth, it would never have worked between us.'

'It wouldn't?'

'No. I couldn't keep up with your wit. You're far too sharp for me.'

He rolled up a paper serviette and threw it at me.

'So about Violet....' he began.

'Forget her,' I instructed him. 'I told you. You're taking me and Tash to the prom. I'll drive us there in Martha.'

'The new super-souped up Mini powerhouse, eh?' said Seth. 'Wicked Egg!'

'Don't you mean Wicked Bad?' asked Tash, arriving at our table and pulling up a chair. She looked different somehow.

'Did you hear that?' I asked her. 'Me, Seth and you are going to the prom together. Just like old times.'

'What about Violet?'

'She's going with Theo.'

'Her brother? Bit weird, but whatever. Suits me.' She frowned, or tried to. 'Damn. If I'd known that, I wouldn't have had Botox.'

I stared at her. 'Please tell me you didn't.'

She grimaced, or tried to. 'I did.'

'I thought your face looked odd,' declared Seth, studying her closely.

'Go away, Seth.' She tried to push him away.

'Go on, frown!' he instructed.

She attempted to wrinkle her brow but failed.

'You look like a robot,' he laughed.

'Shut up, Seth.'

'What does it feel like?' I asked.

'Kinda weird. Like I can't do any proper expressions.'

'Do angry!' said Seth. 'Do surprised!'

'Get lost, Seth. You know I can't. You can be a real pain sometimes.'

Seth put his thumbs and forefingers around his eyes and stretched the skin tight, opening his eyes wide. He put on Tash's voice. 'I want to look surprised, but I can't. My face is frozen. I only have one expression.'

'Stop it, Seth. That is not funny.'

'Oh, Tash, why did you do it?' I asked.

'It's Violet's fault,' she said dejectedly. 'When you're up against supernatural beauty, you need any enhancement you can get.'

'Did you have your lips done, too?' I asked. 'They look strange.'

'Just a teensy weensy bit of collagen.'

'Trout pout!' exclaimed Seth in delight.

'Er, Seth, don't you have rugby practice round about now?' I asked pointedly.

He looked at his watch. 'Oh, shirt balls! You're right. Gotta go. See ya laters, ladies.' He mock saluted us, grabbed his bag and swaggered as fast as cool would allow through the cafeteria.

'Okay,' I said to Tash. 'I want to know exactly what you've had done.'

She sighed. 'A bit of Bo on my frown lines, laughter lines and crows' feet, some collagen in my lips and a spray tan. They said that would take a while to show.'

I stared at her face, which was beginning to have an orangey glow. 'I think it's started.'

She pulled out a small hand mirror and studied her face. 'OMG, I look radioactive. What can I do?'

I shrugged. 'Make-up?'

'I look like a friggin' freakshow. What have I done?' she wailed.

'I guess it'll wear off in a few weeks. At least you won't do it again in a hurry.'

'Too right.' She looked over my shoulder. 'Oh Jeez, just what I needed...'

I followed her gaze and saw Violet standing with a group of girls by the cafeteria door.

'Miss Friggin' Perfect,' said Tash. 'She can't see me looking like this.'

She took a book out of her bag and pretended to read.

'Don't worry. She won't come over here. I'm not her favourite person at the moment.'

'Why's that?'

'She's pee-ed off Seth isn't taking her to the prom. She thinks it's my fault.'

As well as she was able, Tash smiled. "Oh yes! At least some things are working in my favour,' she said triumphantly.

15. **Speed Freak**

Bellynda sat astride her mean machine, helmet on, fingers twitching at the throttle. The Kawasaki Ninja ZX-14R spoke back to her with a throaty, powerful growl.

She lifted the visor of her helmet and spoke, 'You've done well, Joseph. She's going like a dream. Even more powerful than before, if that's possible. I don't know how you've managed it.'

'We aim to please,' said Joseph, smiling broadly.

I sat on Martha's bonnet, watching and waiting. The challenge was on. This was Theo's opportunity to prove his power.

We'd driven out to an old airfield, about seven miles south of Hartswell-on-the-Hill. It was evening time, around 7.30 and the sun was still bright. A slight breeze blew, ruffling the tufts of grass that grew in the long deserted runway. It had once been home to a flying club and the military before that. Now, it was a broad stretch of unused land disappearing into the horizon, long and flat, perfect for speed.

Theo, Joseph and I had arrived in Martha, driving fast, blasting out Radar Love by Golden Earring. On the way, Bellynda had overtaken us, flashing past, all black leather and gleaming metal, at one with her machine, leaving us in no doubt of the power at her fingertips. She was soon far ahead on the carriageway, a rapidly disappearing black speck. I blinked. If I wasn't mistaken, she'd given us the finger as she sped past.

'Did you see that?' I asked Theo, who was once again driving.

He grinned. 'Arrogant as ever. It won't last.'

'Sure you're up to this Theo?' said Joseph, from the back seat, shouting over the pulsing rock music. 'That beast can go.'

Theo, his hands glued to the wheel, smiled grimly. 'Just watch me, Joseph.'

He put his foot on the accelerator and we shot forward, Martha eating up the tarmac with an insatiable hunger.

'You're not in the race, yet, Theo,' I said, holding on to my seat. 'Why not let her get there first? Lull her in to a false sense of security.'

He looked across and smiled at me. 'Nice thought, Emily, but not an option.'

He pressed his foot to the floor, drawing every last ounce of power out of Martha's V8 engine. In no time, we'd caught up the black leather vision and held our position alongside her. Bellynda turned briefly, acknowledging our presence, but couldn't shake us no matter how hard she tried and we arrived at the airfield at exactly the same time.

Now, the challenge was on, feet against wheels. Joseph stood in front of them, acting as starter, Theo on the left hand side, eyes focused on a spot on the horizon, Bellynda to the right, keyed up and ready to go. I watched from a safe distance, leaning on Martha's bonnet, feeling the tension and willing Theo to win. Bellynda squeezed the throttle and the Kawasaki revved up, straining at the bit. Theo looked across at her and smiled. I knew that smile, or rather I knew the temperament behind the smile. He was every bit as calculating and ruthless as Bellynda.

'Okay,' said Joseph, moving to one side and raising his arm. 'When I lower my arm, the race is on. You go to the end of the runway, turn, and come back. The winner is the first to return here. Do you both understand?'

Both nodded in his direction.

'Let the best man or woman win.' He raised his arm higher, and dropped it suddenly.

The Kawasaki powered instantly into action, surging forward like a great black stallion, the engine snarling and fierce, Bellynda crouched low over the handlebars. Its acceleration was phenomenal, hugging the runway and shooting forward with the power of a rocket, achieving a ludicrous speed within just a few seconds. If Bellynda was impressive, Theo was nothing short of mind-blowing. At the off, he shot forward like a bullet, agile and lean, keeping pace effortlessly with the monster Kawasaki. It was all so fast, I barely saw them go, seeing nothing more than a blur of white shirt and blonde hair alongside the speeding black powerhouse, its twin exhaust canisters disappearing in a cloud of dust, its revving engine soon no more than a mosquito buzz.

'Wow, would you look at that,' said Joseph, watching as they disappeared down the runway, so fast it was impossible to see who was taking the lead.

'What's happening, Joseph?' I said, straining to see.

'Can't see exactly. I'd say Theo's holding his position. They should be turning round about now.'

We watched as the tiny figures slowed briefly, turned and began the return leg.

'Come on, Theo,' I screamed. 'Give it all you've got!'

In no time, they came back into focus and I could see there was nothing in it. Both were neck and neck, the motorcycle's throaty engine getting louder as they approached.

'He can do it,' said Joseph confidently. 'He's pacing himself, saving the best for last. You watch.'

Heart in my mouth and adrenalin flowing, I could barely bring myself to look at the final few metres. The two flew towards us, the Kawasaki's engine growling with menace. Unbelievably, as they approached the finish, Theo began to pull ahead, leading first by a pace, then a head, and then by a sizeable gap. Within another split second, they'd flashed past, Theo leading by a length, Bellynda the loser. She applied the brakes and slowed to a standstill, while Theo dropped to jogging pace, circling back towards us. I ran to meet him, throwing my arms around him.

'You did it, Theo. You beat her. You're faster than the fastest machine on the planet.'

He wrapped his arms around me, breathing fast.

'Well done, cousin,' said Joseph. 'That was impressive.'

With one arm around my shoulder, Theo shook Joseph's extended hand.

'Thanks, Joseph. That was fun,' said Theo, smiling. I noticed he'd barely broken sweat and not a hair on his head was out of place.

Bellynda brought her machine alongside us and took off her helmet, shaking out her long black hair.

'Okay, Theo, you win this time,' she said, with her clipped, East European accent, stroking the side of the motorcycle with a soft, caressing motion as if to calm her over-exerted mount. 'It was a good race, but it doesn't end here, okay?'

'Do I detect a bad loser?' asked Theo, raising his eyebrows.

'Not at all. You won fair and square. I take my hat off to you, but Joseph….' She beckoned him over. 'A bit more fine-tuning, I think. If we can increase the torque at lower revs, it will unleash more power.'

'Always up for a challenge, Bellynda,' he beamed.

'Ever thought of working for Formula One?' she asked, 'McLaren could benefit from your services.' And she winked at him.

I watched their exchange astounded. I had to admit, she might be terrifying and she clearly didn't like me, but Bellynda LaDrach was nothing short of magnificent.

16. **True Blue Prom**

The night of the True Blue Prom was upon us and I was in my bedroom, looking at various items of clothing strewn across the bed, realising with horror I had nothing to wear. I groaned, wondering what to do.

Even the day before, I still hadn't been sure I would go to the Prom. Then my mum had received a phone call asking if she'd like to go to Spain for the week. A friend at work was due to go with her husband, but a hostile takeover bid meant he was needed in the office. Faced with the prospect of a week in the sun, staying in a luxury apartment, all expenses paid, my mum didn't think twice. She'd said yes immediately. Straight afterwards, she'd regretted it, not wanting to leave me on my own. Going to the prom was my way of showing her I had things planned and not to worry about me.

But now it was 7pm and I had just half an hour to magic up an outfit. There was a knock on the door, and my mum came into my bedroom.

'Right, I'm all packed and my taxi is booked. Juke's going to come over for a couple of hours before I go. There's food in the freezer, so you should be fine.' She looked at the clothes strewn across my bed. 'You're nowhere near ready, Em, what are you going to wear tonight?'

'I don't know, mum. I was kind of thinking I'd just go casual in my Hollister top and jeans, but I don't think it's quite right. And my only dress is the white one.'

'Why didn't you get a dress when you went shopping with Tash?' she asked sensibly.

'I don't know. I wasn't sure I was going, and every time I thought about going shopping, something seemed to come up. So, here I am, night of the prom, with nothing to wear.'

'I have a dress you can borrow,' she offered. 'I'm sure it'll fit you.'

'Thanks, mum,' I said, nervously. 'Nothing floral.'

'How old d'you think I am, Emily? I don't do floral. Anyway, floral's back in. It's all the rage in vintage boutiques.'

'Yeah, whatever. I'm still not wearing it.'

'Come and take a look. Don't say no till you've seen it.'

I reluctantly followed my mother into her room and watched as she pulled out a coat hanger draped with a plastic clothes protector from her wardrobe. She unzipped it to reveal a beautiful, shimmering, blue strappy gown.

'Wow, mum, it's gorgeous,' I exclaimed in surprise. 'How come you've got this in your wardrobe? Can I try it on?'

'It's something I wore once many years ago,' she said, taking it out of the protective cover and passing it to me. 'I've kept it ever since. Don't suppose I could get into it now.'

I unzipped the dress and put it on. It fitted perfectly, as if it had been made for me, the sheer fabric falling to the floor and catching the light, the straps criss-crossing at the back in an intricate design. I twirled in front of the mirror, thinking how it made me look older and more sophisticated.

'What d'you think, mum?' I asked, holding up my hair.

'Absolutely gorgeous,' she said. 'I've even kept the earrings and choker that goes with it.'

She rummaged in the top drawer of her dresser and pulled out a small box. She opened the lid to reveal a blue velvet choker with a blue crystal droplet hanging at the front, and matching earrings. 'They probably haven't got the properties of Theo's crystal, but they're pretty and they match the dress.'

I put on the earrings, and removed my crystal pendant, now fitted with a clasp after Kimberley Chartreuse had cut through the original chain with her wire cutters, and clipped the choker around my throat. I looked in the mirror. Perfect!

'I love it, mum, thank you.' I gave her a quick hug and a kiss.

'Just as well I kept it all these years,' she murmured. 'It could do with a throw or a pashmina, but I don't have anything suitable.'

'I do,' I said, thinking of the blue cloak that lay at the bottom of my wardrobe

It remained where I'd left it, after borrowing it from the Blue Moon Ball, when I'd first found out what was going on at Hartswell Hall. I shivered when I remembered that night and the old people emerging rejuvenated after they'd bathed in the blue crystal's light, activated by the blue moon.

I went to my wardrobe and retrieved it, shaking out the creases and folds. It was soft, sumptuous velvet, so thick that no creases remained, and I put it on, feeling the heavy fabric fall onto my shoulders.

'That's beautiful, Emily,' said my mother, walking into my room and observing me. 'It matches the dress perfectly. Where did you get it from?'

'Oh, it was a fancy dress party I went to ages ago,' I said. 'I never gave it back.'

'Just as well. You look absolutely stunning.'

As I preened in front of the mirror, she noticed the strange symbol on the reverse of the cloak. It was the circle representing the full moon, crossed through with an infinity sign, signifying eternal youth. 'What's that on the back?' she asked, pulling me round.

'I don't know,' I lied. 'Just some design on the fabric.'

'It reminds me of something,' she said, a frown crossing her brow. 'Something I saw many years ago.' She shook her head. 'No, it's gone. The old grey matter's not what it was. I can't remember.'

She stood behind me in the mirror and I looked at our reflection, noticing for the first time the contrast between my youthful seventeen-year old skin and her forty-year old face. I saw the fine, tiny lines around her eyes, the crow's feet between her eyebrows and the faint jowl lines just beginning, and for a second, I felt a deep fear gnawing at my insides. I didn't want my mum to grow old. I didn't want to stay young forever and watch her age.

'If you had the chance to stay young forever, would you do it?' I asked her.

'What kind of question is that, Emily?' she asked. 'Of course I'd love to stay young. Not sure about the forever bit, that sounds like a long time. But who wants to get old and see everything go south?' She studied her face in the mirror. 'Yep, it's all downhill from now on. She pulled the skin tight around her eyes. 'I guess surgery's the next option. Enjoy your youth while you have it, Emily. It disappears all too quickly.' She glanced at her watch. 'It's 7.20. You've got ten minutes to get your make-up on and do your hair. Better look sharp.'

Ten minutes later, I miraculously emerged from my room looking divine, even though I said it myself, thanks to a little help from my mum. She let me borrow her Forever Youthful skin cream and make-up, and the finished effect was amazing. My skin was glowing, smooth and faintly bronzed; my eyes large and dramatic, with sparkling blue eye shadow and lashings of mascara; and my lips sparking and seductive with luscious pale pink frosted lip gel. My blonde hair was pinned up, with small tendrils escaping here and there, creating a glamorous, film star look, and I couldn't help but stare at myself in the mirror.

'Wow, it doesn't even look like me. I look like someone else,' I murmured at my reflection. I imagined staying like this for eternity, without ever getting old. How amazing would that be?

The doorbell sounded and my mum went down stairs to open the front door.

'Emily,' she called up. 'Tash and Seth are here, both looking fantastic.'

As I left my room, I glanced at the crystal pendant lying on the dressing table. For a second, I hesitated, wondering whether to wear it, and quickly put it in the pocket of the blue cloak. 'Just in case,' I murmured to myself.

I walked down the stairs and encountered the twin visions that were Seth and Tash.

'Wow, look at you two,' I said, smiling. 'You look fab.'

'So do you,' said Tash. 'Love the hair.'

'Cool cloak,' said Seth, running his fingers down the velvety folds. 'Especially the hood. You could have some real fun with that cloak. And I love the weird symbol on the back.'

'Hands off, Seth,' I said. 'Your jacket's great. Where d'you get it?'

He was wearing a deep blue velvet jacket, with a pale blue shirt and blue jeans.

'My mum picked it up in a vintage shop in Soho last weekend,' he said. 'Supposed to be Gucci, I guess it is pretty cool.'

Tash, too, looked beautiful. Her floor length, midnight blue dress luckily had long sleeves, hiding much of the orange tan, and she'd managed to cover the bits that were showing with light make-up, so she looked like she'd just returned from a holiday in the Bahamas rather than a trip to a nuclear plant. Like me, she'd pinned up her hair, with small curls escaping here and there, giving her a look of thrown-together, effortless glamour. She placed a small overnight case in the hallway.

'That's my stuff for the morning, don't want to take it to the prom.'

'Are you sure you girls are going to be okay for a few days while I'm not here?' asked my mum, fluttering around us.

'Of course, Mrs Morgan,' replied Tash. 'We're going to have wild parties every night, didn't Emily tell you?'

'Don't worry, mum, we'll be fine. Just go away and have a lovely holiday.'

Part of me desperately didn't want her to go, especially given this was my last few days before my initiation. But I couldn't tell her that and it seemed selfish to ask her to stay at home. She needed this holiday. It was just that by the time she got back, I'd have changed forever. I wondered if she'd notice. Putting the thought out of my head, I focused on the evening ahead.

'Come on. Selfie,' I said, getting my phone out of my clutch bag. 'You too, mum.'

I held up my phone and we posed while I took the picture. Little did I know it was to be the last photo I took of us all together before events took a much darker turn.

We climbed into Martha, feeling excited at attending our first prom. Okay, it wasn't the genuine thing, with limos and ball gowns and months of planning. That was another year away. But despite it being a quickly arranged showcase evening for the benefit of Miss Widdicombe's son, it was nonetheless a big occasion in our social calendar. Even Tash good naturedly handled Seth's teasing.

'Go on, Tash, show me anger. Show me surprise.'

'Back off, smartass,' she said, her face still strangely mask-like and fixed. 'You're a fine one to talk with your poncey blue velvet jacket. Where did your mum find that? In the Ladies' department?'

'Okay, children, that's enough,' I said as I turned Martha's ignition key. It never ceased to thrill me when I heard the cavernous growl of her engine and felt the power that lurked beneath her bonnet. I rolled down the window and waved goodbye to my mum.

'Have a lovely time,' she called, standing on the front step. 'You all look gorgeous. I wish I was coming. See you in a week's time, Emily. Don't do anything I wouldn't do.'

'That means I can do anything,' I called back. 'Have a great holiday.'

As we drove away, we passed a familiar figure walking up the road. It was Juke.

'Oh, look, Seth, it's your new best friend,' I announced. 'Wouldn't you rather spend the evening with him and my mum?'

'Tempting,' said Seth, 'but not when I have such gorgeous girls surrounding me.'

'Yuk, pass the sick bag,' said Tash. 'If that's the best you can do, I'd give up now.'

I pulled to a halt and rolled down the window.

'Hey, Juke,' I called.

No doubt about it, he was cool. He was wearing a battered old fringed suede bush jacket, with torn jeans, ancient Timberland boots and a crumpled old brown leather bush hat. His guitar was slung over his shoulder.

'Hey, Emily,' he said, his face breaking into a crinkled smile. 'Where you off to all dolled up?'

'It's our True Blue prom,' I said.

'Hence we're all wearing blue,' called Tash from the back seat.

'There's a cool band playing,' said Seth. 'The Blue Walrus. Ever heard of 'em, Juke?'

'Can't say I have,' said Juke, grinning broadly, 'but you have a great evening. I'm going to see your mum before she goes on holiday, Emily.'

'Okay, have fun. See you soon,' I said.

I was just about to roll up the window, when he leant forward and spoke in an undertone. 'You be careful, Emily. Don't be on your own. There are things in this village I don't like. Make sure Tash stays with you while your mum's away, okay?'

'Okay,' I said, feeling a slight chill pass over me. What was he talking about? Surely not the de Lucis family?

But the moment was over. He was waving us goodbye and I was pulling away.

'What did he mean?' asked Tash.

'He's just looking out for you,' said Seth. 'It's called parental anxiety. Affects older people. I get it all the time from my mum. It's like they see danger everywhere. Hey, d'you think I'd suit one of those bush hats? Or even dreadlocks? Who says getting old can't be cool? If I could be half as cool as Juke I'd be happy.'

'In your dreams, Seth,' said Tash. 'You gotta get rid of that furry jacket, first.'

We arrived at college and I parked Martha, feeling the beat of the pulsing music before we got out.

'Sounds more like a rock gig,' said Tash, opening the door. 'D'you think we're a bit overdressed?'

'No, we're fine, I think anything goes,' I said, 'although I'm not sure about a fitted velvet jacket.'

'You may mock,' said Seth, sagely, 'but I think you'll find they're making a comeback. I am uber-trendy.'

'Problem is, you're so far ahead, it hasn't arrived yet,' pointed out Tash,

We all laughed and I wondered if we'd still have this relationship once I'd been initiated. Still, we had the evening to look forward to and I put thoughts of the blue crystal out of my head.

Inside the college reception area, a queue had formed, as people waited to hand in their tickets for admission. The music was much louder now we were getting close and a feeling of anticipation and excitement filled the air. Everywhere we looked were blue-clad college kids, in ball gowns, dresses, jackets, shirts, t-shirts, jeans and trousers.

'Cool cloak, Emily,' called Cassie Patel, from my English class, further down the line.

'Thanks,' I called back.

'Nice cloth,' said Ko Chung Ho, the college maths genius, feeling the lapel of Seth's jacket between his fingers, causing us to turn away and snigger. 'Where d'you get it, Seth?'

'Looks like you got yourself a fan,' whispered Tash, seeing Seth's expression. Attracting the college nerd was not part of his plan.

Soon we were handing in our tickets and walking across the foyer to the hall. As we opened the main door, the sight that met our eyes was amazing. The band was on stage, lit by eerie blue light, playing to a sea of heaving blue bodies that moved as one to the thumping music.

'They only play songs with blue in the title or by a band with blue in the name,' explained Seth. 'Could be interesting, musically speaking. This is Blue Oyster Cult, Don't Fear the Reaper.'

'I don't care what it is as long as we can dance,' shouted Tash. 'Come on, let's get in there.'

She pushed forward into the heaving bodies and we followed, squeezing towards the front to get a better view of the band. The song ended to rapturous applause and they began another.

'Deacon Blue, Real Gone Kid,' shouted Seth over the intro.

'It's quite useful having your own personal DJ,' I mouthed to Tash. 'Not sure I'd know what these songs are.'

Soon we were dancing in the middle of the crowd, enjoying the music, the atmosphere and the occasion. It wasn't long before I realised I would have to take off my cloak. It might look dramatic, but it wasn't made for a rock concert and I was starting to get very hot.

'Back in a minute,' I shouted to Tash, pushing my way to the edge of the dance floor. I quickly untied my blue cloak, leaving it on the back of a chair. Soon I was back in the heaving mass, dancing for all I was worth, losing myself in the moment, transfixed by the guys on stage, each bathed in brilliant blue light. The song came to an end and then the lead singer was asking for volunteers to sing backing vocals.

'Do we have any girls who'll come up and help with this next song?' he called out, his hair seemingly bright blue in the spotlight.

'This is so me,' declared Tash, and began to push her way through the throng of girls crowding towards the stage. Next thing we knew, the singer was helping Tash on to the stage and she was one of a handful of girls being instructed to sing into a microphone.

'This is a song originally performed by Madonna in the 1980s, but we've made it our own,' he announced. 'This is called True Blue. And girls, when you hear "True Blue, baby I love you", that's your bit. So sing out.'

The song began and the girls sang for all they were worth. They looked amazing, especially Tash, with her long blue dress and pre-Raphaelite red hair, now unpinned and falling over her shoulders.

'How are you?' I heard a voice breathe into my ear. Then Theo's hands were around my waist and he was pulling me to him.

'All the better for seeing you,' I turned sideways to see him. He was dressed immaculately in a pale blue linen jacket, with a matching shirt and blue jeans, his blonde hair gleaming blue in the light.

'You look gorgeous,' he said, running his hands down the side of my dress. 'Very slinky. And I love the hair. It suits you.'

He kissed my neck, and I turned back to watch Tash, Theo's arms around my middle, luxuriating in his closeness, feeling fantastic. Feeling safe.

'Thank you, girls,' said the lead singer, when the song was over, 'And now we have one for all the lovers out there.' There was a communal groan at this, which turned to applause when they began to sing 'Guilty' by Blue.

'Come on, Emily, this one's for us,' said Theo, turning me round and pulling me to him.

As the words began, all I could think was how appropriate they were for us and how much I loved this strange, beautiful boy with the clear blue eyes that led to infinity. Theo held me tight and we danced slowly, lost in our own world, forgetting everything and everyone around us. For a couple of minutes, it was just Theo and me and the music. Too soon the track ended and Theo led me by the hand off the dance floor.

'Would you like a drink?' he asked.

'Yes please, I'm parched.' I followed him to the bar area that had been set up in the cafeteria and was soon sipping an orange juice.

'Where's Violet?' I asked, wondering if she would deign to speak to me.

'Over there,' said Theo, pointing to a group of girls to one side of the café area.

I looked across. Violet stood head and shoulders above them and looked incredible. She was wearing a catsuit with flared legs and a halter-top in a dark blue chiffon fabric that moulded itself to her body. The outfit itself was stunning enough, especially given her statuesque figure, but what made it outstanding were the tiny silver stars studded into the fabric, each glinting and shining in the light, making her look as if she was sparkling. Dark blue platform shoes gave her additional height, and her blonde hair was partially pinned up at the back, leaving the rest cascading down her shoulders. I couldn't help but stare. She was a vision and the other girls crowded around her, basking in her glory.

'Come on,' said Theo, 'let's go back and see what the band's doing next'

'Okay,' I said, dragging my gaze away from Violet.

We walked back into the main hall where the band was playing a cover of Blue Monday by New Order. The dancers had thinned out somewhat, most taking a breather at the sides of the room or in the bar, so the dance floor was relatively free. I can only think it was the lure of the near empty dance floor, along with the excitement of the occasion and the need to show off, that made Seth act as he did. To start with, we didn't take much notice of the small crowd of kids down by the stage, thinking they were just watching the band. Then we realised they were surrounding someone who was dancing at their centre.

'Let's take a look,' said Theo and led me down to the stage area.

There in the middle of the crowd, Seth was dancing, dressed in my blue cloak. Round and round he spun, like a whirling dervish, swooping the cloak around him, so that it billowed out dramatically. I started to laugh. He looked so ridiculous. I felt Theo stiffen at my side, as he recognised the blue cloak I'd taken from the Blue Moon Ball.

'Where did he get that cloak from?' he said through clenched teeth.

I looked up at him, his face thunderous in the weird blue light.

'It's my fault, Theo,' I stuttered. 'I'm sorry. I put it on over my blue dress and left it hanging over a chair when I got too hot. Seth must have found it.'

'He'd better take it off quickly or I can't vouch for the consequences,' said Theo tightly, and I saw his hands were balled into fists.

'Okay, I'll make him stop,' I said, realising the situation could get out of hand if I didn't act quickly.

'Seth,' I called out, 'stop dancing. Give me my cloak back.'

But of course, he didn't hear me. The music was too loud and he was enjoying the attention.

I never saw Theo move. One minute he was standing by my side and the next he was alongside Seth, grabbing hold of the cloak and telling him to stop. I could barely bring myself to watch as Seth refused and Theo took action. With a short, sharp jab, he punched Seth in the face, who looked momentarily surprised, and . went down like a ninepin. Theo stooped over him and in one deft movement, untied the cloak and pulled it from him. Groggily, Seth got to his feet and went for Theo, aiming at his face. He might as well have been punching concrete for all the impact he had. He ricocheted off Theo's body and fell backwards. At this point, I realised things could go badly wrong for Seth if the fight continued. I ran towards Theo, begging him to stop.

'No more, Theo, please. He didn't mean any harm. It was only a bit of fun. Let's go.'

'No,' shouted Seth, getting back on to his feet. 'Stay and finish what you started, Goldilocks.' He charged at Theo. 'You should never have come to this village, with your weird ways, taking Emily away from us. Why don't you go back where you came from?' The momentum of his movement was meant to knock Theo over, but Seth was no match for a supernatural being and he bounced back, hitting the deck once again.

'Satisfied, Emily?' said a voice in my ear. 'Now you have two men fighting over you?'

It was Violet. I looked up into her cold blue eyes.

Now Tash joined in the affray. 'Seth's right,' she hurled at Violet. 'Everything was okay until you and your brother appeared on the scene, looking so sophisticated and glamorous. But it's all a front, isn't it? I know what really goes on.'

'Tash, no,' I said, desperately willing her to shut up.

'Why don't you back off, Ginger,' said Violet, spitefully. 'Shame nobody's interested in you. There again, your personality's seriously lacking and as for that fake tan, it looks ridiculous.'

It was too much for Tash. The tension of the last few days came to a head and something snapped in her head. Without warning, her fist flew out and connected with Violet's jaw. She took Violet by surprise, knocking her into the crowd.

'How dare you,' cried Violet, rubbing her jaw and coming back at Tash. She grabbed her hair and pulled her head back. 'You seriously don't want to mess with me, Ginger. You can only ever come off worst.'

'I am so not ginger,' said Tash through clenched teeth. 'Let go of my hair.'

She grabbed Violet's arm and stepped backwards, but missed her footing as she did so, and the two tumbled to the floor, locked in a catfight, clawing and scratching at one another.

A crowd rapidly formed around them, cat whistling and cheering, and I was aware the band had stopped. Over by the stage, I saw Theo pull up Seth, who was looking considerably the worse for wear, blood dripping from his nose, one eye already closing. Next thing we knew, the lights were switched on and Miss Widdicombe rushed into the hall, followed by two other members of staff.

'All right, break it up,' she shouted, attempting to pull Violet and Tash apart. Realising that the lights were on and they had an audience, the two girls stopped fighting. Tash got to her feet, looking daggers at Violet, who was already up and dusting down her catsuit. Both looked dishevelled, hair in disarray, clothes grubby from the floor.

Theo stepped forward, smoothing his jacket and holding the cloak. 'Emily, I suggest you get Tash home before she says or does anything else. Violet, I'm taking you back. I'm sure Miss Widdicombe can look after Seth. He needs to cool down.'

'We can't leave Seth,' I started to say, but Theo interrupted.

'He'll be fine, Emily. Just go home. Aquila is out there, he'll follow you and make sure you get back safely.'

'I thought Aquila would be driving you home,' I said.

'No, we borrowed LaDrach's Kawasaki. Unusually for her, she was feeling generous.'

Seth sat on the edge of the stage, surrounded by a crowd of anxious girls, with Miss Widdicombe tending to his bleeding nose.

'Are you okay, Seth?' I called over.

'He'll be fine, Emily,' said Miss Widdicombe brusquely. 'I'll sort out him out and drop him off later. You and Tash get home. Theo, we'll have words about this on Monday. I expected better of you.' She addressed the crowds hanging round the hall. 'All right, everyone, the prom's over. You've had a good party, now it's time to say goodnight.'

Theo wrapped the cloak around my shoulders, saying quietly 'See you tomorrow, Emily. Don't worry. These two weeks were never going to be easy. Not long to wait now. Goodnight sweetheart.'

He went to take Violet's arm, but she brushed him off abruptly.

'Come on, Vi, let's go,' he said gently. 'It's not worth making a scene.'

Darting a last venomous look at us, she reluctantly followed her brother.

'Come on, Tash, let's go,' I said and together we walked out of the hall.

In the car park, an admiring crowd had gathered around Bellynda LaDrach's motorbike. Tash and I sat in Martha, watching Theo and Violet leave the college reception area. They strode purposefully towards the mean machine, dressed in black leather jackets and shiny black motorcycle helmets, and were soon sitting astride it, Violet as pillion passenger. Theo squeezed the throttle. The engine's deep roar filled the air and they were off, shooting forward like a black missile and leaving the crowd behind, watching open mouthed.

For a few moments longer, we sat in Martha, watching people come and go in the car park. I looked around for Aquila but although I couldn't see him, I knew he would be there somewhere. Much as I disliked him, it was still comforting to know we were being protected.

'Are you okay?' I asked, glancing over at Tash.

'Yes, I'm fine,' she said, rubbing her hand. 'I'll have to put some ice on this. It was like punching granite.' She grinned. 'At least I decked Violet. That was worth getting a sore hand for.'

'I have to admit, it was quite spectacular,' I said, smiling. 'And I've no doubt Seth will be bragging about his altercation with Theo.'

I started the ignition. 'Let's go home. That's enough excitement for one night.'

I turned on the sound system and we drove home to the soothing sounds of Ellie Goulding's Beating Heart.

Neither of us noticed the dark figure crouched on the car's back seat.

I pulled up onto the driveway at the front of our house, and turned to Tash.

'Sorry,' I said quietly. 'I never meant for it to be like this. I just wanted….' I stopped as a sudden movement in the rear view mirror attracted my attention. Too late I saw the dark hooded figure rising up behind us.

'Tash, run,' I shouted, but there was no time.

Before she could open the door, the figure struck. I felt a violent blow on the back of my head and the world went black.

The large bird following the car perched on a nearby branch and watched. Then it silently glided away, its eyes glittering with satisfaction.

PART 2: DISAPPEARANCE

17. Abduction

The bird alighted on the ledge of an upper storey window and tapped at the glass with its beak. A hand pulled up the sash and allowed it to enter. Inside, two figures sat chatting, looking at the bird expectantly. It quickly assumed human form.

'Has something occurred?' asked one of them. 'Why do you return so soon?'

The answer made them smile with satisfaction.

'The girl and her friend have been taken. Our problem is solved.'

'Good,' replied one of the figures. 'There shall be no bargaining. I have my orders. With any luck, they will be dead within days.'

The other figure gave a sigh of relief. She could not have asked for a better outcome.

* * *

Mr Nelson looked at the two unconscious girls in the front of the car and smiled. So far so good. Breaking in to the Mini had been a doddle. Years of street life and living on the edge had given him useful skills. Now all he had to do was deliver his captives. He moved the girls to the back seat and quickly drove the car out of the village, following the country lanes until he reached an overgrown farm track, unused for many years. A few hundred yards up the track, half-hidden by a profusion of vegetation, he located the white van he'd stolen earlier. Now, it was a simple of matter of moving the girls into the van and concealing the Mini beneath the overhanging branches. Shame he'd hit the one who was driving so hard. He hadn't meant to make her bleed. Still, she was alive and that was all that mattered.

With the girls in the rear of the van, he drove back down the country lanes until he was once again in the village. He parked in the church car park alongside the village hall, thankful that work was still going on rebuilding the graveyard's easterly wall. The workmen would be back early in the morning, covering up any tracks he'd made.

Taking a large crowbar and a torch from the passenger seat, he locked the van and walked into the graveyard, searching in the darkness until he found the old rectangular vault, its sides covered with creeping ivy and moss, the lid weathered and worn. He ran his fingers along its smooth surface and around the rough edges, looking for a place where the stone had worn away slightly. Inserting the crowbar, he began to prise up the lid, gradually edging it away from the base. A small gap appeared and he shone his torch inside, a large grin spreading across his face as he saw the old stone stairway, hewn into the rock, leading down beneath the church.

'Bingo!' he muttered, and began to push the lid with renewed vigour until there was a large enough gap for him to climb inside.

The hard graft wasn't over, because now he had to carry each girl from the van, through the churchyard and into the vault, down the old stone steps and into the gloom beneath. Twice he did the precarious journey, until both girls were lying in the dark crypt beneath, where the Dark One waited impatiently. Not that he was grateful.

'Why do you bring me two girls? Only one is of interest. What good is the other?'

'Call it collateral damage,' he answered flatly. 'It'll give you double the bargaining power. Now, there's even more reason for them to release the crystal to you. And if one of them doesn't make it, you still have the other. You can't lose.'

He felt rather than saw the Dark One draw near and shuddered as the filmy figure whispered in his ear, giving him instructions. A deathly, decaying coldness filled the air, making his flesh crawl, and once he'd been told what to do, he didn't wait to hear more. Such a feeling of dread descended on him that he quickly abandoned his victims to their fates and hurried back up the old stone steps. He pushed the vault's heavy lid back into place and ran to the van, reversing out of the car park at speed, desperate to get away from the dark, underground crypt with its heinous secret.

* * *

The speeding van woke Juke from a fitful sleep. He sat upright in bed and rubbed his eyes. A dim remnant of a bad dream played in his head, but the harder he tried to remember, the more the details slipped away.

As his eyes grew accustomed to the early morning darkness, his thoughts became clearer. He got out of bed and walked to the window, pulling back the heavy drapes and staring into the street below. A feeling of oppressiveness hovered over him and he knew instinctively something was wrong. He put his hands over his eyes and focused within, allowing his mind to travel and explore beyond the confines of the small room. What he encountered chilled him to the bone.

'Emily's been taken,' he said to himself. 'I see a dark energy surrounding her.'

He sat on the edge of the bed, thinking deeply. This was bad. His mobile phone sounded, indicating he had a text message. Seeing it was from Emily's mother, he switched off the phone, not knowing what to say.

* * *

Late the previous evening, Larry O'Hanlon, ancient caretaker of Hartsdown College had been taking a quick look round, assessing the damage in the aftermath of the True Blue Prom. Thankfully, he found nothing more than empty cups, items of clothing and a torn banner proclaiming 'Blue Walrus welcomes you to the True Blue Prom'.

'This won't take long to clear up. I'll leave it till the morning,' he declared.

Thoughts of a whisky nightcap and a late night film filling his head, he went to turn off the lights, pausing as he saw something glinting on the floor.

He stooped to pick up the delicate blue crystal pendant, holding it in his palm and letting the light catch its sparkling facets. It made him feel strangely energised, as if he were lying on a beautiful warm beach in the hot sunshine.

'Would you look at that,' he said quietly. 'Isn't that beautiful? Someone's going to be missing it.'

He quickly popped the pendant into his jacket pocket and turned off the lights, closing and locking the door behind him.

18. **Missing**

By 6.30 the next morning, a sombre group gathered at the hall. In the early hours, Juke had pounded the village roads and streets, fruitlessly searching for the cream Mini or any sign of Emily and Tash. Finding nothing, he had walked up the long gravel driveway to Hartswell Hall and, in desperation, pounded on the huge, carved oak door. Viyesha had answered, quickly assembling the family in the library when she heard Juke's news. Now he paced the floor in front of them, unable to calm his agitation.

'Are you sure about this, Juke?' asked Viyesha. 'The girls may have gone to someone else's house for the night. It's what teenage girls do, isn't it?'

'No,' he answered shortly, 'something is wrong. Emily's energy levels are weak. Her Mini is missing and there's no answer at her house. She's been taken. I just don't know where or by whom.'

'I can't believe I didn't see Emily home,' said Theo bitterly. 'You were supposed to be guarding her, Aquila. What happened?'

Aquila looked thunderous. 'Of course I guarded her. I followed her back from the college, as you requested, and made sure she arrived home.'

'And did she?' asked Theo.

'Yes,' replied Aquila, glancing at Pantera and Bellynda. 'She parked on the driveway, then she and her friend went into the house.'

'So where is she now?' exclaimed Juke. 'Something took her. And Tash as well.'

'Has Emily tried to contact you using her crystal, Theo?' asked Viyesha.

'No,' he said, flatly. 'There's been nothing.'

'How about Emily's mother? Does she know her daughter is missing?' asked Viyesha. 'And Tash's parents?'

'Emily's mother is on holiday in Spain for a week,' said Juke. 'She knows nothing. Tash was supposed to be staying at Emily's, so she hasn't been missed yet. It buys us a little time.'

'We must keep this under wraps for as long as possible,' said Viyesha. 'We cannot risk the authorities getting involved.'

'I'd like to know why you're in this village, Juke,' demanded Aquila. 'Why here and why now?'

Theo watched Juke closely, his face white and tense, worry etched into his features. 'Time to come clean, Juke,' he muttered.

'Okay. I admit it. I'm an energy sensor,' answered Juke, holding up his hands. 'I work for the light. I uphold the principles of light and truth. It's my mission to seek out dark matter and destroy it.'

'Very worthwhile,' said Bellynda disparagingly, 'but you haven't answered Aquila's question. Why are you here? Seems strange that Emily disappears just as you arrive on the scene.'

'You can't think I had anything to do with it?' demanded Juke incredulously. 'Believe me, I'm on your side. I'm here to help.'

'I believe you,' said Viyesha calmly, 'but I would like to know why you're here in Hartswell-on-the-Hill.'

Juke looked around the room and chose his words carefully.

'Because I've detected a dark energy building and growing. Here in this village.'

Viyesha watched him closely. 'It's true we had feeders circling in the fields, but Pantera and Aquila destroyed them. Except for one that gained access to the hall. But that was soon eliminated.'

'I'm not talking about feeders,' said Juke. 'This is bigger and more powerful.'

'Could it be Reptilia?' breathed Viyesha softly. 'Seeking what we have in order to achieve human form?'

'If you mean the crystal, then, yes, you could be right,' said Juke.

'How do you know of our crystal?' said Leon, looking at Juke sharply.

'Hey, I'm an energy sensor. Your crystal's been shining out like a beacon. I wouldn't be any good at my job if I didn't detect something as powerful as that. The problem is I'm just one of the many moths it's attracted.'

'At least we know it's not that scum detective who's taken Emily,' said Theo. 'Pantera saw to that.'

'It's true,' said Pantera. 'He was little more than a bloodied pulp by the time I'd finished with him.'

'You're sure it was him?' asked Joseph.

Pantera sneered at him dismissively. 'I'd know his foul scent anywhere.'

'Whoever has taken her is from the dark side,' said Juke. 'I see dark energy all around her.'

'Hey, I'm sensitive too and I haven't seen any darkness,' said Joseph.

'Me neither,' agreed Violet.

'You will,' said Juke ominously. 'It's beneath the surface, getting stronger all the time. That's why we have to get the girls back quickly.'

'You're talking rubbish,' spat out Aquila in his heavy Eastern European accent. 'This is a smokescreen to deflect us from the truth.'

'And that being?' asked Joseph.

'He's taken her himself. We can't trust him.'

They all stared at Juke, suddenly unsure of the stranger in their midst. A loud hammering at the front door distracted their attention.

'Who's that?' said Viyesha, looking worried. 'Joseph, go and see. Could it be the girls returned?' she asked hopefully.

Joseph hurried to the large front door and the sound of angry voices filled the air. Seconds later, Seth burst into the room.

'What's happened to Emily and Tash?' he demanded. 'I just heard they never got home. I should have been there to look after them, and I would have been if it hadn't been for him.' He jabbed his finger at Theo.

Seth's nose was taped across the bridge, one eye was a brilliant purple and his upper lip was swollen and red. His right hand was bandaged, with just the fingertips showing.

'What happened to you, Seth?' asked Joseph. 'You look like you went ten rounds.'

'As good as,' said Seth, glaring at Theo. 'Remind me never to punch your cousin again, I've broken three fingers on my right hand.'

'Sorry,' said Theo. 'It wouldn't have happened if you hadn't been wearing one of our blue cloaks.'

'How was I to know it was yours?' exclaimed Seth. 'It was just something Emily was wearing. I was only having a bit of fun.'

'How did Emily get one of our cloaks?' asked Viyesha. 'No don't tell me. We have more important things to discuss. Seth, as you're here, tell us when you last saw Emily and Tash.'

'At the prom. I was supposed to go home with them, but Theo and I had a fight. I ended up in A&E. That's why they went home alone. This would never have happened if I'd been with them. I thought you were going to see them home,' he said pointedly to Theo.

'After Violet and Tash started fighting, I had to keep them apart…' began Theo.

'Violet and Tash fighting, too?' said Viyesha, raising her eyebrows. 'It appears things got out of hand last night.'

'I'm sorry, mother,' said Violet with tears in her eyes. 'She went for me. There was nothing I could do. It was all about Seth.'

'It was?' said Seth, looking pleased. 'You were fighting over me? How cool is that?'

Feeling their eyes on him, he quickly backtracked. 'Well, it would be if they weren't missing. Do you know what's happened?'

'We think they've been abducted,' said Juke, 'but there aren't any clues.'

'So why aren't you out looking for them?' asked Seth. 'You gotta do something.'

'I agree,' said Leon. 'We need to get out there.' He made some quick decisions. 'Violet, you go to Emily's house and see if the girls turn up. Viyesha, stay at the Hall in case any contact is made. Theo, Joseph and I will search the village. Juke and Seth, you can come with us. Check every road, garage, shed, and outbuilding… Aquila and Pantera, scout round the area. You can cover more ground, see if you can discover anything. We'll meet back here at 12 noon. Bellynda, I'm assuming you'll remain on guard in the Clock Tower.'

They each nodded their assent and one by one silently left the room.

Aquila, Pantera and Bellynda were last to leave.

'You must appear to look for the girls with the rest,' Bellynda instructed them. 'But whatever you do, make sure they're not found. Emily's death will make life so much easier, eh, Pantera?'

Pantera nodded. 'I have waited a long time to settle this score.'

19. **Conduit**

As the family convened in the library to discuss Emily's disappearance, Mr Nelson returned, creeping through the grounds of Hartswell Hall. He'd abandoned the white van in the long stay car park at a nearby mainline railway station, about five miles from the village. Its multi-storey car park was full of vehicles, including a number of white vans. He'd left the ignition key concealed in the wheel arch, just in case, and made his way back to the village on foot. Tired from his earlier exertions and stopping every so often to take a quick mouthful from the small silver hip flask he carried in his raincoat pocket, it had taken him some time to reach the Hall.

'I'm too old for this,' he muttered to himself breathlessly, wishing he hadn't been such a voracious pipe smoker in the last few years. 'Still, I've done everything I've been asked. Soon I can look forward to the pay out.'

His mouth salivated at the thought of what he could do with the promised money. Buy an Aston Martin, he'd always fancied one of those; take a long holiday in the Bahamas, that was a definite; acquire an attractive young girlfriend - he might not be God's gift, but money always had appeal. His face leered at the thought of a pretty young thing hanging on his arm and he was so enamoured of this particular daydream, he almost fell into a ditch.

'Focus, Nelson,' he cajoled himself. 'Time enough for fancies later.'

Hidden by the bushes and keeping to the shadows, he crept up the hall's main drive, taking the path past the rose garden to the old walled garden. Nearly there. All he had to do was get inside. It didn't take him long to find the ancient carved door. He turned the handle, but it was locked.

Quickly, he pulled out a coil of thin nylon rope with a small hook attached to one end. He threw the hook over the wall, watching it arc high and hearing it land with a thud on the other side. He pulled hard until the hook caught. Giving it a sharp tug to make sure it was anchored and donning a pair of suede gardening gloves, he grasped the rope and, puffing loudly, began to pull himself upwards.

He was soon on top of the wall. Now it was simply a matter of swinging down to the ground below.

Inside the walled garden it was dark and shadowy, despite the early morning light. Taking out a flashlight, he discovered an overgrown pathway leading through the jungle of bushes and brambles and slowly made his way forward. After a few hundred metres the pathway opened out into a natural clearing and there before him stood an ornate ruined building, its ancient brickwork silhouetted against the brightening sky.

'A gothic folly,' he declared, staring up at its arched recesses, surprised it hadn't been renovated like the rest of the grounds.

Seeing an old log that had fallen inside the folly's walls, he sat down and took out his hip flask. He drank deeply, feeling the liquor warm his insides. In no time, his body gave way to exhaustion and he fell into a deep sleep.

He dreamt he was back underground, trudging through the sewage pipe, the rancid odour making it difficult to breathe. His feet moved slowly, sucked down by the vile filth that threatened to drag him under. Then he was climbing out of the sewer and into the large vaulted cavern he'd visited before. He listened for the menacing reptilian voice that had previously given him orders, but all was silent. Well, not quite. There was a faint background noise he couldn't quite place. A slipping, sliding sort of sound. With a shudder, he remembered the black creatures lining every surface of the chamber, and strained to see through the darkness. As before, he saw an undulating, moving blackness covering the walls and arches, like a mass of pulsating jellyfishes, and felt a creeping despair start to fill his mind.

Without warning, one of the black shapes dropped.

He barely had time to scream before the thing landed on his back, spreading over his shoulders like a dark cloak and absorbing his vital energy. As he tried in vain to shake it off, another dropped, and another, landing on his back, his front, his head and his arms. Within seconds he was a seething mass of dark matter, feeding on his life force, deleting his thoughts one by one.

Back inside the ruined folly, Mr Nelson's sleeping form twitched and turned. His body suddenly jerked violently and he twisted on to his stomach, his eyes rolling back in their sockets. Slowly, a black shape detached itself from his back, flowing silently across the floor and up the walls of the folly. It was followed by another, and another, until gradually a steady stream of black feeders seeped out of Mr Nelson's back, each finding a place in the folly's old brickwork. Within half an hour, the graceful structure was all but hidden beneath the swarming dark shapes, and yet still more flowed from his comatose figure.

Mr Nelson had become a conduit, enabling feeders to pass effortlessly from the crypt below up to the hall grounds. And having tasted human energy, the feeders wanted more. They might be seeking human form, but their immediate hunger was for human life.

As events in the folly unfolded, Hartswell-on-the-Hill woke bright and early to a vibrant new morning, unaware of the horror in its midst.

20. **Family Council**

At noon, the family assembled back at the hall. Everyone was there except Seth.

'Where's Seth?' asked Violet. 'We can't start without him.'

Theo shrugged. 'Probably still licking his wounds. We don't need him, Violet, I don't see how he can help.'

'I'm sure he'll be here soon,' said Viyesha. ' Now, has anyone found any evidence of how the girls were taken?' She looked around the group.

They all shook their heads.

'There's nothing,' said Theo, in despair. 'It's as if they've vanished into thin air. There's no sign of Martha and nobody has seen or heard anything. We have no idea where they are.'

'Juke, can you detect anything more about this dark energy?' asked Viyesha.

He frowned. 'I get the feeling something's blocking Emily's energy. She has a very bright aura, as I'm sure you know, Violet.'

'Yeah, it's usually bright blue.'

'Well, I get the sense something's being used to conceal her energy, to hold it back from us, which means we're dealing with an abductor who knows about such things.'

'There is another possibility,' said Theo, slowly. 'Emily could be dead. That would stop her energy shining.' He looked at his mother. 'I can't face going through this again,' he said, his face white and strained. 'I'd rather die.'

'We'll have none of that, Theo,' said his mother, sharply. 'She's been taken, I'm sure of it, and is being kept against her will. Someone or something is shielding her.' She turned to Juke. 'How about Tash? Do you detect anything from her?'

He frowned again. 'Maybe a faint glimmer. It's too weak to be sure.'

'So, what do we do now?' asked Joseph.

'Wait until the captors get in touch?' suggested Leon. 'Although we know what they want.'

'The girls for the crystal,' said Viyesha, in a whisper, 'which we cannot do. It would be a death sentence for us all. We are in an impossible situation.'

'We're not in any situation yet,' said Juke pragmatically. 'There's no point jumping the gun. We have to take this one step at a time. For the moment, we must wait.'

'There must be something we can do,' said Theo, jumping up and facing them angrily. 'Aquila, you had a bird's eye view of the area this morning. Didn't you see anything? Emily's car abandoned somewhere? If anyone could see it, it's you.'

Aquila looked at him coldly. 'I saw nothing,' he said, in a clipped, mechanical voice.

'How far did you go?' asked Theo. 'Could you have missed something?'

'I saw nothing,' he repeated with a snarl. 'If there was, I would have found it.'

'Maybe you weren't looking hard enough,' said Theo through clenched teeth. 'It's no secret how much you dislike her.'

Aquila smiled unpleasantly at his words and that proved to be the breaking point for Theo. He flew at Aquila, his hands grasping the chauffeur's shirt collar and pinning him back against the wall. 'You're nothing but a filthy scavenger,' he shouted in Aquila's face. 'I don't believe you didn't see anything.'

'Theo, that's enough,' cried Leon, rising from his seat and placing his hands on Theo's shoulders. 'Calm down, this is not helping. I understand your frustration, but we need to keep a clear head. Fighting amongst ourselves achieves nothing.'

Slowly, Theo let go of Aquila's shirt, and shot him a venomous look. His father might be right, but it didn't mean he had to trust Aquila. He returned to his seat, his shoulders slumped forward in unhappiness and despair.

'Okay, folks, let's go over this again…' began Juke, when he was interrupted by the sound of a moped put-putting up the driveway. It came to a halt outside the hall and seconds later the door was flung open to reveal Seth.

'I've found Martha,' he exclaimed breathlessly. 'I would have called but my phone was out of juice. I came as quickly as I could.'

'Found Martha where?' demanded Theo. 'Any sign of Emily or Tash?'

'Not that I could see,' answered Seth. 'The car's parked up a farm track a couple of miles away, by Sticketts Farm. I only saw her by chance. Her keys are still in the ignition, but the car's empty.' He caught sight of Aquila glowering and couldn't resist a dig. 'I'm surprised you didn't see her Aquila, given your eagle eyes. There again, what match is a bunch of immortals against Super Seth on his moped?'

Violet looked at him in admiration, but Theo rose to the bait.

'Don't push your luck, Seth,' he said angrily. 'I could finish you off like that.' He snapped his fingers to make a point.

Seth was unafraid. 'Ooh, scary boy. Do you want to see where Martha is or not?'

'We're right behind you, Seth,' said Leon. 'Why don't you show us?'

No one thought to ask him how he knew of their immortal status. For the moment, there were bigger issues to focus on.

A strange convoy set off from the hall: Theo, Leon and Juke riding with Aquila in the Jaguar, Joseph riding pillion with Bellynda on the Kawasaki, and Seth leading the way on his moped.

Viyesha, Violet and Pantera remained at the hall, guarding the crystal and waiting for the kidnapper to make contact.

21. **Martha**

'And you found the car how, exactly?' asked Bellynda as Seth led the way up the overgrown track.

'Sixth sense,' answered Seth, turning back and grinning at her. Despite the seriousness of the situation, he couldn't help himself. 'I put out my energy feelers and they led me here.'

She looked at him dubiously. 'I doubt that very much. I repeat, how did you find it?'

'OK, it was eggs,' he answered cryptically.

'Eggs?' she repeated disbelievingly. 'What are you talking about?'

'My mum told me to pick up some free-range eggs from the farm shop and I took the wrong lane,' he explained. 'The farm shop's the next turning. Anyway, next thing I know, King's Tights, I see Martha's bonnet sticking out from the undergrowth.'

'King's Tights?' she queried, baffled.

'Don't even go there,' advised Theo. 'The boy's half-baked.'

As he spoke, the Mini's cream bonnet came into view, partially hidden beneath a raft of branches.

'Whoever did it hasn't done a very good job of hiding the car,' observed Leon. 'Looks like it was done in a hurry. I'm surprised you missed it, Aquila.'

Aquila shrugged and said nothing, while Juke and Theo helped Leon clear the branches.

'The door's open and the key's in the ignition,' said Seth, 'but I didn't touch anything. Crime scene and all, you know.'

'One thing we won't be doing is getting the police involved, Seth,' advised Juke. 'No mention of this to anyone, okay? We deal with this in our own way.'

Seth raised his eyebrows and tapped his nose. 'Hago, sago. Mum's the word.'

'You don't seem to get the seriousness of the situation, idiot,' said Theo. 'Emily and Tash could be dead for all we know.'

'I get it, all right?' answered Seth. 'I've just got a different way of dealing with it.'

'Okay, break it up,' snapped Leon. 'This unpleasantness ends now. We have more important issues to deal with than your petty squabbles.'

'Exactly,' said Theo in exasperation, pulling open the car door.

He peered inside the cabin and gasped.

'There's blood on the front seats.'

Juke opened the passenger door and looked in. He examined the dark stains.

'You're right, but we don't know if it's Emily's or the attacker's,' he pointed out. He reached into the footwell and brought out a dark blue clutch bag.

'Is this Emily's?' he asked, holding it up, over the car's roof.

'Yeah, it's hers,' said Seth. 'She had it with her last night.'

Juke opened it to reveal a set of house keys and a mobile phone. 'We won't be getting a call from her,' he said. 'What about Tash, did she have a purse or a clutch bag?'

They looked over the car and found another mobile phone in the rear footwell.

'It's Tash's,' confirmed Seth.

'Are there any messages?' asked Juke. 'The kidnapper may have left a demand, assuming the phones would be found.'

'Nothing,' said Seth, scrolling down Tash's phone.

'Just a couple from Emily's mum,' said Theo, looking at Emily's phone.

'What about car tracks, Joseph?' asked Leon, 'Can you see anything?'

'There was definitely another vehicle here,' answered Joseph, examining the ground. 'A large van by the look of it. It's my guess the girls were brought here and moved. Which means the kidnapper probably disabled the girls while they were in the Mini and drove it out here, where the getaway van was concealed. It's possible there were two attackers, but I don't think so. I can see only one set of footprints leading from the car.'

'So what do we do now?' asked Theo, ashen faced.

'We take the car back to the hall,' answered Leon, 'and get Pantera to look inside. She can tell us whose blood this is, human or otherwise.'

A look flickered between Aquila and Bellynda but it was gone in an instant and no one else noticed it.

There was no question as to who would drive Martha. Theo sat inside, turned the ignition and carefully eased the car from its resting place. As the cavalcade left for the hall, Seth fell behind, his 50cc engine no match against the Jaguar and Kawasaki. Realising no one was going to wait for him, he decided to collect his mother's eggs from Sticketts Farm.

'Don't suppose you saw anything strange last night,' he enquired of the wizened old farmer behind the counter.

'Strange? How d'you mean?'

'Did you see a van parked up the old farm track just down the way?'

The old farmer scrutinised him closely.

'Mebbe I did,' he replied at length. 'What's it to you?'

Seth thought quickly. 'My friend had her car stolen last night and we found it down there, hidden under some branches. Looks like they used a van too.'

'Aye, they did,' the farmer informed him. 'VW Transporter 2 litre TDI. White.'

'Really? You're sure?' asked Seth, his eyes widening with interest. 'How d'you know?'

'Problems wi' poachers,' the old farmer told him. 'I were out wi' me old gun dog, Sally, last night, layin' low, waitin' and watchin'. Saw the Transporter come out the old farm track. I shouted for it to stop, but it took no notice. Were off down the lane afore I could do 'owt. Packed full wi' rabbit, no doubt, mebbe some sheep, altho' none seems to be missin'.'

'Yowza!' said Seth, his eyes shining, picking up his eggs, 'Don't suppose you remember what time it was?'

'Half past midnight or round about.'

'Yowza, wowza. Thanks for the info, dude.' He picked up his eggs and made for the door.

'Y977 XOJ,' the farmer called after him. 'I never forget a registration.'

'You saw the reg?' asked Seth, amazed, coming back into the shop. 'Got a pen and paper so I can write it down?'

Back at the hall, Viyesha, Violet and Pantera were waiting on the steps.

'Looks like Emily and Tash were taken away in a van,' Theo told them, getting out of the Mini. 'But we've found blood stains on Martha's front seats."

'Pantera, this is your area,' said Leon. 'Take a look, see what you can pick up.' He opened the front door to the Mini and haughtily, she walked forwards, glancing at Aquila and Bellynda. They watched, impassive, as she leant inside the car, inhaling deeply over the bloodstained areas.

'Do you detect anything that's not human?' asked Juke, peering in after her.

'No, I don't,' she said in a superior tone. She inhaled again.

'This is Emily's blood,' she said, at length, 'but there's another scent, too.'

'That'll be Tash, surely?' asked Theo.

'No, it's a scent other than the girls,' said Pantera, stepping back from the car. She looked puzzled. 'I'm picking up that detective trash, Mr Nelson.'

'But that's impossible, said Viyesha. 'You killed him yourself.'

'So I thought,' said Pantera, 'but the car reeks of him. Somehow, this man is very much alive.'

'So the dark forces could be using him,' said Juke. 'This is making more sense. It looks like they got him to snatch the girls. We need to find this Mr Nelson fast.'

No sooner had he uttered the words, than the put-putting of Seth's moped could be heard coming up the drive.

'Why does he always turn up like an annoying pest?' said Theo, looking irritated.

On cue, Seth dismounted from his moped, removed his safety helmet and grinned widely.

'Greetings earthlings,' he said, holding up his hand. 'I am the Soup Dragon. I come from a universe far away where the ground is blue and made of cheese.'

'I rest my case,' said Theo. 'He's a complete idiot.'

'An idiot armed with information,' corrected Seth. 'Like the fact it was a VW Transporter that took Emily and Tash, with the registration Y977 XOJ.'

Theo stared at him open-mouthed.

'Impressive,' whistled Joseph. 'How did you come by that information, Seth?'

Seth tapped his index finger against the side of his nose. 'Need to know basis, my friend. Just take it from your friendly super-sleuth that the information is indeed accurate.'

'This is no time for games, boy,' said Bellynda, towering over him. 'How do you know?'

Seth grinned at her.

'Eggs,' he replied.

'You're right, Theo,' said Bellynda, with a sideways glance, 'the boy's a fool. Can't even come up with an original answer.'

'It's true,' said Seth, enjoying their annoyance. 'You left me behind, so I went to the farm shop to buy my mum's eggs. I got talking to the farmer, asked if he'd seen anything strange last night and wham bam, thank you ma'am, turns out he'd been looking for poachers and saw a van. Even remembered the registration.' He smirked at Theo. 'Not bad for the village idiot, eh Goldilocks?'

Theo frowned but didn't reply.

'Well done, mate,' said Juke, slapping Seth on the back. 'You've done better than the rest of us put together. We know how the girls were taken and who did it. Now, we just need to find out where they're being held. Don't suppose you know that too, Seth?'

'Not yet,' admitted Seth, 'But give me time.'

22. **Entombed**

I tentatively opened my eyes and found myself in oppressive darkness. It was no good. No matter how hard I tried, the blackness was solid and impenetrable.

I wriggled my toes and fingers. Everything seemed to be working, although my head ached from the blow I'd received. Slowly, I took stock of my situation. I was lying on a flat, cold surface. That much I could ascertain without moving. Unable to see anything in the inky black, I found my other senses were working overtime. An earthy, dank smell assailed my nostrils and the air felt damp and cloying. I turned my head from side to side, wincing as the movement put pressure on the wound I'd sustained. Raising my arm, I brought my hand slowly to the back of my head, investigating the damage. My hair was damp and matted, and my fingers rapidly became wet and sticky. Bringing my hand to my nose, there was no mistaking the coppery smell of blood and I flung my hand away in revulsion. As I did so, I touched a hard surface to my right. Thinking it was a wall, I felt it nervously with my fingertips, expecting to feel the rough texture of brick or stone. Instead, I was surprised to find it cold and smooth.

My fingers crept upwards for a few more inches until they reached a corner. Slowly, I traced the smooth surface above me, maybe six inches above my face. I pushed upwards as hard as I could but it refused to budge and only then did the full horror of my situation hit me. I was in a box, a metal box that felt for all the world like a tomb.

As the word tomb came into my head and the full implication hit me, I lost control and hammered on the lid for all I was worth, screaming 'Help, get me out' over and over until my throat was sore. But nothing happened and no one came. It remained as silent as the grave, and I realised with an involuntary sob that this was just what it might become.

I thought of my mother and a lump came into my throat. Thank God she was in Spain and knew nothing of this. She was the innocent victim in all this. I'd gone into it with my eyes open, knowing the danger. I thought of Tash. Was she in another box like mine? Was she injured? Had she even survived?

'Tash, are you there?' I called out, but there was no answer.

I tried to put out of my head the thought that she was superfluous to requirements and may not have survived. I had to focus on us being alive and getting out of here.

Theo, I knew, would be in despair. The thing he feared most had happened and I was sure he would be doing all in his power to save us. I tried to think positively. If my captors wanted me dead, I wouldn't be here now. Which meant they wanted to keep me alive, probably to barter for the crystal. I had to hope Viyesha and the family would negotiate. Except I knew the Lunari didn't care whether I lived or died. I was a passing distraction, nothing more. Faced with a choice between my life or the crystal, it was obvious what Badru would choose. And if I survived this ordeal but missed my initiation, he would still come for me.

Things didn't look great either way.

Just hours earlier, my situation had been so different. I'd had the boy of my dreams by my side and was looking forward to a life of eternal youth and beauty.. How could things have changed so rapidly? I thought about the day I first met Theo, how I'd gazed into his deep blue eyes, falling in love and losing myself forever.

I thought about the story of Ahmes and her untimely death. It was horrible and I hadn't been expecting it. Had I been Ahmes in a previous life? Was it possible to reincarnate? Surely I would have some memory? It all sounded so improbable. But there again, Theo's whole existence was improbable.

I forced myself to be still, feeling the warmth of the blue velvet cloak around me. At least I wasn't cold. Then I remembered the blue crystal pendant in the cloak pocket. That meant I could contact Theo. With trembling hands, I plunged my fingers deep into the pockets of the cloak. But they were empty. Either the crystal pendant had fallen out, perhaps when Seth was doing his ridiculous dance, or my captors had removed it. At the realisation that my protective crystal and only means of contacting Theo had gone, I felt the tears roll down my cheeks. I was in a desperate situation and had never felt more alone.

I recalled my earlier conversation with Viyesha about entering a state of suspended animation. Okay, I hadn't been initiated and my body chemistry hadn't changed, but I could try. I consciously slowed my breathing and tried to calm my racing heart, but it wasn't easy. How did you lower your brain waves? The more I tried not to think about anything, the more thoughts kept crowding into my mind. And the more I tried to be still, the more I wanted to move about.

Viyesha had mentioned remote viewing. If only I could get my consciousness to leave my body, perhaps I could see where I was being held. I closed my eyes tight and concentrated hard on seeing beyond the metal box, but nothing happened.

I wondered how long I had until the air ran out. The thought of suffocation brought on fresh panic and once again I lost control, hammering on the lid with my fists until they hurt and screaming for all I was worth.

But no one came.

And from somewhere within came the small unwelcome thought, lodged like a persistent maggot in my brain that I might never get out. Or they'd find me too late.

Try as hard as I could, I simply couldn't get the song My Boy Builds Coffins by Florence and the Machine out of my head.

23. **Searching**

All the next day they continued to search for the van. They began in the village, checking the roads and lanes, the public parking area by the allotments, the sports field, the cricket ground and the wooded area behind the council estate. Finding nothing, they gradually moved further afield, going to neighbouring villages, searching every street, lane and driveway, but continually drawing a blank.

With no sign of the van or word from the kidnapper, it was a weary, despondent bunch that assembled at Hartswell Hall in the oak-panelled library. Once again, Seth was absent.

'Nothing,' said Theo, miserably, 'absolutely nothing. The van could be anywhere. And if it's hidden away in a garage, we'll never find it.'

'Even if we do, I don't see how it's going to help,' said Violet. 'We know Emily and Tash have been taken. I can't see that finding the van will tell us where they are.'

'It's our only lead,' said Juke, wearily. 'I was hoping it might give us a clue as to their whereabouts.'

'I still can't believe Emily hasn't used her crystal to contact you, Theo,' commented Viyesha.

'Maybe she can't,' he answered, his voice choking. 'Maybe...'

He was interrupted by Seth, making a dramatic entrance.

'Great. This is all we need,' groaned Theo.

'Hail, fellow seekers,' said Seth, in a mock theatrical voice.

'Do you know something, Seth?' asked Juke, recognising the signs from his earlier behaviour.

'I might know why Emily's not getting in touch with you, Theo,' said Seth. He pulled something out of his pocket and held it up. 'Ta dah!'

It was the crystal necklace.

'Where did you get that?' demanded Theo, reaching forward and snatching it.

'Lateral thinking, my dear Watson,' he said smugly.

'Cut the dramatics, Seth,' advised Juke. 'Just tell us what you know, mate.'

'Okay. I went back to college and had a word with the caretaker, Mr O'Hanlon. I asked whether he'd found any jewellery after the prom. Lo and behold, he pulled this out of his pocket.' For a moment, he looked serious. 'I know it's not what you wanted to hear, Theo, but at least it explains why she's not contacting you.'

'You've done well, Seth,' said Viyesha, 'So far, you're the only one giving us any answers. Is there anything else you can tell us?'

'Well, I did ask my dad if he could check out the van registration. He knows people.' He tapped his nose secretively with his forefinger.

'And?' asked Joseph.

'It was reported stolen from a Birmingham address on Saturday morning. That's all I know. Bit of a dead end, I'm afraid.' He looked expectantly around the group.

'How about Emily's mother?' asked Viyesha. 'I take it she still doesn't know what's happened.'

'So far I've managed to stall her by telling her Emily's lost her phone,' answered Juke. 'But she comes back on Saturday...'

'And what about Emily's initiation?' asked Theo. 'If we don't get her back before the full moon, she'll miss it.'

'And Badru will come for her,' said Pantera with satisfaction.

'So, Emily is definitely joining you?' asked Juke, looking at them levelly. 'Is that what she wants?'

'She understands the risks,' said Viyesha calmly. 'We have explained everything. It is her choice. And she has rare gifts. She will be most welcome in our family. '

'I'm aware of her gifts, but I'd like to hear it from Emily herself,' declared Juke.'

As he spoke, Emily's mobile phone, lying on the table, began to ring. Juke glanced anxiously at the screen. 'It's her mother.'

Viyesha glanced at Violet. 'I suggest a little intervention.'

'Are you sure?' asked Violet.

'In the circumstances, yes.'

Violet picked up the phone and pressed the green 'answer' button.

'Hello,' she said, causing Seth to do a double take. She was speaking in Emily's voice. 'Hi, mum. Sorry I haven't replied to your messages. I lost my phone. Silly me, I found it in the laundry basket. Yes, we're fine. No, we haven't had any wild parties. Yes, we're eating well. How's the resort? Great…. Wow… Sounds fab. Well, you enjoy yourself. Don't do anything I wouldn't do. Theo sends his love. We'll see you on Saturday. Love you… Bye.' She pressed the 'end call' button and placed it back on the table, then glanced around at everyone watching her.

'Where did you learn to do that?' asked Seth in admiration.

Just another of my many talents,' said Violet, smiling at him.

'At least her mother's not about to call the police,' said Viyesha. 'I suggest you do the same with Tash's mother, Violet. And let college know the girls won't be in. Say they've gone down with a flu virus. We must keep the authorities and the media away. Are we in agreement?' She looked round the room.

'Absolutely,' said Leon. 'A media storm is the last thing we need. It could jeopardise everything.'

Do as you will,' said Aquila. 'Makes no difference to me.'

'So, what now?' asked Seth. 'What's the plan?'

'There is no plan,' said Theo bitterly. 'We're at a dead end.'

'Not quite,' said Juke, his face impassive. 'There is something I can do. I can visit Dreamtime. See if I can find out more about the dark forces holding Emily.'

'Dreamtime,' echoed Seth. 'You're going into Dreamtime? Cool!'

24. **Dreamtime**

Theo, Viyesha and Seth sat in the ballroom, watching Juke, while the others waited in the library. He sat in the middle of the floor cross legged and pressed play on his iPod. The mournful sounds of a didgeridoo filled the room, conjuring up images of an alien landscape, full of mystery and magic.

'Didgeridoos have the right vibrations,' explained Juke. 'Now, listen carefully. I'll be going into a trance. Whatever happens, don't wake me. Let me come out of it myself. If you wake me too soon, I might not get back, and I don't want to stay in Dreamtime forever. Got it?'

They all nodded.

'Here, Juke,' said Theo quickly, leaning forward. 'Take this. You might need it.' He thrust Emily's crystal necklace into his hand.

Juke stared at it for a split second and closed his fingers around it. He shut his eyes, concentrating on the music and rocking to and fro. As the music became louder and more intense, he started spinning round, shaking his head this way and that. Faster and faster he moved, stooping down then reaching into the air. Suddenly, his body tensed and fell to the floor.

Viyesha put her hand on Seth's arm. 'Leave him,' she commanded. 'He knows what he's doing. We mustn't interfere.'

There was nothing they could do but watch and wait.

In the strange dimension that constitutes Dreamtime, Juke opened his eyes and looked around. He was in an eerie, barren place. A filmy mist hung in the air and the landscape was broken only by the occasional blasted tree, with twisted branches reaching out like tortured souls.

Cautiously, he walked forward. For the moment, he could see little and hear nothing but the low drone of the didgeridoo. To his left, he saw the skeleton of some poor animal, its bones bleached white, partially concealed beneath the pale sand that slowly consumed it. He felt the soft fingers of the cloying mist drift across his face, caressing him in a deadly embrace. This was an empty, godforsaken part of Dreamtime he'd never encountered before and he knew he couldn't stay long. The mist concealed an ancient threat. He could feel it in his bones and shivered. He turned suddenly, aware that someone or something had just brushed very close to him, but all he could see was the eerie mist, closing in all around. He turned and cautiously moved forward. In the distance, voices cried out, screaming as if in torture, and fading as quickly as they had started. Something low and rasping ran across in front of him, scuttling through the sand with a dry, crackling sound, like a large, alien insect. Juke balled his fists, feeling the hard facets of the crystal press into his palm, and forced himself to breathe slowly.

This was a part of Dreamtime where lost souls roamed, unable to find their way out, stuck for eternity in a hellish limbo, and he prayed he wouldn't find Emily here. Still he lingered, feeling there was something in this chilling, empty landscape he needed to see. On he went, almost crying out as he came upon a swinging corpse, a thick cord wound around its neck, suspended from a dead branch that pierced the mist like a twisted javelin. Rotting flesh fell away from the bones and he turned from its grinning cadaverous face in revulsion.

Immediately, he became aware of something standing close to his right side, like a dark, ominous wall, impenetrable yet without form. Instinctively, he drew back, looking up and trying to work out what was towering above him. Waves of despair, empty and hollow, flooded downwards, filling his mind with cold, poisonous thoughts. He tried too late to avert his gaze from the hooded figure that looked down at him, ancient and malign, absorbing anything that was good and wholesome to feed its unholy hunger. He felt the air become tainted and black, and as it bent towards him, the stench of decay filled his nostrils, suffocating and putrid. Every instinct told him to run, but his feet remained rooted to the ground and he was helpless, like a fly in a web. He was aware of an insidious lethargy spreading through his body and tried to distinguish the features of his attacker, but its face remained hidden in shadow.

Juke tried in vain to harness his protective energy field, but the figure's power was too strong and he felt it shrivel around him. His arms were fixed by his side, rendering him helpless, and the misty landscape began to grow dim. 'This cannot be how it ends,' he thought. 'Unless... '

With superhuman effort, he wrenched his right arm from his side, opened his palm and thrust Emily's blue crystal necklace upwards, feeling his energy field ignite like a beacon, white and shining. With a deafening crack, the dark form above him began to crumble and split, breaking into a million pieces, and an inhuman shriek filled the air. As the black fragments fell towards him, threatening to engulf him like a monstrous mudslide, Juke felt himself falling backwards into the seeping mist. Back he fell, until he landed on something flat and solid, and thankfully, for Juke, the nightmare was over.

He opened his eyes and saw the familiar décor of the ballroom around him, and Viyesha, Theo and Seth staring anxiously down at him.

'Hey, you all right, dude?' asked Seth.

Juke smiled weakly. 'Yeah, thanks dude, I'm good.'

He struggled to get up and Theo offered him a helping hand.

'What happened? Did you see anything?' he demanded.

Juke took a deep breath. 'I did, and if it hadn't been for Emily's crystal, I might not be here now.'

He opened his hand to reveal his palm, lacerated and bloody, where the crystal had cut into him, and laughed bitterly. 'That shows how hard I was gripping it.'

'And the thing you saw?' prompted Viyesha.

Juke's face grew dark. 'I couldn't see clearly. But it's powerful and malevolent. If that's what has Emily and Tash, heaven help them. Their chances aren't good.'

25. **Exorcism**

Father James Debonair, vicar of the village church, Saint Michael and All Angels, stood in front of the mirror in his dressing room, tweaked his dog collar and smiled. No, that was too full on. He turned slightly so that his face was three-quarters towards the mirror and tried again. That was better. More understated. With his long tawny hair and piercing blue eyes, he'd been told he had a Jesus look about him. It was a vanity he fought against, although it had never harmed his pulpit power.

A gentle knock at the door disturbed his thoughts. It was Mrs O'Briain, his elderly housekeeper.

'Sorry, Father, I don't wish to disturb you, not when you're writing the sermon for Sunday,' she said in her lilting Irish brogue. 'It's just you have a visitor.'

'Who is it?' he asked, looking at his watch. 'I have the Ladies Prayer Meeting in twenty minutes.'

'Mrs Palmer.'

'Mrs Palmer, eh? I wonder what she wants?' He thought of the comely divorcee who graced his early Eucharist service every Sunday at 8.15am.

'She doesn't look good,' said Mrs O'Briain.

'She doesn't?" he said in surprise. 'What's the problem?'

'I don't know,' admitted Mrs O'Briain. 'She looks stooped somehow.'

'Better show her into my study. I'll be down in a second.'

Mrs O'Briain disappeared and Father James smoothed his hair and adjusted his collar. With one last glance in the mirror, he followed her downstairs.

Mrs Palmer sat in the floral blue armchair to one side of the fireplace. She was very stooped, one shoulder raised alarmingly, the other arm swinging loose, giving her a Quasimodo look. She attempted to stand as he walked in.

'Mrs Palmer, please don't,' he said, seeing her discomfort and moving across the room to her. 'To what do I owe this pleasure?'

'It's nothing to do with pleasure,' said Mrs Palmer, in a strained voice. 'There's something not right with me, Father. I didn't know where else to come.'

'It looks like a back condition. Surely you should see a doctor?'

'I don't think a doctor can fix this problem.' She grasped his hand. 'You have to help me, Father. It's getting worse by the minute. I can't take much more.'

'Why don't you tell me what's happened?' he suggested.

She perched uncomfortably on the edge of the chair.

'It began last night. I'd taken Juicy for a walk, that's my Shih Tzu, and was coming back down the High Street, when he slipped his lead and went running into Hartswell Hall grounds. Something must have attracted his attention. I ran after him, calling his name and eventually found him on the other side of the rose garden, by the old wall that's just been rebuilt. As I bent down to clip on his lead, I felt something land on my back. It was the strangest sensation, as if someone had thrown a coat or a blanket over me. I couldn't shake it off. I felt my back to see what it was, but there was nothing there. When I got home – I'm sorry, Father, this is where it starts to get disgusting - I suddenly felt inordinately hungry, and before I knew it, I was eating Juicy's dog food.' She grimaced. 'And really enjoying it. I opened half a dozen packets and ate it all.' Her voice choked and she stifled a sob.

'It's fine, Mrs Palmer,' he assured her. 'What happened next?'

'I went to bed and fell into a deep sleep. When I awoke, the pain in my spine was excruciating and I was completely hunched over. After that, a hunger came upon me like I've never known. I had to eat. And it had to be raw meat.' She looked at him with tortured eyes. 'Father, I've been a vegetarian for ten years. None of this makes sense.'

'Did you eat meat?' he asked.

'I did. It was as if a bloodlust took over and, I swear, if Juicy hadn't run out of the house, I would have eaten him. He kept growling and barking as if he sensed something was wrong, till he was driving me crazy. I picked up a kitchen knife and would have used it, Father. The thought of slicing him into pieces had me salivating. Instead, I somehow drove to the butcher's and cleared them out of liver and steak. I ate it in the car, the blood running down my chin.'

She stopped, tears streaming down her cheeks, and clasped his hand. 'Help me, Father. It's getting stronger. It's sucking the life out of me.'

'My dear Mrs Palmer, please don't distress yourself,' said Father James, leaning forward and attempting to put his arm around her. As he did so, his crucifix swung forward, almost touching her. The effect was electric. She leapt backwards, crying 'Get that thing away from me.'

Father James stepped away, clutching his crucifix. This was no muscular complaint. It was obvious he was dealing with something dark and unholy, calling for spiritual intervention. He spoke clearly and calmly.

'Mrs Palmer. Do not distress yourself. I believe I know the nature of the problem.'

'What is it?' she asked tearfully, anguish etched into her features.

'I believe it is an Elemental,' he said authoritatively. 'An earth-bound spirit that has latched on to your life force. A sort of spiritual tick.'

'A tick?' she said in disbelief. 'Like sheep pick up in the fields?'

'The same, only this absorbs energy rather than drinking blood. The red meat you've been eating makes your life force stronger and more palatable. I'm afraid it's a case of being in the wrong place at the wrong time. Nothing we can't handle, don't worry.'

'Thank you, Father. I can't tell you how grateful I am.'

Her back went into a violent spasm, as if the thing was tightening its hold, and she cried out in pain. 'Hurry, Father. It's getting worse.'

Father James leapt into action. Striding across the room, he opened the door and called for his housekeeper.

'Mrs O'Briain, cancel the Ladies Prayer meeting, then go to church, fill a jug with holy water from the font and bring back the big crucifix on the altar. Can you manage?'

'Of course, Father,' she said, confidently. 'Is it an exorcism? I've seen them before, you know. The last father was a dab hand at the exorcism. Cast out more demons than he had hot dinners. It was most impressive to watch.'

'Well, I'm not sure how impressive this will be and I'm not licenced for exorcism. This is simply to remove an Elemental from Mrs Palmer's back.'

'An Elemental! How exciting!' she beamed and went scuttling into the kitchen.

Father James went upstairs to find his encyclopaedia of Demons and Spiritual Parasites. In no time, Mrs O'Briain had returned, carrying a large crucifix along with Father James's best cut glass whisky decanter full of holy water.

'Here, Father,' she said, carefully placing both on the desk in his study.

'Thank you, Mrs O'Briain,' he said, feeling a little nervous.

'Keep a steady hand, Father,' she advised him. 'Elementals can be tricky. The blighters rarely want to come out, but you have to be firm. It's like squeezing a large pimple. Just keep the pressure on, and hey presto, they suddenly pop out. But make sure you get the tentacles out. You don't want to leave anything in there.'

'Thank you Mrs O'Briain, I'll remember that. Let's get started.'

Mrs Palmer sat in the pale blue floral armchair, looking thoroughly miserable.

'Just get rid of it, Father, whatever it is. I have a bridge party tonight that I'd very much like to attend.'

Holding the large crucifix in one hand and with the encyclopaedia open at the appropriate page, he began to read:

'In the name of our Lord Jesus Christ, I command you to leave this woman. In the name of He who flung you from the Gates of Heaven to the depths of Hell, I command you to be gone!'

Mrs Palmer screamed as if in terrible agony and seemed to stoop more than ever.

'Very good, Father,' shouted Mrs O'Briain. 'That was straight from The Exorcist if I'm not mistaken. Carry on.'

Holding the crucifix closer to Mrs Palmer, he said loudly, 'In the name of Michael the Archangel, the Blessed Apostles and all the Saints, be gone, you unclean spirit, you infernal invader!'

Mrs Palmer screamed louder than ever and fell to the floor, seemingly convulsing, an unpleasant froth appearing at the sides of her mouth.

'Excellent, Father!' shouted Mrs O'Briain. 'It didn't like that! Keep going.'

Father James bent over the contorted, screaming figure of Mrs Palmer and held the crucifix close to her spine.

'I adjure you to be gone you inhuman creature, in the name of God of Heaven, God of Earth, God of Angels, God of Martyrs...'

Mrs Palmer screeched and writhed and a gust of wind scattered the papers off his desk.

'The Holy Water,' screeched Mrs O'Briain, holding out the whisky decanter.

'You do it,' shouted Father James, beads of sweat breaking out across his brow, 'I haven't got a free hand.'

'Really, Father?' she asked in delight, pulling the stopper out of the decanter, the frenzied wind whipping through her hair.

'Just do it," he commanded, struggling to hold his crucifix over the writhing creature, her piercing screams threatening to burst his eardrums.

Holding on to the chair to keep herself steady, Mrs O'Briain splashed holy water on to Mrs Palmer's spine, muttering in Latin as she did so. 'Exorciamus te, omnis immundus spiritus, omnia incursion infernalis, omnis legio et secta diabolica....'

A hissing and a spitting came from Mrs Palmer's spine and she curved upwards, like a cat arching its back. Father James held the crucifix over her and a black entity slowly disengaged itself from Mrs Palmer's back. He and Mrs O'Briain watched horrified as it rose, black tentacles stretching thinly, snapping upwards as the creature relinquished its grip.

'More holy water,' Father James instructed, and Mrs O'Briain threw the remaining contents of the decanter. With a great shriek as the water touched it, the creature burst into a million dark fragments, each piece hovering in the air, before disappearing completely. The wind calmed, Mrs Palmer stopped screaming and Father James looked at Mrs O'Briain in amazement.

'We did it,' he said. 'Well done, Mrs O'Briain. I didn't know you spoke Latin.'

'I don't,' she admitted. 'Just seen a lot of horror films, that's all. I must admit, I've never seen an Elemental quite like that before.'

'I've never seen one,' said Father James. 'That was a first for me.'

'Well, whatever it was, it's gone,' said Mrs Palmer, getting to her feet, her spine ramrod straight. She smoothed down her purple fitted suit. 'I can't tell you how good I feel. I shall show my appreciation in the collection plate on Sunday. Now, must dash, I have a bridge party to attend.'

Mrs O'Briain showed Mrs Palmer out of the vicarage and Father James sat back in his armchair, feeling exhausted. That was one experience he didn't want to repeat.

Had he been able to see into other homes across the village, he would have been horrified to find a similar complaint affecting his other parishioners. Unbeknown to him, the nightmare was just beginning.

26. **Remote Viewing**

This time, I didn't open my eyes and I didn't panic. I kept my breathing slow and rhythmic, and concentrated on a point between my eyebrows. My third eye. If anything was going to let me see, this was it. I felt my consciousness get clearer and sharper, and kept focusing inwards, willing myself to escape the confines of my metal tomb, concentrating with a force I hadn't known I possessed.

I saw a bright, white light shining all around me, getting more intense as my focus increased. Gradually it formed a tubular shape and I was able to travel along it, gaining speed until the end of the tunnel came in sight. Without warning, it disappeared and the light was gone. I looked around and saw I was in a great underground cavern, dank and dark, with moss covering the lower walls. Huge vaulted arches soared above me and to one side I saw row upon row of coffins stacked high. With a jolt, I realised it was an ancient crypt.

Turning around, I saw a large lead tomb standing on a dais, its surface mottled and patinated with age, a vast lid extending over the base. This was my prison and I realised the immense strength that would be required to open it and release me. I turned back, looking through the darkness to see if anyone was there. To my right, a strange creature slept on the floor, apparently my guard. I found I could move forward, and hovered a metre or so over its black, scaly body. It was like nothing I'd seen before, a semi-human lizard with large legs, a plated tail and a man's torso. I drew closer, trying to see more, backing off in alarm as the creature suddenly opened a large yellow eye and looked straight at me. I guessed it couldn't see me, but it seemed to detect something because it drew itself up and peered through the gloom. I looked in disgust at its hideous face, more lizard than human with its lack of lips, flattened nostrils and yellow blinking eyes. It took a huge yawn, revealing rows of broken yellowing teeth, the remains of rotting meat clearly visible, and long entrails of saliva dripped onto the stone floor. I was glad I couldn't smell anything. Its breath must have been rank beyond belief.

I moved on, traversing the walls of the crypt until I came to an opening that led into a dark passage. Cautiously, I entered the darkness, not knowing where I was headed and reluctant to leave the lead tomb, with my physical body lying inside.

Slowly, I moved forward, coming to another doorway on my right. A large studded door was locked with a massive iron key lodged in the keyhole. I willed myself to keep going and somehow managed to pass through the door. I found myself in a small, squalid room with bare stone walls and a tiny lantern, high up in an alcove, creating a faint flicker of light. There on a low plinth lay a motionless figure and I gasped as I recognised her. It was Tash, still wearing her long blue dress, red hair matted around her face. A heavy iron chain led from her wrists to a large iron ring fixed into the stone walls, pulling her arms above her head. Dried blood showed where the manacles had rubbed her skin.

'Oh Tash,' I said silently. 'I'm so sorry. I never meant for you to get involved.'

Mentally I called her name, hoping to contact her telepathically, but she remained still. I tried to see her face to find out if she was still breathing, and was comforted when I saw the faint rise and fall of her chest. She was alive, but she didn't look in good shape and I didn't know how much longer she could carry on. At least she wasn't entombed, and a bowl of water along with the remains of some bread on a plate indicated they were keeping her alive. For the moment.

I left her sleeping and passed back through the heavy door into the passageway. I continued until I came to a low arch and cautiously peered inside. It was little more than an antechamber, going back just a few feet, with a low ceiling. At first I thought it was empty, then movement caught my eye. Something or someone was in there, sitting silently in the darkness, watching me. I don't know how I knew, but I was aware it could see me. Whatever it was remained in the shadows, cloaked in darkness and mystery, and I was unable to make out whether it was another reptilian creature.

'So you have come to seek me out,' said a faint, whispering voice that simultaneously repelled and fascinated me.

'Yes,' I answered silently. 'I want to know who my captor is.'

'I am here before you,' the voice replied, in soft, sibilant tones that I found both terrifying and enchanting.

'What do you want with me?' I demanded.

'Is that not obvious? I wish to trade you for that which rightfully belongs to me."

'And that is?'

'Do not disappoint me with feigned stupidity. You know.'

'The crystal. You hope to trade me for the crystal. Well, let me tell you, that is not going to happen. The family would never let it go. Even for me.'

'You do not hold yourself in very high regard.'

'I understand the importance of the crystal.'

The voice grew icy and cold. 'You understand nothing of the crystal.'

'Who are you?' I demanded. 'Why do you want the crystal?'

'I want what is rightfully mine, that which was stolen from me centuries past.'

'What d'you mean, rightfully yours?'

'Before Viyesha ever found the crystal, it belonged to me. As did all the jewels of the earth. They were mine until they were taken away and I was cast out, forced to flee from all I loved and leave behind all that gave me sustenance. I, who once had everything, was forced to live in the shadows, a half creature of dust and ashes. But the crystal shall be mine and I shall rise again. And when I do, I shall crush those who sought to destroy me. My revenge will be total and absolute. Without mercy.'

'Who are you?' I asked once again, feeling waves of menace and malevolence radiate from the creature.

'I once shone as brightly as they,' came the reply. 'Brighter. I lit all around with my shining glory. I was the golden one. Untouchable. Favoured above all others. Until I was betrayed and my jewels were taken from me. My fall was absolute.'

'You were a Light Being?' I asked.

The voice laughed with a dry, dead, mournful sound scarred by centuries of suffering.

'I was indeed. Until my form was taken from me and I became nothing more than an abstract thought, capable of wielding power only through men's delusions and weaknesses.'

'I don't understand,' I began to say.

'How could you?' said the voice. 'You are the embodiment of innocence and love, the very things I seek to destroy. I am the one who corrupts and taints, who fills the murderer's heart with enmity and hatred, who prompts the invader to destroy all that is beautiful and good, who sits on your back and insidiously feeds you thoughts of personal gain and glorification... But I am done with abstract vengeance. I seek life form to make my revenge a living reality. And that is why, Ahmes, I require the crystal. They...' he spat the word out, 'use it to bestow youth and beauty on themselves. I need it for life, to rise beyond this vile, reptilian bondage and raise my legions of followers to greatness.'

As I listened to its words, hissing and spitting in the putrid air, I was aware of the creature moving towards me, and I was filled with an all-consuming fear. I felt myself being catapulted backwards, at huge speed, out of the alcove, back down the passageway and into the large crypt. As my consciousness shot back towards my lead tomb, my eyes saw what I had missed on my first glance around the underground cavern. The entire crypt was a living, writhing, seething mass of black undulating shapes. They lined the walls, hung from the ancient arches and littered the old stone floor, black eyes glittering, tentacles at the ready, and I realised with sheer, blind terror that my tomb was in the heart of a feeders' nest.

Then I was back in the sanctity of my metal prison, filled with dread and despair, knowing rescue for Tash and me was impossible and that missing the full moon deadline was the least of my problems.

27. **Feeders**

Strange scenes were going on in Hartswell-on-the-hill Medical Practice. The waiting room was crowded with crooked, hunched villagers, pain etched across their features, most with one shoulder raised alarmingly high, forcing the other arm to swing helplessly.

'Mrs Dewett', announced Doctor Kingsley over the intercom, at the beginning of surgery, and a stooped elderly woman forced herself to stand and limp through the reception area, down the corridor and into his consulting room.

'Looks like a case of advanced scoliosis,' he informed her, after a quick examination. 'You should have come to see me before now. I'll have to refer you to an orthopaedic consultant. Whether there's anything that can be done at this late stage, I can't say.'

'It only came on this last night, doctor,' Mrs Dewett told him. 'I couldn't have come any sooner.'

'Yes, yes,' he said in his 'humouring the patient' voice. 'I'll sort out your referral.'

After ten more patients with the same condition, Dr Kingsley was baffled. All displayed the same twisted, stooped posture. All complained of feeling exhausted and needing to sleep for hours on end, and all spoke of a compulsion to eat red meat. Could it be some kind of collective hysteria? Was there something in the water? In all his years of practice, he'd never encountered anything like it. At the end of morning surgery, he decided to call a colleague who specialised in psychosomatic illness. But the call was never made. No sooner had he reached for the phone than he heard an ungodly shriek from the waiting room. Flinging open the door, he raced down the corridor, wondering what he was going to encounter next.

A crowd of hunched villagers stood around a figure lying on the floor and, with horror, he realised it was Mrs Dewett, his first patient of the morning.

'She won't be needing your referral now, doc,' an elderly man informed him. 'She's a gonner.'

'It's my fault,' said the new blonde receptionist tearfully. 'She rushed in demanding to see you again and I told her she had to make an appointment. I didn't realise how urgent it was. And now she's dead.' She dabbed at her eyes with a paper tissue.

Doctor Kingsley bent over the deceased woman and checked her pulse. There was nothing. 'Alright, stand back,' he informed the crowd of villagers. 'I need to call an ambulance.'

He stood up and attempted to move them back, giving the dead woman a little space and dignity.

'Would you look at that!' exclaimed the grey-haired elderly man, staring hard at Mrs Dewett, causing them all to gaze down at her.

In front of their eyes, her twisted bent spine began to straighten and her anguished grimace to clear. Her brow became less lined, her mouth turned up at the edges as if smiling and a peaceful expression appeared on her face. They stared horror-struck, each wondering if this was to be their fate.

Doctor Kingsley watched in amazement. This was a day of surprises.

No one noticed the silent black shadow slide from Mrs Dewett's back and onto the floor. It passed unseen between their feet, climbing up the surgery wall until it hung suspended above them. Without a sound it moved across the ceiling tiles until it hovered over the reception desk, where the blonde receptionist dabbed her eyes. Silently it dropped, landing neatly in the middle of her back, four black tentacles embedding themselves firmly into their new feeding ground. She shrugged, feeling a sudden unpleasant sensation, as if her muscles had momentarily gone into spasm. Putting it down to the tension of the situation, she rolled her shoulders and attempted to stand tall. But no matter how much she tried, she couldn't get her spine to straighten fully. It was if she were carrying a rucksack on her back. In any other circumstances, she would have asked the doctor to take a look. But today, he simply had too much on his plate. She decided to take a painkiller and keep quiet.

* * *

Over in the grounds of Hartswell Hall, Mr Nelson continued to act as a conduit, oblivious to all that went on around him. Had he been conscious, he would have been horrified to see he now shared the folly with more than five hundred silent black feeders, suspended from the ruined walls and arches, giving the folly a blighted, diseased appearance. As he slept, more feeders emerged from his back, each one hungry for human energy.

28. **Land of Lost Souls**

A sombre group sat in the library discussing Juke's visit to Dreamtime.

'What was this creature you encountered?' asked Leon.

'I don't know. It kept its face concealed,' said Juke, still shaken. 'I thought I was done for. I haven't encountered anything as dark or powerful as that in a long time.'

'Do you think this creature is behind Emily's abduction?' asked Joseph.

'Put it this way, I don't believe I met it by accident,' answered Juke. 'It was waiting for me, and it's sending a clear message.'

'That being?' asked Theo.

'To back off,' said Juke. 'Believe me, that is one creature you don't want to mess with.'

'So, what do we do? Wait for it to demand the crystal?' demanded Theo angrily.

'There can be no negotiation,' said Bellynda in a harsh, dry tone. 'Badru is clear. If it comes to a choice between the crystal and the girls, he will save the crystal.'

Behind her, Aquila and Pantera allowed themselves a brief look of triumph.

'Which means we have no choice,' said Seth. 'We have to rescue them.'

'If we knew where they were,' pointed out Theo.

'You're forgetting one thing,' said Juke. 'This creature isn't human and has no form in this dimension. It's just a spirit, or a demon, or whatever you want to call it. As far as we know, it used Mr Nelson to abduct the girls, which means it could be dependent on him to make contact with us.'

'So, why haven't we heard from him?' asked Joseph. 'There's been nothing. How do we know this Mr Nelson hasn't scarpered? The closest we've come is this evil entity.'

'Which is why I need to go back,' said Juke. 'Find out exactly who we're dealing with.'

There was silence round the room as they took in his words.

'No, Juke, it's too dangerous,' said Viyesha. 'You barely survived last time. It could destroy you.'

'That's a chance I'm willing to take,' said Juke. 'I haven't exactly protected Emily. This is the least I can do for her.'

'It's not up to you to protect her,' said Theo. 'That's my job and I failed. Let me go into Dreamtime. I'm strong enough to stand up to any evil spirit.'

'No,' said Juke firmly. 'I promised her mother I'd look after her. Besides, destroying dark energy is what I do.'

'But we don't want to destroy it,' pointed out Theo. 'Not yet, anyway. It could be our only link to Emily.'

'I know. I'll just gather information. Find out who and what it is '

'A dangerous strategy,' sneered Bellynda. 'Sounds like suicide to me.'

'It's my decision, Bellynda,' said Juke stonily.

There was an uneasy silence, broken by Viyesha.

'Are we all agreed that Juke goes back into Dreamtime?'

'It seems like we've run out of options,' answered Leon.

Bellynda laughed scornfully. 'It's up to you, Juke. It's your funeral.'

* * *

Haunting didgeridoo music filled the ballroom. Theo, Viyesha and Seth sat on the sofa watching Juke, who stood in the middle of the room. It was early next morning, at a time when Juke's energies were strongest and he felt most able to encounter the dark force once again. With still no word from the girls' abductor, it seemed the only thing he could do.

'Take this,' said Viyesha, handing him the large crystal pendant that hung round her neck. 'It was recharged at the last Blue Moon and will give you powerful protection.'

'Whoa, that is powerful,' said Juke, fastening the chain around his neck. 'I don't think there's much could harm me when I'm wearing this.'

He began swaying to the music, his eyes closed, moving faster and faster until his body went rigid, his eyes opened wide and he fell to the floor in a trance.

'He's gone,' said Theo. 'All we can do is wait.'

'And pray,' added Viyesha.

'If anyone can do it, Juke can,' said Seth confidently. 'He is one amazing dude.'

In another dimension, Juke sat up and looked about him. The landscape was familiar, but there was a darkness and heaviness to the rolling mist and the air was chilled, as if a storm was approaching. He shivered, as much from apprehension as the temperature. A pressure was building and he put his fingers between his eyebrows, pressing hard to disperse the tight headache that threatened. Even breathing was difficult and laboured. He moved his fingers to the crystal hanging round his neck and closed his fist around it, feeling comfort from its cold, hard facets. Immediately, his head began to clear and he was able to breathe. He turned, unsure which direction to take, relying on intuition to guide him. Behind, he could see a faint glimmer, as if day was about to break. Common sense told him to turn and walk in that direction, keep going until he found sunshine and green trees and good energy, but he knew that would achieve nothing.

Ahead, the darkness intensified, ominous and heavy. With a terrible foreboding, Juke walked into the blackness.

29. **Meeting Juke**

Inside my lead tomb, I retreated deep within myself to a place that was safe and secure. My body had all but ceased to function, the only indication of life a pinprick of consciousness in my cerebral lobe. The place where I hid was warm and happy, filled with childhood memories: playing with friends, laughing in the sunshine, clinging to my mother's skirt. All around me fresh air and blue skies made me glad to be alive. I felt blades of grass beneath my feet and a gentle breeze caress my skin. I held my face up to the sun, closing my eyes, enjoying the warmth.

As I relaxed into the moment, feeling safe, I became aware of the brightness fading, as if a cloud had passed in front of the sun. I opened my eyes and found to my horror that the landscape had changed. The sky had become dark and ominous. A faint mist hung in the air and the temperature was dropping, making me shiver. I looked for shelter, but the landscape was stark and barren, with only the occasional dead tree to break the monotony. The mist was growing thicker by the second, curling its clammy fingers around my arms and legs, and it was becoming hard to see.

I strained my eyes, detecting movement, and sure enough, I saw a figure moving towards me. Now I panicked. This was my sanctuary, a place where no one could touch me, yet here was an intruder invading my private thoughts. I watched as the figure became clearer, gasping in amazement as it came into view.

'Juke,' I cried, never more glad to see anyone in my life. 'What are you doing here?'

He looked at me in surprise. 'Emily! What are doing here? You're in Dreamtime.'

'So that's what it is. One moment I was in my own special place, the next I was here.'

'Are you okay?'

'I'm still alive, if that's what you mean. And so is Tash, although not good.'

'Do you know where you're being held?'

'No. I was knocked unconscious. When I woke up I was inside a metal coffin. It was pretty scary. The only way I could cope was to close down and go inside my mind. I guess that's how I've found my way here.'

'A metal coffin? Jesus! That's enough to send anyone crazy. No wonder you zoned out. Who did this, Emily? Do you know?'

'No, but he's creepy. Said he wants the crystal back. That it used to belong to him a long time ago and how he was banished to a world of shadows and dust. He said when he has the crystal, he'll rise again and destroy everything that's good and innocent.'

'You've spoken with him?' Juke asked incredulously.

'Yeah, I did some remote viewing outside of the coffin and I found him concealed in the shadows. He said he wants to trade me for the crystal, but I told him he was wasting his time.'

Juke took hold of my shoulders and looked into my eyes.

'Listen hard, Emily. We don't have much time. I think I know who this creature is and you need to be prepared. He's the de Lucis family's old enemy, an ancient and powerful force from the dark side, who craves the blue crystal more than anything. It would enable him to achieve physical form in the human world.'

'I know,' I said. 'He told me.'

'Did he say anything else?'

I was about to mention that he'd called me Ahmes, but stopped myself. It seemed too personal somehow, in view of what Theo had told me, and I wasn't prepared to repeat that story. 'Not really.'

'Okay. Is there anything else you can tell me?'

'There was a strange reptilian creature keeping guard. And another one guarding Tash in a cell. And black feeders everywhere, clinging to the walls, hanging from the arches.'

'A feeder colony,' declared Juke. 'Like a nest of vipers, only a million times worse.'

'I've been attacked by a feeder before,' I said. 'I know they feed on human energy.' I looked steadily at Juke. 'The family can't trade the crystal, I know. It would be a death sentence for them. And even if they knew where we were, they couldn't rescue us, not with all those feeders and reptilian creatures guarding us.'

'We're going to get you out, Emily,' said Juke firmly. 'Think carefully. Is there any clue as to where you are?'

'Only that it's a crypt,' I said. 'There are coffins stacked up on shelves. And it's underground, I'm sure.' My voice dropped to a whisper. 'That's all I know.'

'I think that is enough,' hissed a voice, its sibilant tones slicing through the mist. We both froze, trying to see where it was coming from. But the mist was too dense. Juke stood close to me, his gaze darting around.

'Very touching,' said the voice, 'but what makes you think you can protect Emily, Juke? You don't have the power. I can destroy you in an instant.' It began to laugh a deep, low, menacing chuckle. 'That would be some compensation for all I have suffered over the centuries, a minor distraction from my woes.' The voice grew steely. 'But it's not what I want and you know it. I suggest you leave, Emily. Juke and I have business to discuss.'

'He's right,' said Juke, turning to me. 'Go, Emily. Get out now.'

'I'm not leaving,' I said defiantly. 'We'll face him together.'

The voice laughed again. 'You think you are a match for me? Do you have any idea of my power?'

To prove a point, a bolt of lightning flew through the mist, hitting one of the gnarled old trees and blasting it with flames.

'Please go, Emily,' said Juke urgently. 'I need to know you're okay. Go while you can.'

Another bolt of lightning shot past us, reducing a nearby tree to a burning husk.

'Time to go, Emily,' mocked the hissing voice. 'If you stay, Juke's next. It's up to you.'

'I can't leave you, Juke,' I said hopelessly.

'Don't say I didn't warn you,' it taunted.

'No,' I screamed, as a figure began to emerge out of the mist. Whatever it was towered above us, its face concealed amidst the swirling eddies, its breath reeking of death and decay.

'You need just enough life to tell Viyesha who she's dealing with, Juke,' it said viciously. 'Let her be in no doubt. Tell her to give me the crystal or I will give the girls to the feeders.'

The figure raised an arm from the cloak draped around it and for a split second I saw Juke holding up a bright blue crystal pendant, his whole being lit up with bright white energy. Once more, a lightning bolt shot from the creature's fingers, blasting Juke's energy field into smithereens, the impact throwing him into the air like a rag doll. He fell to the ground a lifeless puppet, the remnants of his energy field hanging like burnt rags from his singed, burning body. A demonic laugh echoed across the barren landscape and I screamed.

30. **Crystal Healing**

Viyesha, Theo and Seth watched in horror as Juke's inert form began to burn before them. Smoke poured from his body as flames flickered around him and he began to twist and writhe in agony.

'What's happening to him?' cried Seth. 'He's burning.'

'Don't touch him,' cautioned Viyesha. 'They're flames from another dimension. If you touch him, you'll do more harm.'

'We have to do something, mother,' shouted Theo, in panic. 'He's dying before our eyes.'

'Wait,' said Viyesha again, holding out her arms on either side of her to stop the two boys moving forward.

Gradually, Juke stopped moving and lay still. The flames petered out and wisps of smoke gently rose from his body.

'Is he dead?' asked Seth.

'I don't think so,' said Viyesha. 'Let him come round in his own time.'

Gradually, Juke's eyes flickered open and he looked around the room trying to focus.

'You're back at Hartswell Hall, Juke,' said Viyesha. 'Can you tell us what happened?'

Juke opened his mouth, but his lips were charred and no sound came out.

'He needs water,' said Seth, reaching into his backpack and pulling out a bottle of Evian. He splashed some into Juke's mouth and they watched anxiously as he swallowed and tried to speak again.

'Emily,' he managed to say. 'She's alive… being held in a lead tomb…'

'And Tash?' asked Seth.

'Alive but not good.' He tried to sit up but fell back to the floor. Viyesha bent down and cradled his head in her arms.

'Where are they, Juke? Do you know?' asked Theo.

'Underground crypt. Don't know where.'

He struggled to speak and Seth gave him more water.

'Who did this to you, Juke?' asked Viyesha. 'Did you meet their captor?'

'Yes. Wants to trade the girls for the crystal…'

'Who, Juke, who?'

The words appeared to stick in his throat and she lent forward trying to hear. Juke clutched her arm and with one last effort, managed to whisper faintly in her ear. 'Your worst nightmare, Viyesha... The Fallen Angel.'

He closed his eyes and fell back, unconscious.

Viyesha gasped, a look of horror etched into her perfect features and her hands shook. No one else had heard his whispered message.

'Is he dead now?' asked Seth.

Viyesha looked at him, uncomprehending. 'What? No. He's badly injured. Theo, run and get Joseph.'

Theo ran from the ballroom, while Seth and Viyesha looked anxiously at Juke, now barely breathing. A loud ring tone sounded from Seth's backpack, startling them both.

'It's my mobile,' he explained, fumbling for his phone. 'Oh no, it's my mother,' he groaned, glancing at the screen. 'I forgot, I'm supposed to take her to the station.' He pressed the receive button. 'Hello? No, I haven't forgotten. No.... No... Okay... Yes, I'll be there. Give me ten minutes.'

He hung up and glanced at Viyesha. 'I'm sorry. Gotta go. I promised her, but I'll be back as soon as I can.'

'It's all right, Seth,' said Viyesha, with a faint smile, 'There's nothing more you can do. Juke will be fine once Joseph has worked his magic.'

As she spoke, Joseph ran into the ballroom. He dropped to his knees and put his hands on Juke's body, moving them around to assess the damage.

'His energy field's all but destroyed,' he announced. 'Who did this? It takes superhuman strength to do this level of damage.'

'An old enemy has returned,' said Viyesha informed him in hushed tones. 'The Fallen Angel is back. We will speak of it later. Now, can you save him, Joseph?'

For a moment he simply stared at her in shock, before focusing on the task in hand.

'He still has a faint pulse. We need to get him up to the Clock Tower. If I can harness the crystal's power, there's a chance I can bring him back. But we must hurry.'

On cue, Leon strode into the ballroom.

'I heard,' he informed them. 'I'll carry him.'

He picked up Juke as if he weighed no more than a bag of sugar and strode out of the ballroom.

Seth watched them go. Reluctantly, he slung his backpack over his shoulder and walked through reception.

'Where are you going, Seth?' called Violet, seductively.

'I have to take my mother to the station,' he said grimacing.

'Are you coming back?' Violet asked hopefully.

'Yeah, I wanna check Juke's okay.'

'Oh,' said Violet, unable to hide her disappointment.

Seth quickly realised his error. 'And see you, of course.'

She smiled at him. 'Would you like me to come with you?'

'Probably not a good idea. You don't want to meet my mother just yet. Especially when she's late for a train. She's evil. Catch you later, okay?'

'Okay,' said Violet, her blue eyes twinkling at him.

* * *

Leon got to the Clock Tower room in record time and Viyesha unlocked the carved oak door. In no time, she'd opened the secret panel, taken the silver casket from its hiding place and was holding the blue crystal, rivulets of blue energy criss-crossing her palms. She passed it to Joseph, who took it in his hands, letting the cascading blue light run across his fingers. Leon laid Juke in the centre of the room over the faintly glowing hieroglyphics and Joseph moved the crystal over his body. Gradually, Juke's energy field began to respond. A small flicker flared up here and there, as tears and rents began to mend, and a dim white glow appeared around him.

'You might want to look away,' Joseph advised the family, putting on Ray-bans. 'Don't forget, Juke's an energy sensor. His energy field will be intense.'

They took his advice, shielding their eyes with their hands, as Joseph continued to work with the crystal, his eyes protected by his dark glasses. Juke glowed ever brighter and soon he was shining with a blinding intensity.

'Perfect,' said Joseph in satisfaction. 'Lit up like a Christmas tree.'

He noticed the crystal necklace hanging round Juke's neck, emitting a brilliant blue light. 'I think that may have saved you, my friend,' he said, smiling at Juke. To his amazement, Juke moved his head and opened his eyes, looking up at Joseph.

'Where am I?' he muttered, trying to sit up.

'Don't move too quickly,' advised Joseph. 'You've had a near miss and I've just put you back together again.'

He placed the blue crystal back in its casket and handed it to Viyesha. She quickly returned the casket to the alcove, sliding the secret lever into its upright position and moving the wall panel into place. Gradually, Juke's bright white energy dissipated and he stood up.

'Don't know what you've done to me, Joseph, but I feel fantastic, all shining and new. I haven't felt as good as this in ages. Thanks, mate.'

'You've been lucky, Juke,' Joseph cautioned him. 'The crystal necklace gave you some protection and we were able to get you to the large crystal in time. You'll live to fight another battle.'

As Juke remembered his ordeal, his face darkened. 'Have you told them, Viyesha?' he asked.

'Not yet,' she faltered. 'There was no time.'

'Told us what?' demanded Theo.

'We know who has the girls,' she said. 'Juke met him in Dreamtime.'

'Who is it?' asked Leon.

'It would seem our worst nightmare has returned,' said Viyesha in a faint voice. 'The Fallen Angel is back, desperate for human form. He wants to trade the girls for the crystal.'

There was a momentary silence as they took in her words.

Theo looked at Viyesha with agony in his eyes. 'I'm never going to see Emily again, am I? Just as we were so close to being together.'

31. **White Van**

Seth got back into his mother's new Ford Fiesta. It had been touch and go whether his mother would make her train, but she'd caught it with seconds to spare, giving Seth a quick peck on the cheek, telling him she'd see him in a couple of days.

For a while he sat listening to his favourite Katy Perry track, Dark Horse, appreciating the words all the more after the events of the last few days. Idly, he glanced across to the station's long stay multi-storey car park, where rows of parked vehicles stood waiting for their owners to retrieve them, and wondered what would happen if you forgot to collect your car, if you had an accident or died and couldn't come back for it. Perhaps it would just stay there for years, gradually rusting away. He saw a new Mercedes drive in and mentally made a note that was the car he'd buy as soon as he'd made some money, then did a double take as he watched a white van follow it into the car park. A thought formed in his mind. Where's the easiest place to offload a van for which you had no further use? Where could you dump a stolen van without drawing any attention?

Realising he might be on to something, he leapt out of his mother's car and sprinted over to the entrance, where he discovered the enormity of his task. Hundreds of cars were parked on every level and on the ground floor alone there were any number of white vans. He decided to take a look.

The old farmer had been convinced he'd seen a Volkswagen Transporter 2 litre TDI, and the registration definitely had 977 in it. Shame he'd left his notebook at home, where he'd written down the details. Still, he had something to go on. The first van a Ford Transit and so was the second. The third was a Vauxhall and the fourth a Toyota. By the time he'd covered half the ground floor level and looked at a dozen more, he began to think he was wasting his time. Noticing a van tucked away in the shadows at the far end of the car park, he felt his pulse quicken. The van was covered in dried mud as if it had been driving down country lanes.

He hurried towards it, feeling excited, and looked at the registration number. Yes! He punched the air in satisfaction. Y977 XOJ. A VW Transporter 2 litre TDI. This was the vehicle that had been used to move Emily and Tash. He tried the driver's door but found it locked. Same with the rear doors. Remembering TV detective programmes, he put his hand inside the wheel arch on the driver's side and ran his hand over the tyre. To his amazement, his fingers closed around a key.

'Yowza!' he exclaimed loudly.

In two minutes, he was sitting behind the driving wheel, looking for clues or anything that might give the slightest indication of Emily and Tash's whereabouts. There was nothing, apart from the parking ticket left on the dashboard. He unlocked the rear doors and searched the back of the van, again finding nothing except a few dried bloodstains.

'May as well drive it back to the hall,' he said to himself. 'One of them might find something I'm missing.' He turned the key in the ignition, pleased to hear the engine roar into life, and putting on the seat belt, cautiously reversed, cringing as he scraped against a concrete post.

Thankfully, he had just enough money for the ticket machine, then he was driving out of the car park and along the lanes back to Hartswell Hall, leaving his mother's car behind.

He found Juke sitting on the hall steps, taking in the afternoon sunshine, a mysterious glow surrounding his body.

'Juke, you're back with us, man,' he said, climbing out of the van.

'Sure am, Seth, thanks to the crystal and Joseph's healing hands. What's with the van, mate?'

'This is the van that was used to transport Emily and Tash,' said Seth proudly. 'I found it in the long stay car park at the station.'

'No kidding, Seth,' said Juke, coming down the steps and looking over the van. 'You're a man of surprises. Does it yield any clues?'

'I haven't found any,' said Seth, 'but I thought the family, with their 'supernatural skills',' he made speech marks with his fingers, 'might detect something.'

'Good thinking, Seth. This could be the breakthrough we need.'

Soon, the family was clustered round the van, while Aquila, Pantera and Bellynda watched suspiciously from the steps. Seth handed the van key to Leon and once again, found himself the centre of attention.

'I don't know how you do it, Seth. You are truly amazing,' said Violet flirtatiously.

'Natural brilliance, my dear, some of us have it. Some of us don't.' He looked pointedly at Theo, who raised his eyebrows, but wisely kept silent.

'We are indebted to you, Seth,' said Viyesha. 'Time and again you have demonstrated exceptional abilities. Now, let's see if the van yields any secrets. Pantera, see what scents you can pick up."

Leon opened the rear of the van, revealing the empty interior with the ominous darkened bloodstains on the wall, and reluctantly Pantera climbed inside.

'Mr Nelson was here,' she informed them. 'There are traces of him in the cab, and Emily and Tash were held in the rear. This is Emily's blood, but it's nearly a week old, and I can detect nothing that would suggest where they're being held.'

'Nothing?' said Viyesha in dismay. 'So, we're at a dead end once again?'

'Wait a second,' said Joseph, examining the tyre treads. 'There might be something here.' He pulled a penknife from his pocket and began loosening some material embedded in the rubber. He placed the contents into his palm.

'This grit has a pink tinge to it. The van must have been in a location where pink grit is on the ground. It's not much to go on, but it's something.'

'Great,' said Theo, sarcastically. 'We're looking for somewhere with a pink driveway. That could be anywhere. Where do we start looking?'

'A pink driveway?' asked Seth. 'It's obvious, dudes.'

'It is?' asked Joseph.

'The village hall car park,' announced Seth. 'They've just had it covered with this weird pink grit. My mum was moaning about it the other day after her keep fit class. She said it got into the tread of her trainers.'

Joseph looked at him in amazement. 'Mr Nelson parked the van in the village hall car park, then carried the girls somewhere close by?'

'Emily thought they were in a large underground crypt,' said Juke. 'She saw coffins stacked up. Is there a crypt at the church?'

'There is,' answered Theo. 'I've been there. Except it's nothing but a small dry room with no coffins in sight. You said Emily was in a cavernous place with vaulted ceilings. It's nothing like that.'

'There has to be somewhere else,' said Juke. 'This all fits together. I told you I've been detecting dark matter around this location, but I couldn't work out where.'

'We need to ask the vicar,' said Viyesha. 'There may be an old underground vault that's no longer used. Let me phone him.'

'Don't tell him any more than you have to,' cautioned Leon. 'We cannot risk outside intervention now we're so close. If the authorities were to become involved it could be disastrous. Tell him you're researching the history of the place.'

They waited anxiously while Viyesha made the call. Five minutes later she had the information they needed.

'Father James believes there may be an underground crypt that's been unused for years,' she informed them. 'He thinks entry is via a large tomb situated next to the new vestry. Apparently, one of the churchwardens told him a few weeks ago it's not a tomb, but a stairway leading down into the church vaults.' She looked at her husband. 'You need to take a look as soon as possible, Leon.'

* * *

Theo, Joseph and Leon walked briskly along the pathway to the old church. As they crossed the village hall car park, Joseph bent down and picked up some of the small pink grit covering its surface.

'It's the same as I found on the van tyres,' he said. 'We're getting close, Theo.'

They took the path into the graveyard and stopped when they reached the large stone tomb by the new vestry.

'This must be it,' said Leon, running his hands along its large stone lid.

'Look here,' said Joseph, examining the side of the tomb. 'These marks have been made recently by a crowbar.'

'This is it,' said Theo, his face white and strained. 'I know it. They've been here all the time and we had no idea. We have to get in. Every second counts, Father.'

157

'We have to prepare, Theo,' answered Leon. 'If we go barging in, things could go wrong. We' need to go in under cover of darkness.'

'Can't we just take a quick look? At least we'll know if we're in the right place.'

Leon saw the agony on his son's face and agreed.

'Alright. Keep watch while I move the lid.'

He placed his hands around the ancient stone lid and slowly inched it aside. Joseph shone a torch into the opening and peered inside. He whistled softly.

'There are steps, leading down,' he said. 'It's definitely an entranceway.'

Leon and Theo peered into the gloomy interior at the flight of ancient stone steps leading down into the earth.

'I think we've found what we're looking for,' said Leon. 'Let's put the lid back and return to the hall. We need a plan if we're going inside.'

'Not without me, you don't,' said a voice behind them, causing them spin round in alarm, as Father James appeared out of the vestry. 'Tell me what's going on, Mr de Lucis. This is sanctified ground.'

Leon stared at him for a second, and made a decision.

'Father, we have reason to believe that two village girls have been abducted and are being held prisoner in this vault.'

'Dear God, are you sure?' asked Father James. 'We must call the police.'

'No,' said Leon briskly, 'that would not be advisable, given the nature of the creatures we're dealing with. It would be better if you allowed us to handle this.'

'Creatures? What creatures? What are you talking about?'

Leon considered his words carefully. 'How can I put it, Father? These are beings to which the laws of physics don't apply. The police would be powerless against them. Only my family and our retainers have the necessary skills to deal with them.'

'I see,' said Father James, giving Leon's words some thought.

Expecting ridicule, Leon was taken aback by his next words.

'I've been encountering strange manifestations myself over the last couple of days,' he said. 'I know something unholy is going on in this village. Could the events be linked?'

Leon glanced at Theo and Joseph. 'Strange manifestations?' he queried.

'Some kind of demonic possession, a dark shape that attaches to people's backs and drains the life force out of them. I've exorcised half a dozen now. I thought they were Elemental spirits, but now I wonder if they're something darker.'

'Feeders,' said Leon. 'This is worse than we thought. If there are feeders in the village, it means he's amassing forces on the outside as well as beneath us.'

'He?' asked Father James. 'Who is this 'he'?'

'Let's just say an ancient demon whom we've encountered before,' said Leon. 'The feeders are his minions, preparing the way for him to return. What you've seen is nothing. The real threat is still to come.'

'And the abducted girls?' asked Father James. 'Where do they fit in?'

'He's holding the girls as leverage,' answered Leon 'He wants something we possess. Something that will give him human form, which we can never allow.'

'Dear God! Who are these girls?' asked Father James. 'You say they're from the village?'

'Emily and her friend Tash,' said Theo, speaking for the first time.

'Emily Morgan? I only buried her grandfather a few weeks ago.'

'You'll be burying Emily as well if we don't get her out quickly,' said Theo, 'Time is running out, Father.'

'If it's true what you say,' said Father James, 'then we must get them out.'

'We?' questioned Leon.

'Absolutely. I'm coming with you. No question about it. It's my church and these are my parishioners. I have to know what we're dealing with.'

'It's too risky, Father. With respect, you don't know what you're up against.'

Father James held his ground. 'It's non-negotiable, Mr de Lucis. If you wish to go into the crypt, you take me with you.'

'Very well, but it's at your own risk,' said Leon. 'Our first priority is to rescue the girls, but we also need to destroy whatever evil we find down there, and it won't give up without a fight. I can't vouch for your safety. '

'I'll take my chances,' said Father James. 'Do I need to bring anything?'

'Holy water and a crucifix might come in handy,' said Leon.

'Tools of the trade,' said Father James. 'How about you?'

'We have own resources,' answered Leon. 'Don't worry about us.'

PART THREE: RESCUE

32. The Crypt

By nightfall, the tomb team was ready. A low, cloying mist, created by Pantera, swirled around them, concealing their actions and giving the graveyard a sinister, mysterious atmosphere.

Aquila, Pantera and Bellynda went first into the tomb, knowing however much they disliked Emily, it was their duty to protect the family. They were followed by Leon, Theo, Joseph and Juke, with Father James bringing up the rear. Viyesha stood guard at the tomb entrance. Against her better judgment, she had allowed Seth to remain at the hall with Violet, guarding the crystal. It was a marginally better option than letting him go into the crypt, which he'd wanted to do.

Silently, they descended into the earth, the three shape shifters finding their way with ease, the others using torches to see the old stone steps.

'Take care, Father,' called Viyesha, as he disappeared into the gloom. 'If the situation looks bad, come back. There's no glory in dying down there.'

'Don't worry, I don't intend to play the hero.' He looked back at her, his face taking on an eerie, otherworldly glow in the torchlight, his crucifix glinting.

Down they went, the steps seemingly endless, the air stale and musty, as if undisturbed for many years, and getting noticeably cooler.

'I shouldn't be here, Leon,' muttered Bellynda. 'My job is to guard the crystal.'

'It could get ugly, Bellynda. I need you with us,' he answered. 'You're our secret weapon.'

She snorted. 'I suppose the prospect of a fight does have its attractions.' Her yellow eyes glinted and she cracked her knuckles, her long nails curling over the tips of her fingers.

The steps ended abruptly, leading into a passageway, a couple of metres wide with a high ceiling, stretching ahead into the darkness. Aquila led the way and they followed him in single file. Drops of water fell from above and a putrid stench filled the air making Father

James wonder if the crypt was full of decomposing bodies. He pushed the thought from his mind and concentrated on putting one foot in front of the other. They sensed rather than saw the passageway coming to an end, feeling the air brush past them like a flimsy, gossamer veil.

'Looks like we've reached the crypt,' said Aquila.

A further flight of steps, hewn into the rock, led downwards and they followed him into a vast, vaulted, subterranean chamber. Their torches revealed huge pilasters and columns rising to a great height, supporting massive ribs and pointed arches that spanned the width of the enormous cavern, all decorated with ornate, ancient symbols.

'Jesus, would you look at that?' exclaimed Juke, as his torch picked out rows of mouldering coffins, stacked against the crypt wall.

'Corpses can't hurt us,' said Bellynda. 'Where are the feeders? That's what I'd like to know.'

'Emily said they were everywhere,' said Juke.

'Not anymore,' snapped Bellynda. 'I don't like the look of this. It's too quiet. And too empty.'

'They've definitely been here,' said Pantera, wrinkling her nose. 'Their stench is everywhere.' She sniffed the air. 'Reptilia, too, and not too long ago.'

'Something's not right,' said Leon. 'We need to find the girls and get out.' He shone his torch towards a large lead tomb on a raised dais at the head of the crypt. 'That must be where Emily is. But why no guard? It doesn't make sense.'

'Unless it's a trap,' said Theo. 'Or she's not there.'

'Or the whole thing is a diversion,' said Bellynda. 'I should never have left the crystal unprotected. I need to get back.'

'No,' said Leon firmly. 'We get the girls out first. Then we return to the hall. Violet is protecting the crystal.'

'Come on, what are we waiting for?' said Theo impatiently. He moved towards the lead tomb, but Leon pulled him back.

'Careful, Theo. We don't know what nasties are waiting for us.'

'Do we have a plan?' asked Aquila, looking around suspiciously.

'Yes. You and Bellynda take a look around,' said Leon. 'Your eyesight's better than ours. See if anything's hiding in the shadows, keep Theo and me covered while we go to the tomb.'

He shone his torch around the crypt, revealing steps leading up to a dark opening in the rock face directly opposite them. 'I'm guessing that's where Tash may be held. Pantera, take Joseph and Juke, and check it out. That could be where Emily met the Fallen Angel, so be careful.'

He turned to the priest. 'Father, stay by the entrance and keep a look out. Shout if you see anything and have your cross and holy water ready.'

Father James went back up the steps and took his place, looking nervously around, while Pantera led Juke and Joseph towards the far passageway, their torches flashing in the dark.

Aquila and Bellynda walked cautiously into the crypt, looking behind every shadowy arch and pillar with razor sharp vision.

'Do you have Emily's crystal?' asked Leon.

Theo nodded and, gripping the crystal tightly, followed his father.

At the tomb, Leon placed his fingers under the lip of the heavy lid and slowly began to lift. No sooner had he done so, than a loud cracking sound cut through the silence, echoing across the cavernous chamber.

'What was that?' he asked, dropping the lid back into place and looking around.

'It came from up there,' said Theo, shining his torch into the vaulted roof and straining to see in the dim light.

Aquila and Bellynda were with them in an instant, looking into the expanse above.

'Do you see anything?' asked Leon.

'I'm not sure,' said Bellynda, screwing up her eyes.

'There,' said Aquila, pointing upwards. 'The arch has cracked.'

Theo pointed his torch where Aquila indicated and sure enough a massive crack had appeared in the stone arch directly above them. An ominous black substance was slowly seeping through the gap.

'I don't like the look of that,' said Bellynda. 'You need to get the girl out fast and leave.'

Leon needed no further prompting. In one deft movement, he curled his fingers beneath the massive tomb lid, lifted it upwards and sent it crashing to the crypt floor. With a brief glance upwards, Theo climbed onto the dais and peered inside the tomb.

There she lay, eyes closed, face pale and drawn, wearing the blue cloak. Relief turned to panic as he looked for signs of life, but saw nothing.

'She's not breathing, Father. We're too late.' He lifted her towards him, finding her hair matted with blood.

'What have they done to you?' he cried, tears falling onto her pallid face.

Leon put a hand on his son's shoulder. 'Put the crystal pendant around her neck,' he said calmly.

With trembling hands, Theo fastened the necklace and placed the crystal on her breastbone.

'Time to wake your sleeping beauty...' said Leon.

Comprehension dawned in Theo. 'You mean...?'

Leon nodded. Quickly, Theo leant into the tomb and placed his lips on hers, finding them cold and lifeless. Gently he kissed her, feeling the energy flow from his body to hers. Beneath him, the blue crystal pendant started to glow and Theo became aware of a searing heat that burnt his chest.

* * *

I felt I was being woken from a long, death-like sleep and dragged into a life that was little more than a dim memory. I took a sharp intake of breath, my lungs filling with air, and as the oxygen woke my brain, I heard a familiar voice say: 'She's alive. Emily's alive!' I forced my heavy eyelids open, struggling to focus after so long in the dark. I took in Theo's deep blue eyes and tousled blonde hair and wondered if I was dreaming or still lost in that hidden place within my mind.

'Is it you, Theo?' I asked, my voice dry and faint.

'Yes,' he said. 'I'm going to get you out. Thank God I've found you.'

I felt strong arms lift me out of the lead tomb and wrap the blue cloak around me. My eyelids fluttered and I turned my face towards Theo's chest, feeling his heart beat beneath his white linen shirt. I inhaled deeply. I couldn't trust what my eyes were seeing, but my sense of smell wouldn't lie. This was real. This was happening. Theo was here at last.

I heard Leon's voice say 'Take her back to the hall as fast as you can.' Then my eyelids closed and sleep claimed me again.

* * *

'Move, Theo!' shouted Bellynda, as he stepped off the dais. Holding Emily tightly in his arms, he moved with lightning speed towards the entrance. Directly above, the seeping black substance began to drip from the arch, landing in the tomb beneath, making the lead blister and buckle as if touched by acid.

'Get back, Leon,' shrieked Bellynda. 'This stuff is lethal.'

Leon moved backwards as more drops fell, splashing into the tomb and running down the dais onto the floor. He leapt over the spreading black liquid, as further drops landed where he'd been standing. Rapidly, the blackness covered the crypt floor, causing the old stonework to hiss and steam.

Shining his torch into the expanse above, Leon saw with horror a spider's web of cracks spreading across the vaulted ceiling and down the supporting columns. Each crack sounded like gunshot in the echoing chamber, and blackness oozed wherever a crack appeared, seeping over the ancient carvings as if the stone was bleeding. In seconds, the whole structure began to disintegrate, as arches and pillars fractured, and large black drops rained down, eating into the stone floor below.

'We need to get out,' shouted Aquila. 'The whole place is starting to go.'

Stepping over the hissing, spitting pools of blackness and dodging black droplets and falling masonry, Aquila and Bellynda ran across the crypt towards the entrance. Leon wasn't so lucky. A falling brick knocked the torch from his hand and everything plunged into darkness. He stood stock still, not daring to move, aware of the lethal black liquid's destructive power. One step in the wrong direction could be his last.

'I can't see,' he shouted into the chamber, his voice lost in the unfolding mayhem.

Miraculously, a shining light appeared from the entrance, lighting his way through the mayhem. It was Father James holding up his crucifix, which shone with the intensity of a lighthouse.

'Follow the light, Leon,' called Father James.

Needing no prompting, Leon followed the shining pathway, leaping between black pools and avoiding droplets and fragments of stone, until he was climbing the steps to the crypt entrance, where Aquila, Bellynda and Father James were waiting.

'Thank you, Father,' he gasped. 'You saved my life. How about Theo? Did he make it?'

'Yes, he did. He's gone into the passageway, with Emily,' said Father James.

'And what about Pantera and the others? Did they find Tash?'

'No sign of them,' said Father James.

He held up his crucifix once again, lighting up the bubbling, seething sea of black that now covered the crypt floor, and they looked in vain for Pantera, Joseph and Juke.

'There,' said Aquila, pointing into the gloom.

Leon strained his eyes and could just make them out on the other side of the crypt, in the mouth of the passageway. Joseph came first, holding Tash in his arms, followed by Juke and Pantera. They stood at the top of the steps, looking out on the unfolding disaster and the rising blackness beneath.

'Stay where you are,' shouted Leon, but his words were lost amidst the hissing and cracking.

He turned in desperation to Bellynda.

'They're trapped. What can we do? We're running out of time.'

As he spoke, one of the major archways groaned and collapsed, crashing into the morass below.

Bellynda paused for a second, as if weighing up her options, and said, 'Okay. Stand back. I need space.'

As she spoke, her yellow eyes began to elongate and the pupils turned to narrow slits. Her black leather jacket and trousers began to melt, spreading across her body and fusing into smooth, scaly armour. Her chest moved forward and she dropped to all fours, black wings sprouting from her back. Her legs and arms became muscular and reptilian, and her long curled nails turned into vicious talons. A huge black tail snaked out behind her and her neck extended upwards, becoming crested and curved. Her nose and jaw extended serpent-like into a long, pointed snout with two large nostrils, and opening her mouth she revealed rows of jagged, pointed teeth.

Flexing her wings, she exhaled a fireball of flames.

Father James watched, eyes wide in amazement, crossing himself and holding his crucifix tightly.

With no time to waste, the huge black dragon flew upwards into the chamber, lethal black drops bouncing off her body like rain off a duck's back.

'What a woman,' said Aquila, transfixed. 'Look at that wingspan.'

Dodging the falling rocks and stonework, the dragon came in to land by the passageway, skimming over the bubbling black sea, and clinging with powerful talons to the stone steps. They watched as Joseph placed Tash's inert form over the dragon's back, and climbed on. Once more, the dragon rose into the air, wings beating back the dripping blackness, carrying Joseph and Tash across the crypt to safety.

'Thanks, Bellynda,' said Joseph, as he dismounted. 'We owe our lives to you. We'd never have made it otherwise.' He gently lifted Tash from the dragon's back.

'Is she okay?' asked Leon.

'No, she's failing fast. I need to get her back to the hall.'

'Go,' instructed Leon. 'Theo's already gone with Emily. We'll meet you there.'

Joseph needed no further bidding. He disappeared into the passageway, Tash in his arms.

The dragon flew again across the crypt, the scene now resembling a war zone, broken arches and pillars crashing to the ground, the air thick with black matter and the black liquid sea rising fast. Just as it reached the upper steps, the dragon landed, and Pantera and Juke climbed on to her back. Then she was flying back through the devastation and destruction.

'Jesus. It's like World War Three,' said Juke, as they came into land. 'Did you get Emily out, Leon?'

'Yes. Theo's taken her back to the hall and Joseph's following with Tash. Did you find the Fallen Angel?'

'Long gone,' answered Pantera, 'although his filthy scent was everywhere. I guess this is his way of saying hello.'

'Goodbye, more like,' said Aquila. 'If it wasn't for Bellynda you'd never have made it.'

'We are indebted,' said Pantera, as Bellynda quickly assumed human form, dusting down her leather jacket. She nodded in Pantera's direction.

'I was expecting to fight feeders, not fly through black acid rain,' she muttered, examining a small burn mark on her jacket with a look of irritation.

'It's black anti-matter,' said Juke. 'I've seen it before. Totally lethal. Destroys everything in its path.' He shone his torch over the desolation, and did a double take. 'Actually, not everything. I don't want to panic you, guys, but we have company.'

They turned to look in the direction of his torchlight and stared open mouthed as a dark figure rose silently out of the bubbling black matter. It looked like a man covered in thick, steaming tar, his features concealed. Juke shone his torch across the crypt, revealing more figures, rising sinister and silent from the bubbling black liquid.

'What are they?' asked Leon, horrified.

'Some kind of walking dead,' said Juke, thinking fast. He banged his head with his hand. 'Of course, put anti-matter with a dead body and it reverses the process. These are the inhabitants of those old, mouldering coffins.'

'Oh, please,' said Bellynda. 'Zombies? You have to be kidding.'

Further dark figures emerged, rising up from below into the shadows. Faceless and menacing, they all moved in one direction. Towards the crypt entrance.

'Don't try any heroics,' cautioned Juke. 'If they touch you, you're done for. Even you, Bellynda.'

'What can we do?' asked Father James, holding his crucifix tighter than ever.

'We need to get back to ground level and close the vault lid,' said Juke. 'You immortals go first. You're faster. Get back up the steps and make sure the vault lid is ready to close. Father James and I will be right behind you.'

Already, the first black figure was just metres from the lower steps, black gloop seeping from its empty eye sockets, its teeth just visible in a chilling grin.

They didn't stay to see more. As one, they turned and ran down the passageway towards the exit. Unable to match the supernatural speed of their companions, Juke and Father James fell behind.

'Come on, Father, we'll be fine as long as we keep running,' said Juke, hearing Father James's ragged breath. 'As you might have noticed, these creatures don't move fast.'

They continued running along the passageway, Juke flashing his torch ahead, willing the stone steps to appear.

But a surprise awaited them. As they neared the end of the passageway, Juke's torch picked out a crowd of figures. It was Leon, Aquila, Pantera and Bellynda. Behind them, stood Joseph with Tash in his arms and Theo holding Emily.

'What's wrong?' he called. 'Why don't you go up the steps?'

'What steps?' shouted Aquila. 'They've gone. There is no way out.'

Juke shone his torch forward. Instead of the ancient stone steps, there was a solid rock face, smooth and impenetrable, blocking their way.

'He's sealed us in,' said Theo, unable to keep the despair out of his voice.

'It was a trap,' came Bellynda's steely voice through the darkness. 'He's played us and we fell for it. He knew we'd never trade the crystal. He's used the girls as bait, knowing we'd come to rescue them. While we're stuck down here, he's stealing the crystal. Violet will be no match for him.'

'I knew we should never have come,' muttered Pantera.

From the passageway came the sucking, sloshing, slopping sounds as the anti-matter zombies approached.

'I guess this is what's called being stuck between a rock and a hard place,' said Juke. 'Any ideas, anyone?'

33. Under Attack

'Why don't we sit in the ballroom?' Violet suggested to Seth.

'I thought we were supposed to be looking after the crystal?'

'The crystal will be fine,' she said, opening the double doors and pulling him in. She walked over to one of the large sofas and sat down, patting the place next to her. With her long, golden hair, flawless ivory skin and cornflower eyes, she was irresistible.

Seth grinned widely. He didn't need further encouragement and sat by her side.

'D'you want a drink?' she asked.

'No, I'm good.' He smiled and she smiled back, both suddenly nervous.

'Don't you have guests in the hotel?' he asked, for want of anything better to say.

'No, my mother cancelled the guests. We were supposed to be having a family event and she needed time to prepare.'

'If you mean Emily's initiation, I know all about it,' he admitted.

'You do?' asked Violet, frowning. 'You're not supposed to know about these things. It could be dangerous for you…'

'Violet, I know everything,' he said, enjoying her surprise. 'I know about the crystal and its powers, I know about Badru and the Lunari, and I know Emily was supposed to go through her initiation at the full moon.'

'She's told you a lot, hasn't she? The Lunari could kill you for less, you know.'

'The Lunari don't scare me,' he said nonchalantly. 'At the moment, I'm the least of their problems.'

'I hope the others are okay,' said Violet, 'Who knows what's waiting for them in the crypt?'

'I wish they'd let me go with them,' said Seth. 'I wanted to be part of the action.'

Violet smiled coyly. 'You are part of the action, Seth,' she said softly, leaning a little closer.

He looked into her eyes, mesmerised by their changing colours. One minute they were blue as a summer's day, the next dark as the deepest ocean, flecks of violet flashing brightly, tantalising and teasing. He found himself leaning in towards her, then her lips were upon his and he was getting lost in the most amazing kiss of his life. He could literally feel the sparks fly. He closed his eyes, never wanting the moment to stop, surrendering to this bewitching girl who offered him delights he'd never even dreamed existed. She broke off and looked at him.

'You have beautiful eyes, Seth,' she said, 'smouldering and sensual. Has anyone ever told you?'

'Yeah, all the time,' he said breathlessly. 'It's what comes of having Greek Cypriot parents.' And he pulled her back towards him, hungry for the exquisite taste of her lips, wanting to touch her perfect flesh, smooth, toned and tempting.

'The others will be back soon,' she whispered. 'We don't have long.'

'Better make the most of it,' he answered huskily, finding her lips again, and running his fingers through her golden hair.

Neither of them noticed the dark shadows at the ballroom windows, cutting out the light, like storm clouds passing in front of the sun. They accumulated rapidly, pressing against the glass, watching and waiting for their opportunity. At the front of the house, silent dark shapes passed into the entrance hallway, finding the huge oak door open and inviting. An insubstantial glass door was all that kept them from entering the reception area. More dark forms flowed up the driveway, drawn by the power of the crystal, silently creeping up the exterior walls, seeking out windows where they could enter. Gradually, the hall's honey-coloured brickwork became hidden beneath a sea of moving, creeping blackness. All natural light was quickly obliterated and inside it became dark as night.

'What's going on?' asked Violet, suddenly aware of the darkness. 'Look's like a storm's coming.'

She opened her eyes, mid kiss, and looked over Seth's shoulder, stifling a scream. In the gloom, she could just make out dark shapes pressed against the windows, black eyes glittering, watching their every movement. She pulled away from him, forcing herself to stay calm.

'Don't turn round now, Seth,' she whispered, 'but we're being watched. We need to get out of here quickly.'

'What d'you mean? Don't stop now. I was enjoying that.' He tried to pull her close again, then seeing her frightened face, turned and followed her gaze across the room.

'Holy moley,' he muttered. 'What in Spock's name are they?'

'Feeders,' said Violet in a panic. 'Oh my God, what have we done? We were supposed to be protecting the crystal. What if they've got in to the hall? We have to get up to the Clock Tower.'

She leapt up and grabbed his hand.

'Come on, Seth. This is bad and we're on our own. Did we close the front door?'

'I can't remember,' he said. 'What happens if they get in?'

'The crystal is lost and we're dead,' she cried, pulling him out of the ballroom.

'Let me go first,' he said, feeling invincible after the amazing kiss.

'No, Seth. It's too dangerous. They'll finish you off in seconds. Whatever you do, don't turn your back on them.'

She opened the ballroom door a fraction and peered out.

'The coast is clear. If we can get up the main stairway, there's a chance we can get to the crystal.'

'Can't you summon the others telepathically?' asked Seth, 'I mean you're a mega being. Isn't that how you communicate?'

'Very funny, Seth. Not my talent. I wish I could. All I can do is call my mother on my mobile. Not that there's much she can do on her own. And I don't want her to know we were kissing and cuddling while feeders were gathering outside. Let's get to the Clock Tower first.'

She opened the door wider and stifled another scream as she saw the feeders pressed against the glass door leading from the entrance hall into reception. More feeders covered the outside windows, cutting out the light, making it eerie, dark and silent.

'Oh my God, Seth. We must have left the front door open.'

Seth walked up to the glass door and used the torch app on his phone to look at the feeders. 'Yowza. They are mean-looking dudes. They've got tentacles and mouths full of teeth, like piranhas. There must be hundreds out there.'

'Seth, come on. We don't have long,' said Violet, urgently. 'We don't know how long the glass will withstand their pressure.'

She grasped his hand and pulled him towards the central stairway.

'You go first,' she said.

'Whoa! You're the immortal. You go first,' he quipped.

'Seth, I'm serious. Your back is your vulnerable point. It's safer if I go behind.'

'What if there are feeders upstairs?'

'Just keep going. We have to get to the Clock Tower.'

They ran up the stairs to the central landing. So far, the upper levels appeared to be feeder-free.

'To the right,' instructed Violet.

'Yeah, I know,' said Seth.

'How? You haven't been up here before.'

He turned and grinned. 'Long story. Don't ask. I just know where we're heading.'

Violet looked at him strangely. 'Okay, lead the way. You can tell me later.'

Seth ran towards the old servants' stairway and began climbing the steps two at a time, Violet close behind. Downstairs, they heard the sound of breaking glass and Violet screamed involuntarily.

'Hurry, Seth. They're in. We have to reach the crystal.'

Quickly, they ran through the old servants' quarters until they got to the stone spiral stairway. Further sounds of smashing glass came from below.

'Oh my God, we're not going to make it,' screamed Violet.

'We will,' said Seth. 'Don't worry. I've been in worse situations.'

'You have?' she asked hopefully.

'Not really,' he admitted. 'I just thought it might make you feel better.'

'Seth!' she said in exasperation. 'Just keep going.'

Seth led the way up the old spiral steps, the muscles in his legs burning and tight.

'This is like one of those never-ending nightmares,' he said, breathlessly, 'where you keep running and your legs get heavier and heavier and you never reach the end.'

'Shut up,' said Violet. 'You're making it worse.'

Then the old carved doorway was before them, Seth was removing a loose brick from the wall and taking out the key.

'How did you…..' she started to say, and thought better of it. 'Give it to me.'

She snatched the key and unlocked the door, looking back over her shoulder. Gliding silently up the steps appeared the first of the feeders, black tentacles reaching forward, drawn irrevocably towards the crystal.

'Get in, Seth,' she shrieked in panic.

She grasped his arm and pulled him over the threshold into the room, slamming the door shut and locking it. She turned to face him.

'Oh my God, Seth, we did it. Let me call mother and tell her what's happened. She'll know what to do.' She looked at his face. 'What's the matter?'

He took a deep breath. 'Sorry, Violet. I think I've brought one in with me. I think I've got a feeder on my back.'

She opened her eyes wide in disbelief.

'This is no time for joking.

'I'm not. It feels weird, like something's hanging there and digging in its claws.'

He turned to show her.

'I can't see anything,' she said, 'but you are quite hunched. You could have picked one up, I suppose. I told you not to turn your back on them.'

'How else could I get in?' he asked, indignantly.

'Okay, let me think. I need to call mother and warn her what's happened. She's standing guard at the entrance to the tomb. Hopefully, she can get word to Bellynda. If anyone can sort out the feeders, it's her.'

'One woman against an army?' asked Seth. 'How does that work?'

Violet laughed. 'She's no ordinary woman. The clue's in her name. Bellynda means serpent, LaDrach means dragon.'

'Dragon Woman!' said Seth. His eyes lit up, then he winced as his back went into spasm. 'This doesn't feel good, Violet. I need to get this thing off me.'

'Okay, I'm calling now.' She waited impatiently for her call to be answered. 'Hi, mother. It's Violet. You have to help us. We're in the Clock Tower and the hall is crawling with feeders. Seth is…'

She stared at the phone in disbelief. 'It's dead. The signal's gone.'

'Try mine,' said Seth, getting out his mobile phone.

It was the same. No signal.

'Anything to do with the feeders?' asked Seth.

'Could be,' said Violet. 'Maybe dark matter blocks the signal. I just hope mother heard enough.'

'I hope so, too,' said Seth, grimacing. 'I don't feel great. This thing is strong.'

'Sorry, Seth. I don't know how to remove it. We'll just have to wait for help to come.'

'Typical,' said Seth. 'I get a girl and a feeder gets me. Just my luck.'

34. Zombies

Juke shone his torch down the underground passage. Ten metres away the first of the anti-matter zombies approached, squelching and deadly.

Father James held up his crucifix, shining brightly once again.

'I don't think that's going to save you, Father,' said Juke. 'We need a plan.'

'I can break through the rock face,' called Leon, 'but it's going to take time. You'll need to stall the zombies, Juke.'

'Hurry, please,'' sounded Joseph's voice. 'Tash is fading fast. I need to get her to the surface.'

The squelching got closer.

'I need to think like a zombie,' muttered Juke.

'Shouldn't be difficult,' he heard Bellynda say.

'Zombies are pretty stupid,' continued Juke.

'I rest my case,' came Bellynda's sneering voice.

'You're not helping, Bellynda,' he called back. 'And don't even think of turning into a dragon. There isn't room. You'd squish us all.'

More zombies appeared, filling up the passageway behind the leader. Now, they presented a solid front, moving slowly forwards. The first was nearly at Father James, its arms extended, dripping with sludge.

Father James pressed himself against the passageway wall, holding the glowing crucifix up in front of him. To Juke's amazement, the creature shrank back in horror.

'Well, I'll be damned. Try throwing some holy water, Father,' he suggested.

Father James pulled the stopper from the bottle and hurled a few drops at the creature. The effect was immediate. It let out an inhuman wail and its body began to hiss and steam, melting down like a burning candle. Its head dropped inwards, its arms and legs fused into its body and it fell to the floor, a sticky black pool of bubbling gunge. As they watched, it shrank inwards and disappeared to nothing, leaving a hole in the passageway floor.

'Wow,' said Juke. 'That was unexpected. Try again.'

Father James threw water over the next creature, with the same results. Screaming and screeching, it melted into the ground and disappeared, leaving another hole in the stone floor.

'Are you thinking what I'm thinking, Father?' asked Juke.

'I'm thinking I can't keep this up for much longer. I only have one bottle of water,' answered Father James.

'I'm thinking if they can dissolve a stone floor, they can do the same to a rock face. It'll be much quicker than waiting for Leon to break us out,' said Juke. 'All we have to do is lure one to the end of the passageway.'

'One problem,' called Aquila. 'We're in the way. We can't disappear.'

'That's where you're wrong,' declared Juke. 'These mists you create, Pantera, are they zombie-proof?'

'They keep bad energy away,' she answered. 'I guess so.'

'A zombie won't attack if it can't see you,' said Juke, thinking fast. 'This might just work. And it's worth a try, given that we're running out of options. Father, hold that cross high and keep the zombies back. Everyone else, get as close to the side of the passageway as you can. Stand in single file. Make room for a zombie to walk past. Theo, if we make it out, get a bucket of font water from the church as fast as you can. Have it ready at the entrance to the tomb. Now, Pantera, do your mist thing.'

Pantera took a deep breath and exhaled. A thick swirling mist came out of her nostrils, curling around them and concealing them from view, quickly settling on their side of the passageway and reaching down to Father James. Juke positioned himself in front of the rock face, holding Father James's bottle of holy water.

'Okay, Father,' he called out. 'Let one through.'

Further down the passageway, Father James stepped to the side and was immediately swallowed by the mist. He hid his crucifix beneath his jacket and watched as a zombie went past, heading straight towards Juke, arms outstretched. As soon as it was past, he stepped out from the mist wielding his crucifix, holding the remaining zombies back, cowering and screeching.

'Come on, boy. Come and get me.' Juke taunted the approaching zombie.

Slowly, it walked forwards, heading towards him.

Everyone stood still, holding their breath, their super powers helpless against the deadly black matter. Theo and Joseph held Emily and Tash tightly in their arms, Bellynda tried to make herself as small as she could, Leon and Aquila stood alongside Pantera.

At the last second, just as the zombie's outstretched hands were about to touch him, Juke stepped sideways into the mist. The creature continued forward and Juke threw the holy water. There was a terrible hissing, spitting and screaming as the water hit its body, and the zombie began to melt, black matter splattering forward into the rock face, corrosive as acid. Within seconds it had disintegrated, leaving a hole, through which the stone steps were just visible.

'Who'd have thought it?' said Bellynda begrudgingly, stepping out of the mist. 'The plan actually worked, Juke. I guess you do think like a zombie, Juke. Now, let's get the hell out of here.'

'Wait till the anti-matter's evaporated,' advised Juke. 'This stuff kills.'

As soon as the black sizzling gloop had gone, Leon punched through the rough edges of the hole, making it large enough for them to step through. Then they were climbing the old stone steps to the graveyard above, Leon carrying Emily, while Theo sped ahead to the church.

Deep in the passageway, Father James continued to hold the zombies at bay, waiting until everyone was out. Slowly, he edged closer to the hole in the wall, holding his crucifix high as he climbed through and backed up the steps. To his horror, the zombies followed, moving relentlessly forward, through the hole and up towards ground level. As he reached the top, he felt Leon's strong arms pulling him out, and with no time to lose, hurled his crucifix down onto the nearest zombie. Screeching and crying, it fell back on the others.

'Now, Theo,' shouted Father James. 'Pour the font water.'

Just in time, Theo appeared with the holy water. He balanced it on the edge of the tomb and poured it inside.

The sound was deafening. There was a terrible screaming as the zombies fell backwards, followed by a loud crack and a deep rumble as the stone steps split and cascaded down in to the darkness, clouds of dust rising up. Leon quickly pulled the lid over the open tomb, sealing it shut, and restoring peace once more to the quiet graveyard.

'You okay, Father?' asked Juke.

'I'm fine,' he replied. 'I'll live to fight another day.'

'We owe you, Father,' said Leon. 'We couldn't have done it without you.'

'Thank God you're all safe.' Viyesha's voice sounded in the darkness. 'But we need to go. The hall is under attack. I just pray we're not too late.'

35. Fighting Back

'Violet called,' explained Viyesha. 'She said the hall is crawling with feeders.'

'Did she mention the crystal?' asked Bellynda.

'No, just that she and Seth were in the Clock Tower room. Then the line went dead.'

'I must get back,' said Bellynda. 'I should never have left the crystal.'

While Joseph and Father James took Emily and Tash to the vicarage, the rest gathered in front of the hall. Its honey-coloured stone was completely covered by feeders, swarming all over it like great black slugs, forming a moving, pulsing skin.

Viyesha spoke. 'Bellynda and Aquila, take the outside. Strike quickly and destroy every last one. They're forming a force field around the house, that's why Violet's phone went dead. Once it's strong enough, there will be no way in. Only the Fallen Angel will be able to enter and the crystal will be his to take.'

'He's here,' said Pantera, sniffing the air. 'I can smell him. His stench is everywhere. But I don't sense he's in the hall. He's getting his minions to do his dirty work for him.'

'As ever, ' said Viyesha, 'but that buys us time. Pantera and Theo, you take the inside. Kill all the feeders, while Leon and I get to the Clock Tower to secure the crystal. Be on your guard everyone, we are fighting for our survival.' She turned to Juke. 'I applaud your courage, but this is too dangerous. You must stand down.'

He looked at her steadily. 'Trust me, Viyesha, I'm the ally you can't do without. I'll go with Pantera and Theo.'

'As you will,' she answered. 'But it's at your own risk.'

Bellynda and Aquila needed no further orders. They assumed their shape-shifter forms: she a magnificent black dragon, spewing fire, and he a massive black eagle, the ultimate bird of prey. They rose into the air, flying close to the walls and striking with deadly accuracy. Time and again, Aquila flew in for the kill, talons outstretched, beak at the ready, tearing and ripping at the living wall of black, littering the air with dark confetti.

Bellynda flew close to the hall, her great wings outstretched, dowsing the feeders with a wall of flame, scorching, burning and destroying huge numbers at a time. Taking aim, she flew fast and furiously towards the upper levels, giving her onslaught even greater power, until the air became full of screeching feeders, wounded and dying, their black incinerated bodies and smouldering remains dropping to earth like flies.

Pantera, now a great black panther, leapt towards the entrance, powerful muscles rippling beneath her gleaming coat. Ripping and tearing with teeth and claws, she relentlessly shredded feeders into tiny pieces. As soon as the way was clear, Viyesha, Leon, Theo and Juke followed her into the hall. Feeders were everywhere, hanging from the doorframes, clinging to the walls, attached to furniture. Pantera was unforgiving, clawing and biting with savage ferocity, while Theo set about destroying feeders with his bare hands, grabbing, twisting and smashing his fist into their rows of tiny, vicious teeth.

'Make for the Clock Tower, Leon,' Viyesha called over the noise of the shrieking, mangled feeders, and together they disappeared up the main stairway, kicking and swiping as they went.

'Protect yourself, Juke,' called Theo, seeing a feeder latch on to his back, tentacles outstretched.

As he spoke, Juke's body began to shimmer and glow with a faint silver light, and for a brief second, Theo was distracted from the fight. The glow grew into a brilliant white light, blinding and intense, forcing Theo to shield his eyes, and when he looked again, a strong, white energy field had surrounded Juke, beams of light radiating out like rays of sunshine. In his hand was a shining silver sword.

'You're no energy sensor,' gasped Theo. 'I've seen beings like you before. You're from the angelic realm.'

Juke laughed. 'Urban angel more like. I'm one of the lesser beings. I can't be doing with all that higher plane stuff. Too highbrow for me.'

He moved his sword suddenly over his back, slicing with speed and precision, and cutting through the feeder lodged there. It dropped to the ground in two pieces.

'Welcome on board,' said Theo, smiling widely. 'We had no idea.'

He watched in amazement as Juke slashed at the feeders surrounding him, his sword moving at speed, striking and cutting in an arc of light. Pantera briefly acknowledged Juke's presence and by some silent agreement they launched into battle, a strange and deadly duo, all sinewy black muscle and flashing light. Relentlessly, they went from room to room, Theo fighting alongside them, felling and destroying feeder after feeder, until the ground floor was secure.

They moved up to the first floor, opening door after door, cutting, savaging and fighting feeders, ensuring every room was free before moving on to the next.

Outside, Bellynda and Aquila continued their attack, systematically destroying feeders on every piece of wall, window, arch and pillar, until the honeyed stone showed once again, scorch marks emblazoned across the stonework. In and out, Bellynda weaved, soaring through the night sky, her black scaly body glinting in the moonlight. Where her fiery breath failed to destroy, her massive spiked tail flicked back and forth, cutting through the feeders' dark matter with the same precision as Juke's angelic sword.

Leon and Viyesha approached the spiral stairway, dismayed to see the steps and walls lined with feeders. Leon went first, swiping feeders to left and right, and treading them underfoot, making the creatures shriek and screech as he plunged his feet into their dark membranes. Viyesha followed close behind, knocking feeders off the walls with powerful gestures, blue energy crackling. At last, they reached the top of the spiral stairway and the Clock Tower room was before them, its ornate carved door barely visible beneath feeders two and three deep, all drawn by the crystal.

Leon glanced at Viyesha. 'It's too risky to open the door. They'll crowd in before we can stop them.'

'A little trickery should solve the problem,' said Viyesha. 'These creatures are hardly intelligent. They react purely on instinct.'

She unclasped the small blue crystal pendant hanging round her neck and began spinning it round, sending small blue sparks into the air. Faster and faster the pendant spun, creating a moving circle of blue. The feeders watched, fascinated, their black eyes glittering. Viyesha placed her fingers into the circle and pulled it away from the pendant, rolling it in her palm into a ball of sizzling energy.

Gradually, she pulled out strands of energy, expanding the ball until it was the size of a small grapefruit. Mesmerised by the sparkling blue light, the feeders crowded around her. Slowly she walked down the steps, holding the energy ball aloft, leading the feeders away from the Clock Tower room. As soon as they'd left the doorway clear, she threw the energy ball down the spiral stairway and the feeders followed, desperate for its light and power.

'Now, Leon,' she called, running back up the steps.

He knocked on the door and spoke to Violet. Immediately, the door opened and they were in.

'Mother,' cried Violet, closing the door quickly and embracing Viyesha warmly. 'Am I glad to see you. Are the feeders still out there?'

'Yes, but they're being destroyed as we speak,' said Viyesha. 'Is the crystal safe?'

'It is,' said Violet. 'I didn't dare take it out, not with Seth being the way he is. He has a feeder on his back.'

Leon and Viyesha turned to Seth, lying awkwardly on the floor, his body curled forward, his spine almost forming a letter 'C'.

'Hi, Mr and Mrs de Lucis,' he said weakly, raising his hand. 'I would stand up but I can't.'

Viyesha bent down to look at him.

'Hi Seth,' she said gently. 'We're going to get that thing off you. But not here. Feeders move quickly and we cannot risk it getting to the crystal. '

'And we can't get out until the feeders are gone,' added Leon.

'Great. Doesn't look like I have too many options,' said Seth, gritting his teeth.

'Hang on in there,' said Leon, patting his shoulder.

Violet knelt down next to him and gently smoothed back his unruly black hair.

'You're very brave, Seth,' she said in a soothing voice.

Seth attempted to turn his face and grin at her. 'Relatively speaking, it's not as bad as having needles stuck in your eyeballs. Or being hung, drawn and quartered. Or being flayed alive. Or….'

He was interrupted by a loud roaring and screaming outside the windows. Moonlight spilled into the room and they saw a dark shape flying past, flames shooting up against the windowpanes.

'It's Bellynda,' cried Violet, rushing to one of the long, arched windows.

They watched with delight as the huge dragon flew past, a torrent of fire shooting from her mouth, dowsing feeders with flames until the night sky was littered with bits of dark matter, falling like pieces of charred newspaper to the grounds below.

At the same time, there was a knock on the Clock Tower door and they heard Juke's voice.

'All okay in there? You can come out now, the coast's clear.'

Viyesha flung open the door to reveal Juke, still bathed in brilliant white light standing on the threshold. She smiled as she finally understood his earlier words. 'Juke! You are indeed the ally we can't do without!'

'All feeders destroyed, ma'am,' he said, with a mock salute. 'Theo, Pantera and I made a formidable team. Shame you missed the action.'

'All feeders but one.' She stood back so he could see Seth. 'Our friend here needs assistance.'

'Hey, dude,' said Seth, trying to turn his face towards Juke, and holding his hand in front of his eyes. 'Youza, that's bright. What's with the Christmas tree lights, mate?'

'Didn't ya know? I'm the fairy at the top of the tree,' said Juke, stepping into the room, 'Lucky for you I have a magic wand.'

He walked over to where Seth lay on the floor, contorted and twisted, and looked at his back.

'What's the diagnosis, doc?' asked Seth.

'Looks like you're carrying a passenger, mate. Just give me a second…'

He plunged his hands beneath Seth's jacket and after wrestling for a moment, pulled out a squirming black form. The creature wriggled and writhed, trying to get free, snapping at Juke's hands with small razor teeth, its tentacles still attached to Seth's back. Holding the creature tightly, Juke moved slowly across the room, stretching the tentacles taut. Unwilling to release its prey, the feeder hung on, but Juke's grip was too firm. With the sound of an elastic band snapping, its tentacles shot back into its body. Juke threw it to the floor and raised his sword, swiftly cutting it to pieces. Tiny bits of dark matter covered the floor for a second, before evaporating into the air and disappearing from view. Seth straightened out his back, exhaling with relief.

'Wow, can't tell you how good that feels. Thanks, dude.'

He turned to take a good look at Juke's shining form, and blinked in disappointment as he saw the familiar dreadlocks, battered brown leather waistcoat and faded jeans tucked into old Timberland boots.

'Whoa, where's all the bright stuff gone? You were shining like a beacon.'

Juke winked at him. 'Just a party trick, Seth. Comes in useful once in a while.'

'Whatever it was, that was awesome,' said Violet, linking her hand in Seth's. 'Thanks, Juke. We owe you.'

'She's right,' said Leon, 'We can't thank you enough for your help today, Juke.'

Juke mock-saluted once again.

'Glad to be of service. Like I said, it's what I do.'

36. Emily and Tash

I hardly dared open my eyes, for fear of what I might see. Or rather, what I might not see. I couldn't bear the thought of being back in that box. I wriggled my fingers, feeling for the smooth cold surface that I'd lain on for so many days, but finding instead soft, silky fabric. I gripped it in my hand, not sure if I was hallucinating. Things had become so strange, I was no longer sure what was real and what was in my head.

'Emily,' I heard a voice say. 'Can you hear me?'

It was Joseph.

'Yes.'

'Can you open your eyes?'

'No. If I do, you'll disappear. You're not real. You're in my head.'

'Emily, listen to me. You've been rescued. You're not in the coffin. You're at the vicarage.'

'Are you sure?'

'Yes. Take a look.'

I opened my eyes and took in the strange bedroom, with its dark oak furniture, flock wallpaper and chintzy curtains, and Joseph sitting on the edge of the bed.

'Welcome to the world of the living,' he smiled.

'Joseph. Thank God you're here,' I said, reaching for him, and looking around wildly. 'Where's Theo? I need to tell him I'm okay.'

'He's kind of busy at the hall right now, but you'll see him soon.'

'Does he know I'm alright?'

'It was Theo who rescued you Emily.'

'It was? I can't remember. How about my mum? Does she know what's happened? Is she back from holiday?'

'She's not back yet and thanks to Violet's mimicry, she has no idea what happened. She thinks she's been chatting to you all week.'

'Oh,' I said, confused.

'Violet pretended to be you when she called. She did the same with Tash's mum. We couldn't risk them calling the police,' he explained.

'Tash! I exclaimed, trying to sit up and feeling weak and dizzy. 'Where is she?''

'Over there.' He indicated a bed on the other side of the room and I saw Tash's red hair spread across the white pillowcase.

'Is she okay?'

'She will be,' answered Joseph, 'with a little help.'

He gently touched the back of my head and I winced.

'That hurts, doesn't it?'

'A little. I think I was hit on the head.'

'Judging by the wound, you were. We found a lot of blood in your car. For a while, we didn't know if you were alive or dead. We need to get that wound cleaned up. Here, let me bathe it.'

I saw he'd placed a silver bowl filled with water by the side of the bed and he gently dabbed the back of my head with a gauze pad.

'You found my car?' I asked, in surprise.

'Yes. Or rather, Seth did. It had been dumped down a country lane.'

I frowned. 'I can't remember what happened. It's all a blur. I remember getting hit on the back of the head and next thing I knew I woke up inside that box.'

I shuddered at the memory.

'Don't think about it now,' advised Joseph. 'Just relax.'

The door opened and an elderly woman entered the bedroom. She was vaguely familiar.

'Emily, you've woken up,' she said in a broad Irish accent. 'I've brought you some chicken broth.' She set down a steaming bowl on the bedside cabinet. 'Homemade and nutritious, just what you need after your ordeal.'

I stared at her, finding it difficult to think clearly.

'It's Mrs O'Briain,' said Joseph, seeing me struggling, 'Father James's housekeeper.'

'Oh, yes, I remember. Thank you,' I said, feeling odd and out of place. 'It smells delicious.'

'How is Father James?' Joseph asked Mrs O'Briain.

'He's sleeping. Getting over his experience in the crypt.' She looked over at Tash. 'I see your friend hasn't come round yet. It's Natasha, isn't it?'

'Yes.'

'Was she the victim of one of those creatures?' she asked. 'She doesn't look too good.'

'No Mrs O'Brian,' answered Joseph, walking over to Tash's bedside. 'She was attacked and imprisoned. She's very weak. As soon as I get her back to the hall, I'll treat her, but for now, we need to keep her comfortable.'

He looked anxiously at Tash's face and carefully smoothed back her hair.

'Can I get her anything?' asked Mrs O'Briain.

'She's very dehydrated. Some water would be good. And perhaps some weak soup.'

'Coming up,' said Mrs O'Briain, beaming. She scuttled out of the room.

I sat up, propped up against the pillows, eating my chicken broth and feeling my body respond to the nourishment. Joseph sat with Tash, willing her to wake up.

Without warning, her eyes suddenly flickered open and she stared at him.

'Am I in heaven?' she asked, weakly. 'Have I died?'

'No,' said Joseph, gently. 'You're at the vicarage. You've had a bad experience but now you're safe. We've rescued you.'

Her large green eyes filled with tears as she remembered what she'd been through.

'I was chained to a wall. Kept prisoner by a hideous reptile, fed bits of old bread and water. And it was cold, very cold.'

'It's okay,' said Joseph. 'You and Emily are safe now.'

'Emily,' she said, trying to get up, but finding herself too weak.

'I'm over here, Tash,' I called. 'I'm fine. Joseph will get you better.'

'Joseph?' she queried.

'That's me,' he answered. 'Theo's cousin.'

'Emily said he had a cousin.' She smiled up at him. 'You're even better looking than Theo. I think I'm hallucinating.'

Joseph couldn't help himself. He smiled from ear to ear. A noise at the door heralded Mrs O'Briain's arrival and she came back in to the room carrying a tray.

'Natasha, thank the Lord, you've woken up. Here's water and some soup for you.'

She bustled out of the room and Joseph held the glass to Tash's lips. 'Drink this. Your lips look very swollen. It must be the dehydration.'

'It's the collagen implants,' I informed him. 'She doesn't normally have a trout pout.'

'Why did you have collagen implants?' asked Joseph, astounded.

'Same reason I had Botox,' she answered. 'I wanted to look as good as Violet and as good as Emily's going to look.'

'But you're beautiful,' said Joseph. 'You don't need these treatments.'

'Thank you. I think I'm falling in love with you, Joseph. Too bad you're not real.' She smiled to herself. 'Mind you, the Botox had its benefits. The creature couldn't understand why I didn't look scared. Truth was, I was terrified but I couldn't show any expression. My face was frozen.'

I stifled a smile. Tash's surgical enhancements had benefits after all. Who would have thought it?

She managed to eat most of her soup before falling back asleep. Joseph carefully took the bowl away and pulled up the covers, a look of tenderness on his face I hadn't seen before. Suddenly, he frowned and felt her forehead.

'What is it, Joseph?' I asked.

' She's running a fever. I really need to get her back to the hall.'

'So, why don't we go? I don't understand why we're here.'

'Because it's too dangerous. The hall has been attacked by feeders. The others have gone to fight them.'

I felt what little colour was in my cheeks drain away.

'That's what Theo's doing, isn't it? Fighting feeders?' I struggled to get out of bed. 'I have to go to him.'

'No, Emily,' began Joseph, when the door opened.

It was Theo.

There were scratches on his face and hands, and his jacket was torn. His face lit up when he saw me.

'Emily.'

He sat down on the bedside and took me in his arms. 'Thank God you're okay. I'm never leaving your side again. Not after what you've gone through.'

'I'm okay,' I murmured, melting into his embrace and luxuriating in the feel of his arms around me. This is what I'd dreamed of during the worst moments of my ordeal, when I'd thought I might never see him again. I touched one of the cuts on his face. 'You're hurt. What happened at the hall? Joseph said it was overrun with feeders.'

'It was,' he said grimly. 'The place was crawling. But thanks to Bellynda, Aquila, Pantera and Juke, we got rid of them all.'

'Juke?' I said in surprise, drawing back. 'What did he have to do with it?'

'Your mother's new boyfriend is full of surprises, Emily. Let's just say he has hidden talents, especially where fighting feeders is concerned.'

'Wow, a warrior as well as a world traveller.'

'Something like that. The important thing is that you're alright.'

'I am.' I smiled at him, looking into his deep blue eyes, still not quite believing I was here with him, safe. Then I frowned. 'What about the Fallen Angel? You didn't trade the crystal, did you?'

'No. That was never his plan. The whole thing was a trap. He knew we'd never trade the crystal and that we'd try to rescue you. He lured us into the crypt and while the hall was left unprotected, the feeders attacked. Fortunately, we got back before he had time to get to the crystal.'

'So it's safe?'

'Yes.'

'And my initiation can still go ahead?'

'Yes. It's the full moon tomorrow night and Viyesha has everything prepared. As long as you're sure?'

'Theo, I was never more sure about anything. The past few days have made me realise that. This is what I want more than anything in the world. To be with you forever.'

He linked hands with mine and kissed my forehead. 'Your wish is about to come true. We've beaten Badru, the feeders and the Fallen Angel. All that remains is for you to have a good night's sleep. Tomorrow night you'll fulfil your destiny.'

I snuggled under the bed clothes and smiled. I was on the threshold of my new life with Theo. Roll on tomorrow!

If only it could have been that easy.

37. **Next Morning**

Early next morning, Leon and Viyesha walked through the corridors of Hartswell Hall accompanied by Juke and Pantera.

'We are eternally in your debt,' said Viyesha. 'Without you, Aquila and Bellynda, we could not have destroyed the feeders.'

'You may not thank Bellynda when you see the exterior of the hall,' said Pantera. 'But that's dragons for you. All hot air and no consideration.'

They walked outside to the gravelled car park. The hall stood before them, burnt and blackened, its honeyed stonework sooty and grey, some window frames little more than charred wood.

'Superficial wounds,' said Viyesha, smiling at Pantera. 'We'll have it restored within a week. With Joseph's help the hall will soon regenerate.'

They heard voices and Bellynda and Aquila came into view, talking animatedly.

'Thank you for what you did last night,' said Leon, as they approached. 'You were invincible.'

'If a little over-enthusiastic,' said Pantera, glancing up at the fire-damaged building.

Bellynda shrugged. 'If I hadn't been there, it might have ended differently. That's twice I've come to your rescue. My job is to guard the crystal, not fight your battles.'

'But you enjoyed it nonetheless,' said Aquila, giving her a rare smile.

She smiled back at him. 'True, my friend, there is nothing more satisfying than a good torching and I so rarely get the opportunity.'

'You've checked the crystal?' asked Viyesha.

'I have and all is well. The crystal is intact.'

'And you?' asked Viyesha, 'Did you incur any damage?'

Bellynda shrugged. 'One broken nail and a burn on my jacket. I'll live.'

Before anyone could reply, Violet and Seth appeared in the front doorway.

'Mornin' all,' said Seth.

'Good morning,' said Violet in a bright voice.

Seth seemed to have made a full recovery. He stood upright and straight.

'How ya doin' mate?' asked Juke.

'Never better, mate, thanks to you,' answered Seth. He put his arm around Violet and she smiled up at him.

Viyesha gave Leon a worried glance. 'I trust you found our guest room comfortable, Seth?' she asked.

'I had a great night's sleep,' answered Seth, grinning at them.

'We thought we'd make the most of the morning and take a walk round the lake,' said Violet. She looked at Seth adoringly. 'Shall we go?'

'Lead on, baby.'

Arm in arm, they walked down the pathway, the others watching silently as they went.

'How long has that been going on?' demanded Bellynda. 'Badru will not approve.'

'Badru need not know,' pointed out Leon. 'It's a teenage flirtation. It'll be over in a few days.'

'The boy knows too much,' said Bellynda, her yellow eyes glinting.

'I'll sort it, Bellynda,' said Viyesha firmly. 'Leave it to me. I will not allow my daughter to be harmed.'

Bellynda was prevented from saying more by the arrival of Theo. He came from the vicarage, looking tired and strained.

'Theo, darling,' said Viyesha, embracing him. 'How's Emily?'

'Amazingly, she's none the worse for her ordeal,' he answered. 'I sat with her all night while she slept. She says she survived by putting herself into a state of suspended animation after you'd told her what to do. Is that right?'

Viyesha looked surprised. 'It's true I told her we were capable of entering such a state. But I never told her how to do it. She is an unusual girl, Theo, with special talents.'

Theo looked anxiously at his mother. 'Can she be initiated, mother? It's the full moon tonight.' He couldn't hide the tension in his face.

'If she's strong enough, I see no reason why not,' answered Viyesha. 'The crystal is prepared and the room attuned. What do you think Bellynda?'

Bellynda shrugged nonchalantly. 'It's not up to me. The girl has caused you more than enough problems already. Personally, I can't understand what you see in her, Theo. Might be easier to let Badru dispose of her.'

'Never,' said Theo. 'She must be initiated. I will not let Badru harm her.'

Bellynda smiled lazily. 'Ah, young love. Or should I say, old love? You don't have much success with women, do you Theo?'

'That's enough, Bellynda,' said Leon. 'Emily will be initiated tonight. Theo, why don't you go and tell her? Make sure she's ready.'

Theo needed no further prompting. He left for the vicarage immediately.

'I hate to say it folks, but this isn't over,' said Juke. 'The Fallen Angel won't give up that easily.'

'Do you sense him near, Juke?' asked Viyesha anxiously.

'He's close by. I can feel him,' answered Juke.

'Then we must search until we find him,' said Leon.

'Unless he finds you first,' said Juke, ominously. 'He's here, hiding in the shadows, waiting for his opportunity.'

As he spoke, a figure appeared out of the shadows from around the side of the house, making them start. It was Joseph, carrying Tash.

'Help me, Viyesha. Tash is in a bad way. She needs the crystal.'

Viyesha looked at Tash and frowned. 'It's too dangerous, Joseph, you know the risks. Especially with the full moon due. It's all ready for Emily. We don't want to initiate Tash by mistake.'

'As long as I channel the crystal's power through my hands, the risks are small,' he answered. 'Please, Viyesha. It's her only chance.'

Viyesha looked at Tash's hot, feverish face and Joseph's anxious, eager expression.

'Very well,' she relented. 'Take her to the Clock Tower room, Joseph. I'll join you there.'

38. **Light Bodies**

Joseph carried Tash into the Clock Tower room, placing her on the wooden floor over the blue hieroglyphics. Viyesha opened the silver casket and shards of blue light filled the room. Carefully, Joseph picked up the crystal, holding it in his open palms over Tash. He closed his eyes, praying to the healing entities.

Silently, the faint outline of other beings materialised around them, each one glowing white, sunbursts of energy forming haloes of light around their heads. Viyesha tried to make out their features, but their brightness was too intense. Joseph raised the blue crystal higher and the light beings linked hands, creating a closed circle. A beam of blue light appeared from above, passing through the crystal and on to Tash, spreading over her body like blue gauze. Joseph kept his eyes closed, channelling the energy. As one, the light bodies placed their hands into the gauze, making it glow and pulsate.

They held their hands steady, and just as quickly as they'd materialised, they began to fade until only a faint residue was left hanging in the air. Joseph opened his eyes. The blue beam of light and gauzy film disappeared instantly. He took a deep breath, silently thanking the angelic bodies, and placing the crystal back in the casket. Immediately, the room seemed drab and colourless.

'I didn't realise how badly the dark matter had infected her,' he said, looking at Tash's sleeping form.

'She was touched by the Fallen Angel and not many survive that,' answered Viyesha.

'The light bodies came quickly. I have never seen them come so fast.'

'Love is a powerful healer, Joseph. It was thanks to your feelings for Tash they came so quickly.'

'You know?' he asked, amazed.

'Yes,' she answered gently. 'I could see straight away.'

'But it's hopeless, isn't it?' he said bitterly. 'Badru would never let us be together. It would be a death sentence for her.'

Viyesha placed a hand on his arm. 'Let's concentrate on getting her better, Joseph. We'll work the rest out later.'

As soon as Tash was comfortably installed in one of the first floor bedrooms, with Viyesha looking after her, Joseph went into the grounds, seeking herbs to complete the healing process. It was now dusk, and the air was heavy with the scent of honeysuckle, jasmine and roses. The moon was already rising in the sky and it promised to be a beautiful evening.

For the next hour, Joseph searched the kitchen gardens, hedgerows and meadows, finding the herbs and plants he needed: feverfew for headaches and fever, vervain for exhaustion, jasmine for stress and lemon balm for the nervous system; astralagus for boosting energy; borage for stimulating the adrenals; cleavers and juniper for cleansing; and lavender for restoring balance. Thanks to the full moon, their healing power was at its strongest.

Finally, Joseph required just one more herb: angelica, used since ancient times to protect against evil spirits, and he knew just where to find it. It was growing in abundance inside the secret walled garden. He walked through the rose garden, thick with scent, to the old brick wall, now rebuilt, and turned the key in the carved oak door. As soon as it opened, he encountered a deep silence that was ominous and foreboding. No birds sang and the hidden world seemed darker than ever as he peered through the trees and undergrowth. Feeling suddenly afraid, he quickly found the patch of angelica he'd seen on previous visits. Cutting a number of stems rich with seeds, he placed them in his bag.

Against his better judgment, he walked along the overgrown pathway into the centre of the garden, stepping over brambles and holding back branches. He was soon at the ruined folly, strangely dark and silent, dappled with moonlight.

Coming into the clearing, he saw a sight that nearly stopped his heart. The old brickwork of the Victorian folly had become a heaving, seething mass of feeders that clung to every broken wall and arch. The luxurious green grass that once formed a rich carpet beneath the sweeping arches was now a treacherous sea of black, and as he watched, more feeders appeared every second. Instinct told him to run, but he forced himself to look further, trying to see where they were coming from.

Three more steps gave him the answer. There, face down on the ground lay the figure of a man. Whether he was asleep or dead, Joseph couldn't tell, but feeder after feeder appeared to be coming out of his back. Joseph watched repulsed yet fascinated as another began to take shape, starting as a black bubble and gradually getting bigger before breaking away with a popping sound and sliding over the ground to join the others.

To one side of the folly, too far away to see clearly - and Joseph had no intention of getting any closer - a number of feeders had joined together, forming a large, pulsating mass.

Joseph was so absorbed by the scene before him, he quite failed to see a feeder sliding towards him, and it was almost upon him, black tentacles reaching forward, before he saw it. Kicking the thing away, he turned and ran, taking no notice of the brambles and branches that slashed across his face. Once outside the garden, he pulled the door closed behind him and locked it with trembling fingers. Looking up, he realised the feeder had scaled the wall and was hovering on the parapet above, threatening to drop.

Backing away slowly and not taking his eyes off the creature, Joseph put as much distance as he could between himself and the walled garden before turning and running in the direction of the hall. Speed was not one of his superpowers, but it took less than a minute to get back to the gravelled forecourt, where he found Aquila talking with Bellynda.

39. Preparation

His breath ragged and uneven, clearly shaken by what he'd encountered, Joseph told them of his discovery.

'Found a feeder nest… in the old folly… more coming every second… from a man lying on the ground…'

Bellynda listened, a grim expression on her face. 'I believe you have discovered the Fallen Angel's conduit, Joseph. This is how he is able to bring such large numbers of feeders into our world. Gather everyone together in the library. He is too close for comfort and we must attack while we can.'

She glanced at Aquila. 'There will be no initiation tonight. We have the mother of all battles ahead of us.'

In the library, a council of war took place, with Bellynda at its head. She was in her element.

'The last two battles, if we can call them such, were practice missions. They gave us a feel for the enemy and his tactics, but that is all. This is the real thing. And it is a fight we have no choice but to win. If we don't…' she made a cutting motion across her throat.

'Can't we send for reinforcements?' asked Viyesha.

'No time,' said Bellynda. 'We need to strike within the hour. This time, we'll make sure the crystal is properly protected and we'll lead the attack with our best warrior.' She smiled at them all. 'That's me.'

'And Emily's initiation?' asked Theo.

'It cannot take place,' said Bellynda brusquely. 'We are under threat and must fight tonight or pay the price.'

'I'm sorry, Theo,' said Viyesha, seeing her son's face. 'The Fallen Angel is close and we must fight him. Emily will have to wait until the next full moon. Badru will see that we had no choice.'

'Badru will kill her,' said Theo in a whisper.

'I will intercede on her behalf,' said Viyesha.

Seeing the situation was hopeless, he fell silent.

'This is the plan,' continued Bellynda. 'Aquila and I will carry out air strikes. Pantera and Juke, you're on the ground. Leon, Theo and Joseph, I need you to create an energy seal covering the folly.

This is key to the mission's success. You must prevent any feeders or Reptilia escaping. As long as they're trapped, we can pick them off one by one.'

They each nodded, accepting their role.

'And the Fallen Angel?' asked Joseph.

'He may or may not show,' said Bellynda. 'Our main objective is to destroy his conduit and disable him. He is sly and insidious and rarely chooses to fight. He gets others to do that for him. I advise you to be on your guard. If he shows, do not tackle him alone. We must work together. There is strength in numbers.'

'What about mother and me?' asked Violet. 'Can we fight too?'

'No. Viyesha, you will stay in the Clock Tower room and guard the crystal. Form an energy shield around it. Violet, keep watch over the mortals. We cannot risk them getting in the way. They could jeopardise everything.'

'That's not fair, man,' said Seth, sprawled on the sofa next to Violet. 'I can crush feeders with my bare hands.'

'With due respect, little boy,' said Bellynda, raising one eyebrow, 'you'd be wise to recognise your limitations. Foolhardiness will lead to instant death. You will stay out of the way. Got it?'

'Aw…' began Seth. Then Violet smiled at him and he melted, miraculously changing his mind. 'Yeah sure. I'll look after the girls. Someone has to.'

He looked pointedly at Theo, who said: "Yeah, and someone has to fight.'

'That's enough,' said Viyesha. 'We all have our roles, and it's important we play them.'

'We're wasting time,' said Bellynda, rising to her feet. 'Everyone to their stations. We have a battle to win.'

Joseph hastily made a tincture from the herbs he'd collected, instructing Violet to place drops on Tash's lips throughout the night. They moved her into the large bridal suite on the first floor and she lay, sleeping peacefully, in the huge four-poster bed, with Seth and Violet at her side.

'You need to keep up with the tincture, Vi,' said Joseph. 'She needs extra protection, especially with so much dark matter around.'

'I'll do it, don't worry,' said Violet, looking curiously at Joseph. She hadn't seen his energy glow so brightly as long as she could remember.

With a heavy heart, Theo left for the vicarage to tell Emily the news and bring her back to the hall.

40. **Disappointment**

I stared open-mouthed at Theo, not taking in his words.

'What d'you mean I can't be initiated?' I demanded angrily. 'It's what I want. I've made the decision.'

'The decision's been taken out of our hands,' he said flatly. 'It appears there are more pressing matters.'

'Like what?' I asked, my face draining of colour. This could be my death sentence.

'Like the Fallen Angel creating a conduit in the secret garden and filling it with feeders.'

'A conduit?' I repeated stupidly. 'What d'you mean?'

'He's created a means of transporting feeders from his dimension into ours. They're multiplying at a rapid rate in the folly and if we don't act now, he'll use them to pave a way to the crystal, allowing him to assume human form. We have to act tonight, destroy the feeders before they destroy us. It's as simple as that.'

'No it's not,' I cried. 'It's not simple at all. Surely, they can still initiate me.'

Theo shook his head, sadly.

'Viyesha is guarding the crystal, while Violet guards the mortals and the rest of us do battle. There isn't the time or the opportunity. I'm sorry, Emily, there's nothing I can do. Mother said she would intercede on your behalf, explain the circumstances to Badru.'

'And he'll be interested? I doubt it. Killing me will give him great pleasure. You know that.'

'Sorry, Emily. I'm here to take you back to the hall. You need to stay there tonight. Violet will keep you safe.'

'And you?'

'I have to fight.'

He took hold of my hands, tears forming in his eyes.

'Emily, it's not what I want. But what can I do? The crystal is under threat and I must fight with my family.'

'So, that's where your loyalties lie, is it?' I laughed bitterly and picked up my coat. 'Come on, let's go. You have a battle to fight. And I have an execution to attend. My own.'

* * *

Violet peered out of the window.

'There they go,' she said. 'I'm glad Juke's with them. If anyone can see off the enemy, it's him.'

'Juke?' I repeated. 'Theo mentioned something about him being a warrior. What did he mean?'

'Seems like Juke is not who he says he is,' she answered cryptically. Her voice dropped to a conspiratorial whisper. 'He's no energy sensor. He's an urban angel.'

'An urban angel. What's one of those when it's at home?'

I had never felt so flat or disappointed. All my questions and doubts, choosing Theo over Seth, being imprisoned and rescued. It all seemed so pointless now my initiation was cancelled.

'He turns into this awesome light creature,' said Violet. 'Shining with a bright white light and wielding this amazing sword.'

'He is one cool dude,' said Seth. 'All lit up like a beacon. Pulled a feeder off me, no sweat. Sliced it in two. Just like that.' He made a chopping motion with his arms.

'Just as well he's on our side,' I said disinterestedly.

'Emily, you'll be okay,' said Violet, kindly. 'Mother will explain to Badru and he'll give you an extension. You'll be initiated at the next full moon. It's only another month to wait.'

'You wouldn't be so cheerful if it was you, would you Violet?'

'Probably not. But what do you want me to say?'

'You're just as bad as Theo,' I snapped. 'He didn't seem too bothered, either.'

'You're wrong,' said Violet. 'He was gutted. But what could he do? This is serious, Emily. If we don't protect the crystal, we'll all die.'

'And we don't want that, do we?' I snapped. 'Doesn't matter if Emily snuffs it. That's unimportant.'

'Hey, chill, Em,' said Seth, putting his arm around me, 'So, you'll be mortal for another month. That's not so bad, is it?'

'You don't get it, do you?' I said, turning on them. 'I don't have another month. I've met Badru. I know what he's like. There are no extenuating circumstances. Feeders or no feeders, if I don't get initiated, he's coming for me. End of.'

I stomped to the far side of the room, where another large window looked out over the grounds. I saw Leon, Theo and Joseph disappearing into the grounds, a blue energy glowing around them. There was no sign of the shape shifters and Juke and I guessed they'd gone before. I willed Theo to turn around but he didn't.

From the bed, Tash moaned and cried, holding up her hands up as if shielding something away.

'She's having a nightmare,' I heard Violet say, running to her side. 'Come on, Tash, you're okay. Have some medicine. It'll make you better. You have to be better for Joseph.'

I turned round.

'What do you mean, better for Joseph?'

Violet smiled at me.

'It's so sweet,' she said. 'He's fallen for Tash. I've never seen him like this. All these years, he's been on his own, then Tash comes along and he falls headlong in love. Which is great, because it leaves Seth for me.' She made doe eyes at Seth, who winked at her.

'Oh, please,' I said. 'Spare me the sentimentality. This just gets worse and worse. Now my two best friends have found the love of their lives, just as I'm about to lose mine, through no fault of my own. Talk about rubbing salt in the wound. I was supposed to have it all. And now I have nothing.' I drew the curtains angrily, not wishing to be reminded of what was going on in the grounds.

An hour later and I was in no better mood. Now fear replaced anger. I wondered how Badru would come for me, what he would do, whether my death would be painful and slow. Or merciful and quick. I didn't think Badru did merciful and quick.

Suddenly, I missed Theo more than anything else. His absence cut through me like a knife. We'd come so far, only to be knocked back at the final hurdle. I thought of all the pain he'd been through, how he'd waited through the centuries, sure I would come, and now he was about to lose me all over again. I thought how it felt when he held me, how I'd never again look into those blue eyes and get lost in their intensity, never feel his touch again or kiss his lips. Missing him became unbearable.

I glanced over to the four-poster bed. Tash was fast asleep. Violet and Seth were in the en-suite bathroom. Through the open door, I could see them laughing and joking, whispering sweet nothings to each other, eyes only for each other. Now was my chance.

I crept to the door, opened it silently and walked out on to the landing. I had to see Theo one last time. It was nearly midnight, which meant I didn't have long. I walked down the stairs and out of front door.

41. **Into Battle**

Bellynda, Aquila, Pantera and Juke strode purposefully into the night, heading for the walled garden. Leon, Theo and Joseph followed, their intense blue energy shining in the moonlight. Up in the Clock Tower, Viyesha anxiously watched them leave and set about creating a powerful energy seal around the crystal.

They crept into the secret garden, staying low in the undergrowth, until the folly was in sight: Bellynda and Aquila crouched on one side, Pantera and Juke on the other. Leon positioned himself adjacent to the entrance, while Theo and Joseph crept around the walls, one in either direction to form a triangle around the folly. When they were in place, they held out their arms, palms facing upwards, each generating a bolt of blue energy linking them together. Keeping their outstretched hands steady, they extended the blue energy upwards, stretching it higher and higher a hundred or so metres into the air over the folly, before bringing the top to a point, so that it formed a great pyramid of shimmering blue energy, enveloping the folly within.

At the same time, inside the pyramid, the shape-shifters began to change, skin and clothing becoming scales, feathers and fur. By the time the blue pyramid was complete, their human shapes had gone, replaced by a huge black dragon, a fierce black eagle and a lithe black panther. Juke too, had gone through a metamorphosis and was once again an urban angel, shining sword at the ready, starbursts of energy shooting in all directions.

Flying upwards to the apex of the pyramid, Bellynda hovered, took aim, and dropped suddenly, diving fast and furiously towards the folly walls. She dowsed the feeders with powerful plumes of fire, scorching huge numbers, while Aquila struck with deadly accuracy, picking feeders from the tops of the arches, shredding and tearing relentlessly with beak and talons. Soon, the air was filled with the sickening sound of screeching, shrieking feeders, as they fell injured, burnt and dying to the grass below. At ground level, Juke plunged into the feeder nest, swiping and cutting with his shining sword, with Pantera close behind, savaging and tearing with fangs and claws, destroying any dark matter within reach.

Time and again, shrieking feeders flung themselves against the blue energy shield in a bid to escape, but Leon, Theo and Joseph held fast, using every ounce of energy to keep the protective pyramid in place.

The attack appeared to be going well, feeders dropping like flies and the folly's grey brick walls showing once again beneath the sea of black.

'This is too easy,' Juke called to Pantera. 'Where are The Reptilia? Where is the Fallen Angel? Why are they not fighting back?'

No sooner had he spoken than the battle took a menacing and dangerous twist. As the burnt and lacerated feeders fell, disintegrating and disappearing from view, their small razor-sharp teeth dropped into the earth, settling for a second on top of the grass, before burrowing beneath like hard, white maggots. Juke indicated for Pantera to get behind him and she dropped back, yellow eyes glancing nervously around.

Wherever the teeth fell, mounds of earth began to push upwards like tiny molehills, and out of each appeared a small lizard-like creature, a mutant combination of man and reptile, growing rapidly until achieving full height, a good head taller than Juke. Black scales glistened as the creatures stood erect on two legs, powerful tails thrashing, hooked claws flexing and lizard eyes staring without blinking. Putrid saliva dripped from their open jaws, revealing rows of yellowed, pointed teeth, lethal as a chainsaw.

Quickly, their numbers multiplied and the area inside the folly's ruined walls became a mass of scaly bodies, snarling mouths and jagged teeth, all primed for the kill. There was no doubting their capability or power. These were lethal, killing machines, intent on destruction.

Bellynda swooped low, breathing fire, but her flames failed to have any impact on their fireproof bodies. As she flew close, one creature swiped at her wing, drawing its claws through her shining black scales and, with a howl, she fled, wounded, to the top of the folly. Splashes of dragon blood fell from her injured wing onto the Reptilia below, and she saw with revulsion that the creatures opened their mouths to drink it or fell to their knees, noisily lapping it up where it pooled on the ground.

Juke and Pantera watched with horror how the Reptilia changed as they drank, their bodies growing larger and their nostrils exhaling fire. All they needed now were wings and, slowly but surely, small lumps appeared on their shoulders, sprouting into winglets. Immediately, they began to flutter and gain height. Bellynda crouched on the uppermost arches, her wounded wing hanging broken and useless, drops of blood still falling. Aquila swooped and clawed, inflicting damage where he could, but he was ineffective against such numbers.

'Bellynda's blood has given them dragon power,' shouted Juke to Pantera. 'If I don't act now, it'll be too late. Stand back.'

He rapidly drew himself up to full height and inhaled deeply. He held his breath as the oxygen flowed through his body, bringing fresh energy to every cell, and exhaled rapidly with a great sighing sound. Immediately, his body began to glow and his aura to expand, the energy flicking outwards in bright, white tongues of light. He appeared to ripple and fragment, as if he were standing in a heat haze, and first one, then another replica Juke split from his body.

As the process gathered momentum, the phantom figures multiplied quickly until an army of shining Jukes, each wielding a glinting silver sword, faced the evil creatures before them. There was a second of stillness, as both sides took the measure of each other, before the bloodbath began, and the shimmering Jukes ploughed into the scaly black monsters, silver swords flashing in the moonlight, cutting, chopping, slicing and hacking with superhuman speed.

Dragon-like Reptilia swooped from above, breathing fire on the crusading Jukes, but they were powerless against the shining angel fighters, and each was smitten with a single blow from a glowing sword, heads severed from bodies, with a spurt of black blood.

Pantera too, played her part, raking her claws through scaly skin and sinking her teeth into the vulnerable neck areas, tossing reptilian carcasses aside and leaving behind her a trail of black pulp, splintered bone and teeth.

Seeing the carnage, some attempted to flee, flying upwards into the energy field, but Leon, Theo and Joseph held steady, blue energy flowing from their hands, making escape impossible. The Juke figures moved forward with relentless efficiency until not one black reptile remained and the grassy area was a mass of reptilian body parts and sticky black blood.

When the job was complete, just as quickly as he'd divided, Juke's alter egos concertinaed back into one, and once again he became a single glowing urban angel.

'Now, let's see what you were defending,' he cried, stepping through the mangled mess towards the rear of the folly. Pantera followed and Aquila hovered, watching keenly. On a stone plinth lay the facedown figure of Mr Nelson, another feeder emerging from his back. Juke quickly sliced through it, cutting its body in half, and turned his attention to the smooth, pulsing black thing that lay on the other side of the plinth.

'What is it?' asked Pantera.

'A heart,' answered Juke. 'It's a living, beating black heart. And no reward for guessing whose.'

'The Fallen Angel's,' said Pantera in a low voice. 'He's come this close to achieving human form.'

'All he needs now is the crystal to manifest totally,' said Juke, looking at it in disgust.

'We must destroy it,' instructed Aquila.

'Don't worry, mate,' said Juke. 'I intend to.'

He lifted his hand high, holding his sword aloft and with a huge blow, smote the heart in two. A fountain of black blood rose up high and a terrible screaming filled the air. For a brief moment, a black figure appeared, gauzy and faint, over the place where the heart lay bleeding.

A gargoyle-like face, dark and menacing, shot forward in Juke's direction. 'You may have won but you have not triumphed,' it hissed malevolently. 'I will return and retrieve what is rightfully mine. You can never destroy me and you know it.'

A swirling black mist converged around the filmy figure, spinning faster and faster until it formed a vortex. As its power increased, it shot upwards with deadly speed, trying to pierce the blue energy shield. Time and again, it slammed into the blue pyramid, seeking a weakening in the energy wall.

'Hold fast,' yelled Leon into the night.

'I'm trying,' shouted Theo, bracing his arms against the waves of energy that ricocheted down the sides of the pyramid with every fresh onslaught.

'It won't hold much longer,' screamed Joseph. 'He's too strong.'

Sensing a weakening in the pyramid's strength, the black wraith increased its efforts.

'It's coming adrift,' screamed Theo, seeing the energy field begin to tear away from his hand.

It was the chink in their armour the Fallen Angel had been seeking. He crashed into Theo's body with the force of a ten tonne truck, ripping the blue energy away from his hands. Theo flew backwards with the impact and the black vortex was free, blasting into the night and disappearing from sight.

The blue pyramid lay shredded and tattered, hanging like a broken parachute over the folly walls, wisps of blue energy rising up before disappearing into the night.

Leon and Joseph stood still for a second, too stunned to move, their energy fields depleted, their bodies exhausted. Anxiety, twisting within them like a knife, brought them back to their senses, and they ran around the folly in Theo's direction.

'There,' cried Joseph, pointing into the undergrowth.

Theo's body lay blackened and scorched on the ground, his blonde hair smoking and singed, his eyes open and unseeing. Remnants of blue energy fluttered in the moonlight.

As they ran towards him, they saw another figure burst through the bushes, screaming his name and running to his side. Then the Clock Tower struck midnight and a further figure, silent and hooded, appeared alongside.

42. Badru's Deal

I opened my eyes. I was in Badru's chamber, torch lanterns creating flickering patterns on the ancient stone walls, the roof of the cavern high above, the air chilled and dry. Before me stretched the huge, oval, black granite table, a circle crossed by the infinity sign etched into its surface. A large iron lantern, suspended above, cast light from hundreds of small twinkling candles.

I tried to move my hands, but they were stuck to the arms of the stone chair in which I sat. Numb with shock, I looked across the table at Badru.

He was exactly as I remembered him. Ivory skin and cruel mouth. A dark blue cloak over his shoulders, blonde hair showing beneath the draped hood, eyes concealed by dark glasses. His hands were on the table, exquisitely manicured with long pointed fingernails, and adorned with huge jewelled rings. As before, he was flanked by his silent assassins, the twins Atsu and Ata.

'Emily,' he spoke in icy tones, sending a shiver down my spine, 'how nice to see you. But I guess the pleasure's all mine. You know why you're here, of course?'

I looked at him dully. 'Because I missed the initiation.'

'Exactly. And you know my terms.'

'The family weren't able to initiate me,' I said flatly. 'The crystal was under threat. They were fighting to save it.'

'Oh, please,' said Badru in a bored voice. 'The de Lucis family is always fighting to save the crystal. D'you think this hasn't happened before?'

I thought of Theo, lying lifeless by the walls of the folly.

'Theo didn't make it,' I said slowly, 'so, whatever you have planned, Badru, why don't you get on with it? I don't want to live for eternity. Not without Theo.'

'Oh, how sweet. Juliet doesn't want to live without her Romeo. You think he's dead.'

'Stop mocking, Badru. Just get on with it.'

He regarded me for a second, but it was impossible to know what he was thinking behind the dark glasses.

'I want to show you something, Emily,' he said softly.

From a pocket in his cloak he drew out a blue furry creature. It was a huge spider.

'This is my new pet,' he said proudly. 'It's a cobalt blue tarantula. I call her Blue Moon. Isn't she beautiful?'

He let the spider walk across his hands, stroking the fur on its back, and I couldn't help but flinch. Spiders in any shape or form made my skin crawl.

'Here's the thing,' said Badru, 'tarantulas like their food fresh. Atu?'

The hooded figure on the left placed a small box on the table. Badru opened it and took out a tiny white mouse. He held the wriggling animal by its tail. In one rapid movement, the spider pounced, biting into its prey with two razor-like fangs, and began to feed.

'Very nice, Badru,' I said through clenched teeth. 'Is there a point to this?'

He looked at me coldly. 'Of course, Emily, there's always a point.'

I was tired of his cryptic comments. Whatever he had in store for me, I just wanted it over.

He picked up the spider and stroked its back. 'You see, I have another pet. Somewhat larger, which also likes live prey.' He frowned. 'And that was what I had planned for you. Until Theo made a request.'

'Theo? What d'you mean?' I asked.

'Take a look at this,' he answered.

The surface of the large granite table began to mist over and I was looking at the folly. I saw Theo sitting up, his clothes burnt and blackened, his hair singed, fragments of blue energy curling around him. In his arms he held my unconscious body. My eyes were closed and my skin pale. He shouted into the night, his face tense and angry. 'I know you've taken her, Badru, but she doesn't deserve this. Give me a chance to save her. It's the least you can do, especially after tonight. You owe us. And you know it.'

The picture faded and once again I was looking at black granite.

'Theo isn't dead?' I asked, unsure if this was another of Badru's tricks. 'I don't understand. I saw him on the ground.'

'Oh, Theo is very much alive, Emily. He's tougher than you think. The thing is, what do I do?' Badru put his hands together and sat back. 'It was a vicious fight. And it was with my archenemy. I must admit it gave me great delight to see his plans thwarted. But do I give Theo the chance to save you? I've never been one to give in to demands.' He continued to stroke the blue spider.

My mind was spinning. If Badru could be believed, Theo was alive and there was everything to play for. I held my breath, not daring to speak.

'So, I've been thinking,' continued Badru. 'Why not turn the tables? Allow you to save him? Far more entertaining.' He paused and smiled. 'So, here's the deal, Emily. Double or quits. Save Theo, and you get a stay of execution till the next full moon. Fail, and the Cherufe gets you both. What do you say? Are you in?' His eyes lit up at the prospect.

I stared at him with dislike.

'Come on, Emily, if you win, I'll even back off your friends. I've been watching them. I know all about Violet and Theo, and Joseph and Tash. It seems we have more young lovers on our hands. So, what's it to be?'

My words came out clearly, even though my hands were shaking. 'You give me no choice, Badru. I don't like your games. They stink. And I don't know what the Cherufe is. But if Theo's alive and there's a chance we can be together, and I can keep my friends safe into the bargain, then yes, I'm in. If it's a trick, I hope you burn in hell.'

Badru clapped his hands in delight and started to laugh.

The stone walls began to ripple and melt. The lanterns grew dim and the table fell away. The cavern extended around me and I realised I could move my arms. I heard Badru say: 'Oh, Emily, how deliciously appropriate…'

Then he and the twins and the chamber were gone.

43. The Cherufe's Lair

I looked around. I was in a vast cavern that made Badru's chamber seem minuscule in comparison. I shivered, feeling cool air blowing around me and took in my surroundings. I was standing on the tip of a small precipice that jutted out over a deep crevasse. Warily, I looked over the edge and felt immediately sick and giddy. Beneath me, thousands of metres below, fire burned and molten rock gleamed red and golden. It was like looking into the depths of a massive, active volcano. I'd always thought I had a good head for heights, until now. I glanced down again and immediately drew back, feeling the heat of the inferno below. If I fell, I'd be instantly incinerated. I looked behind, wondering if there was a way out, but a pile of fallen rock made me realise going back was not an option. Of course not. That would have been too easy. I looked across, realising the other side of the crevasse was closer than I thought, may be twenty or thirty metres away.

Feeling a sense of creeping desperation, my eyes darted around, taking in the sheer cliff faces all around, the roughly hewn rock surfaces disappearing into the fire pit below and the tiny ledge that mirrored my own across the crevasse. And then I saw him. Theo was on the opposite ledge, tightly bound by huge metal chains wrapped around his arms, legs and body.

'Theo,' I called, not knowing if he'd seen me. I could barely make out his face in the dim light. He failed to acknowledge me and I called again, shouting as loud as I could. This time, he lifted his head.

'Emily?' he called back, doubt in his voice.

'It's me, Theo. I'm here on the opposite side.'

'Is it really you? Or is it you, Badru, playing games?'

'No, it's me, Theo.' I touched the crystal round my neck. 'Can you feel that?

'I feel it,' he exclaimed. 'It is you, Emily. Are you okay?'

'Yes. Badru told me you'd asked for a chance to save me.'

'I did. Only I didn't have this in mind. I can't get out of these chains. There's some kind of enchantment on them.'

'It's up to me, Theo,' I shouted across. 'I have to save you. That's the deal. If I succeed, I get a stay of execution until the next full moon. If I fail, Badru plans to feed us both to the Cherufe. Double or quits. That's what he said.'

There was movement below. I looked down into the swirling, molten mass and gasped. Amidst the flames shooting upwards, spewing up pieces of white-hot rock, I saw the giant figure of a man emerging, fiery and deadly, arms reaching upwards, hands grasping at the sides of the crevasse.

'What is it?' I screamed.

'That's the Cherufe,' answered Theo. 'It lives in the molten magma. Only appears when Badru tempts it out with bait.'

I watched horror-struck as the creature pulled itself out of the erupting flames and slowly but surely began to climb towards us. Or rather, towards Theo, because it was on his side that it climbed.

'What can we do, Theo? There must be something. Try the chains again.'

Theo tried with all his might to break free, but the chains refused to give.

I looked down. The creature was climbing relentlessly upwards and I realised it would reach Theo within minutes. No wonder Badru had given in to Theo's request so easily. He was giving the Cherufe two meals instead of one. At that point, I hated Badru more than I ever thought it possible. Frustration and anger boiled up inside me at the hopelessness of our situation and I stared panic-stricken across the crevasse, my mind working overtime, desperately thinking of a way to get to Theo.

I could see him more clearly now and noticed it was getting light. Maybe day was breaking. I looked up, seeing that it wasn't a cavern at all, but a steep gorge, the sheer rock faces opening to the sky high above us through a narrow gap. Without warning, the cavern was suddenly flooded by a brilliant shaft of light, shining down like a spotlight through the opening, as the sun found the gap in the rocks. It was blinding in its intensity and for a second I stood mesmerised, my eyes adjusting to the brightness.

'Emily, look,' shouted Theo. 'Stepping stones!'

The shaft of light was shining on a line of golden stepping stones that spanned the ravine, suspended in mid-air, stretching from my ledge across to Theo's. All I had to do was walk across them.

I took a step forward, all too aware of the vast drop and molten flames that burned beneath. Out of the corner of my eye, I saw the Cherufe climbing higher, a brilliant, burning figure, rapidly gaining ground and intent on pulling Theo and me into the inferno below.

Pushing my feelings of panic away, I took a deep breath and placed my foot on the first stepping-stone. Although it looked as though my foot would pass straight through, it was surprisingly firm.

'Look ahead, Emily,' called Theo, trying to control his voice. 'It's like walking across stepping stones on a river.'

'Yeah, right," I answered. 'Only this river is thousands of metres below and it's made of molten rock.'

'Don't look down,' he shouted. 'Keep moving forward.'

I took his advice, blocking my mind to the vast drop below, the fiery monster scaling the walls and even Theo himself. I was in the zone, focused on the golden pathway ahead. Fixing my attention on the next glowing stone, I stepped forward and I was on my way. I didn't dare look down or acknowledge the possibility of falling. Speed and balance were all that mattered. I moved quickly and deftly, placing one foot on the next stone, and then the next, moving forward until I was in the middle of the ravine, the far side clearly in view.

For a second, I lost my nerve and nearly my balance. Sweat dripped from my brow and I felt nausea rising. I was going to fall. I couldn't do it. My head was swimming and my vision was blurry. I didn't know how long the shaft of light would last. If it disappeared now, I was dead. Quickly, I forced myself to regroup. I couldn't let Theo down. I could do this. I had to.

Concentrating on the glowing stones ahead and exhaling slowly, I held out my arms and regained my balance. Moving my weight forward, I swung my right leg forward onto the next stepping stone. Theo watched silently, too afraid to speak. I was aware of the heat rising from beneath and the incredible sensation of space all around. I'd never felt so small or vulnerable. A gust of wind blew through the cavern, whipping my hair back, and I stopped until it passed. Carefully, I brought my left leg forward.

Now, just the last few stones were ahead. I was so nearly there, so close to Theo, when the beam of light disappeared as if someone had flicked a switch. The sudden darkness brought the fiery figure of the climbing Cherufe into focus, flames sparking furiously, and I looked down into its eyes. Or what should have been its eyes.

Instead, there were two black holes, like pools of dead energy drawing me in and I felt my balance going.

'Jump, Emily,' screamed Theo.

For a fraction of a second, my foot rested on the surface of the stepping-stone. Just as it faded, I pushed with all my might, propelling myself forward through the air for the last couple of metres. With superhuman effort, I gripped the rough edge of the ledge with my fingertips. Beneath me, I felt the heat of the Cherufe rising upwards.

'Pull yourself up, Emily,' cried Theo.' He strained against the chains, trying desperately to reach me.

Adrenalin pumping and heart beating wildly, I hung on for dear life, my feet trying to find a foothold on the rock face. But the rocky ledge jutted outwards, forming a lip, making it impossible to find leverage. Frantically, I moved my fingers around, clutching wildly, trying to find something to hold on to.

'To your right,' shouted Theo. 'A couple of centimetres. There's a small outcrop.'

I moved my fingers to the right, as he instructed, until they closed around a small lump of rock. As the fingers of my right hand closed around it, I swung my other hand forward, and hung sloth-like for a moment. Somehow, I managed to swing my left leg on to the ledge and lever myself up, feeling my skin graze against the pitted rock surface.

As I scrambled on to the ledge, the small rocky outcrop came loose in my hand, falling through my fingers into the fiery depths below. I watched as it bounced off the sides of the crevasse and disappeared into the flames, realising just how close I'd come to following it down.

Now, there was just the Cherufe to contend with. With horror, I realised the massive tips of its fiery fingers were clutching the ledge. The heat was intense and I felt sweat running down my brow and into my eyes.

'Get the chains, Emily,' shouted Theo in panic.

'How?' I screamed, seeing the huge padlock that held the chains tight. 'They're locked. I need the key.'

The Cherufe's fingers were reaching for Theo's legs, ready to pull him off the ledge, when I saw it. Hanging just above Theo, on a small hook jutting out from the rock, was a silver key.

'I see it,' I said, lunging forward.

I grasped it as the Cherufe grabbed at Theo's chains, pulling him over. Feet manacled together, he kicked with all his might, taking the Cherufe by surprise and knocking it back momentarily, sparks flying. Hysteria rising within me, I struggled to get the key into the padlock and was aware of a screaming sound coming from my lips. Furiously, I turned and twisted the key, feeling my skin burn and my hair singe. Seeing its prey about to escape, the Cherufe let out a huge roar that echoed all round the cavern, causing a shower of rocks to fall from above. It drew itself up and fell on Theo, flames engulfing him, red hot and burning.

'No,' I screamed, seeing Theo's blue eyes in front of me and feeling tears of rage falling from my own. We were so close to freedom, so close to having it all. This couldn't be the end.

My tears splashed on to the Cherufe's fiery body and where they landed, they began to hiss and spit like fat in a pan. It let out a scream of agony, its huge mouth opening wide, causing the walls of the cavern to shudder and shake. Rocks rained down and I realised the hidden weapon at my disposal. As my tears fell, searing into its body, it continued to twist and turn, flecks of fire breaking away and disappearing into the darkness. Rolling away from Theo, its fiery body steaming and smoking, it toppled off the ledge and fell, showering sparks into the air, down and down, until it was swallowed by the inferno below.

Hardly able to touch the hot metal, I finally turned the key in the padlock and the chains binding Theo fell away. Then his arms were around me and I was safe at last.

I closed my eyes, trying to calm my beating heart.

44. **Demise of the Conduit**

I opened my eyes and looked around. I was still in Theo's arms, but the full moon shone above us, illuminating the night sky and I saw the walls of the old folly to one side. I was aware of a sound in my ears and realised it was the Clock Tower striking the final chimes of midnight. Theo looked down at me, the moonlight catching his scorched hair and clothes. He smiled.

'Never knew you had such a head for heights, Emily.'

'Neither did I until tonight.' I smiled back. 'I guess that's what you call coming back from the brink.'

'Yep. Badru certainly turned the heat up.'

'What are you talking about?' began Joseph, but Leon caught his arm.

'I take it you've sorted things out with Badru,' he said.

'We have,' I said, sitting up and feeling suddenly very good, despite the nightmare we'd both been through. 'I have a month's extension. After that, I'm definitely joining you.'

'Glad to hear it,' he said, giving me a hand up. 'Come on Theo. You need to get tidied up. You look like you've walked through an incinerator. It's been an eventful night in more ways than one.'

I caught Theo's look and turned away, smiling.

* * *

Back in the folly, Juke, Aquila and Pantera gathered around the wounded dragon. Slowly, she began to assume human form, her left arm hanging wounded and useless by her side, a large rip in the sleeve of her black leather jacket.

'Would you believe it? she muttered in disgust. 'Succumbing to one of those creatures. With my reputation.'

'I suggest you get some angelica on that, fast,' said Juke. 'You'll soon be good as new.'

A noise behind them attracted their attention. It was Mr Nelson. He sat up, rubbing his eyes and blinking.

'Who are you?' he asked blearily. 'And where am I?'

Pantera regarded him with disgust. 'You're at Hartswell Hall,' she answered icily. 'And if I'm not mistaken by your scent,' she wrinkled her nose in distaste, 'you are the vermin who has caused us so much trouble.'

Mr Nelson got down shakily from the plinth and faced her.

'Nothing we can't smooth over, dear madam. I'm always available to the highest bidder.' He looked at her hopefully.

'Indeed,' she answered. 'It seems you are causing us a lot of trouble, all for the sake of our crystal.'

At the mention of the word 'crystal' his eyes lit up and a drop of saliva appeared on his lip. 'What I wouldn't give to see this crystal they're all so desperate for.'

'That can be arranged,' said Pantera softly, glancing at the others. She turned back to Mr Nelson. 'Why don't you come with me?'

* * *

She led the way up the spiral stone staircase, Mr Nelson following like an obedient puppy. When they reached the top, she opened the door to the Clock Tower Room, signalling to Viyesha to remove the blue energy shield.

'This is Mr Nelson,' she announced, 'He wishes to see the crystal for himself.'

Viyesha understood at once and stood back to let the private detective into the room.

'Welcome, Mr Nelson,' she purred. 'Come and see our crystal.'

She took the silver casket from its hiding place and opened the lid, revealing the crystal in all its glory, blue light filling the room.

Mr Nelson's eyes opened wide and he stepped forward.

So this is what all the fuss is about,' he said in his flat Brummie voice. He reached in to the casket. 'May I?''

'Of course,' said Viyesha, glancing through the window at the full moon still riding high in the sky.

Mr Nelson's hand closed around the crystal and a huge grin mushroomed across his face.

'Oh my,' he gasped. 'Now I understand.'

Rivulets of blue energy pulsed down his arm and criss-crossed his body, and a beatific look came across his features.

'I've never felt so wonderful in all my life,' he informed them. 'If you could bottle this, you'd make a fortune.'

Briefly, they saw the man he'd been before greed, avarice and skulduggery had corrupted his mind and body. A youth with clear blue eyes, blond hair and slim physique stood before them, a world of possibilities ahead of him. Then the crystal's power reversed and, concentrated by the power of the full moon, the ageing process hit with full force.

Before he had time to speak, his skin was shrivelling, his lips were pulled back and his hair became white and sparse. His spine curved over and an old man on the brink of death stood before them. Uncomprehending, he stared at his gnarled and skeletal hands.

'What…?' he started to say, but his vocal cords collapsed and he fell to the floor, the skin pulling tight across his bones, eyes sinking back into their sockets, rotten teeth falling to the floor. His demise was dramatic but quick. In just a few seconds, his body disintegrated, turning into a crumbling pile of bones that rapidly became dust, a pile of old clothes the only evidence of his existence.

* * *

With the demise of the conduit, villagers all over Hartswell-on-the-Hill found their spines were straightening and they were feeling better than they had in days. The affliction that had mysteriously affected them vanished in an instant and all those surviving were soon back to full health, eating a normal diet. All except for old Steve Creasey, who found he'd developed a penchant for black pudding he'd never had before.

45. Aftermath

Viyesha sat in the ballroom, completely still, as if meditating. A small fire was burning in the fireplace, casting dim shadows across the room, and pale blue candles flickered all around her. She was wearing a long, pale blue gown with a bright blue crystal on a silver chain shimmering at her neckline. As I walked into the room, she looked up and smiled. It was a tired, forced smile, without her usual warmth.

'Emily, how lovely to see you. I hope you've put your ordeal behind you.'

'Which ordeal is that, Viyesha?' I asked. 'The one in the crypt or the one at Badru's hands last night?'

'Badru? What do you mean?'

I briefly told her all that had happened the previous night, how Theo had tried to save me and Badru had turned the tables, so that I was the one who had to cross the ravine to save Theo from the Cherufe. When I had finished speaking, she stared at me white-faced.

'He placed you and Theo in the Cherufe's lair? Oh, he has excelled himself this time. I'm sorry, Emily. The events of last night overshadowed everything. I never thought Badru would come so quickly. Your survival is testament to your courage. You have been tested to the limit and not found wanting.' She looked into the distance, speaking more to herself. 'He has changed. The Badru of old would never have played such sadistic games.'

Once more she looked at me. 'Power corrupts, Emily. Once upon a time, Badru was a creature of the light, a force for good. Now it seems he is not so different from the Fallen Angel. But enough of that. You have beaten him and will be initiated at the next full moon. Our plans are on hold for a month, that's all. Perhaps you should move in to the hall and let us keep you safe. What do you say?'

Before I had a chance to reply, my mobile phone rang. I looked at the screen. It was my mother and I took the call, never happier to hear her voice.

'Hi Mum, had a good holiday?'

'Brilliant. How are you, Emily? What have you been up to?'

'Nothing, really. Just your average week. How are you getting back from the airport?'

'Juke's coming to pick me up. He's on his way. I'll be home in half an hour.'

'Can't wait to see you. Love you.'

'Love you too. See you soon.'

I hung up, Seth's description of Juke flashing through my mind. He'd said Juke was lit up like a beacon and had removed a feeder from his back with a sword. Violet had called him an urban angel. I made a mental note that Juke and I needed to have words. He had some explaining to do, but I guessed it meant my mum was in safe hands. Violet also said that Joseph had feelings for Tash, and Badru himself had mentioned it. That was something else I needed to sort out.

I turned to Viyesha. 'My mother's on her way back. I should get home.'

'Of course. But think about what I've said Emily. Our old enemy will stop at nothing to get the crystal. I need you where I can see you.'

'Okay, I will.'

I opened the double doors to the ballroom to find Theo sitting on one of the sofas in reception. He got up when he saw me. Then his lips were on mine and I was experiencing the best kiss of my life, all the anguish of the last few days dispersing in an instant. I was safe and my future was assured. Everything was perfect.

We were interrupted by Violet's anxious voice from the top of the stairway.

'Theo, where's mother?' she called.

He pulled away and looked up at his sister.

'In the ballroom. Why?'

'I'm here,' said Viyesha, appearing through the double doors. 'What's wrong?'

'It's Seth,' answered Violet. 'He can't walk because of the pain in his back. He's in a bad way.'

'Tash too,' said Joseph, appearing next to her at the top of the stairs. 'The fever has returned.'

'What's going on, mother?' asked Violet, a tremor in her voice. 'I thought they were better.'

'They have both been exposed to great evil,' said Viyesha, looking troubled. 'I feared this might happen. If we are to save them, I'm afraid there is only one option open to us.'

'And that is?' I asked.

'They must be initiated at the next full moon,' said Leon, walking into reception.

'What?' I said, turning to face him, uncomprehending. 'Initiate my friends? So they live for eternity? You can't. It's not what they want.'

'I was hoping they would both be strong enough to make a full recovery,' said Viyesha, 'but it appears the evil is too strong. I'm sorry, Emily. There is no alternative.'

'Apart from that, they know too much,' said Leon. 'Badru would never let them live.'

'Badru said he wouldn't touch them.'

Leon laughed dismissively. 'And you believe him?'

The goal posts were moving in front of my eyes. And I couldn't work out if it was a good or bad thing.

Whether they liked it or not, my friends were going to be initiated with me. The decision was out of their hands. Seth, who could barely commit to a brief flirtation, let alone eternity. And Tash, who'd bewitched Joseph, but was in no fit state to know her own mind. How would they feel when they found out? And would they blame me?

Another thought occurred to me. 'The next full moon is a month away, Viyesha. If they're so sick, how will they survive until then?'

'We can give them crystal healing until they are initiated,' she answered. 'But we need to start now.' She clapped her hands. 'Come Joseph, come Violet, let's get them to the Clock Tower.'

I sat on one of the sofas, my mind reeling, Theo and Leon either side of me.

Five minutes later, Viyesha was back, running down the stairs, blonde hair adrift, panic in her eyes.

'Leon,' she cried.

'What is it, my love?' he said, jumping up.

'Our worst nightmare,' she said in a trembling voice. 'The crystal is gone. Someone has taken it.'

I glanced at Theo and felt for his hand. It was icy cold.

Suddenly, everything went into free-fall, our future together uncertain, his family's existence under threat and my friends' survival unlikely.

After everything we'd been through, is this how it would end?

EPILOGUE

In the hall gardens, concealed in the shadows of the secret garden, three clandestine figures met.

'She is stronger than we thought.'

'Do you think it possible she could be Ahmes?'

'Never! Do not insult her memory.'

'Have no fear. The battle for the crystal is just beginning. We will align ourselves with the stronger side. She and her friends are history.'

'Ahmes will be avenged.'

Thank you for reading True Blue

If you have enjoyed reading True Blue, please leave a review on Amazon/Goodreads. Thank you! Pat Spence

Into The Blue (Blue Crystal Trilogy Book 3)

Coming Soon!

Follow The Blue Crystal Trilogy:

On Facebook at https://www.facebook.com/bluecrystaltrilogy

And on Twitter at https://twitter.com/pat_spence

See the Blue Moon trailer at

https://www.youtube.com/watch?v=SFvsXlPem4Q

Acknowledgements

Thanks go to ...

...Steve for reading through the many drafts, Andrew Aske for cover design, Amelia for help with formatting, Bel Friedman for proof reading, Peter Buckman for copy editing, Lynda & Tim O'Rourke for help and advice, Kirsty Kinmond for on-going support and all the friends and family who have provided encouragement. Not forgetting George the cat, for general calming ambience.

Other titles by Pat Spence

Blue Moon (Book One in The Blue Crystal Trilogy)
Into The Blue (Book Three in The Blue Crystal Trilogy) Coming soon!

Abigail's Affair (A quirky love story set in the UK and Australia
Rediscover Your Razzle Dazzle (The 30-day Sparkle Programme)
A self-help guide to looking good and feeling great. Coming soon!

Pat Spence is a freelance writer and previously a magazine editor. She has also worked as a copywriter in advertising agencies, a freelance trainer in personal development and jobsearch skills, and a massage therapist/aromatherapist. She is married with one child, has a degree in English Literature, reads Tarot and is learning banjo.

Made in the USA
Charleston, SC
23 June 2015